THE SEAGULL SOCIETY

THOMAS IAN DOYLE

For Lakey

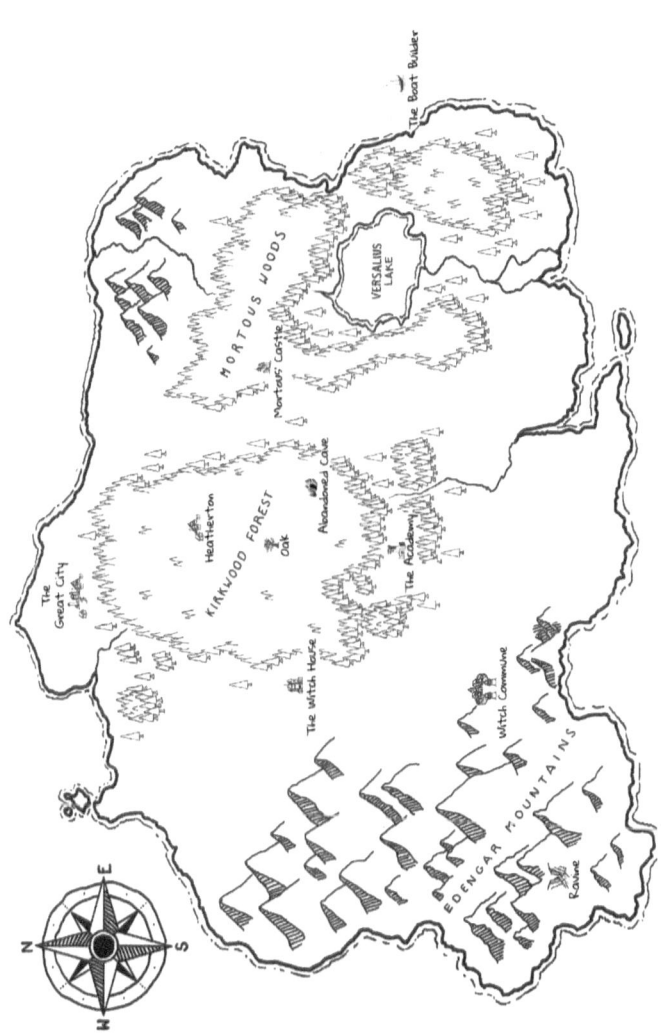

NALDY
The Seagull Society
Thomas Ian Doyle

Book Two

Chapter One

THE WIZARD ARRIVES

Another jumble of yellowed books and worthless trinkets. There was a broken quill, half a tarot deck, a foul-smelling hat, and a silver pin of a seabird—but not the thing Naldy was looking for.

She lifted the wooden box above her head, returning it to the top of the wardrobe.

'Ugh—no! Naldy!'

Ralph placed his silver tray, laden with mint biscuits and a freshly boiled pot of brew, onto the wooden floor of the study. He put his hands on his hips and shook his head in dismay.

'We need to keep it ordered,' said Ralph, exasperated, eyeing the room's mountain of junk. 'If we don't, we'll never get through it all.'

'*Arcesso,*' said Naldy, and the box lifted from the top of the wardrobe, gliding down to join the trunks Ralph had already searched and attempted to stack in a neat pile.

They had spent the better part of two months sifting through boxes, trunks, and mounds of miscellaneous items. Ralph was convinced that hidden amongst the accumulated junk—thanks to the hoarding habits of Naldy's ancestors—they might find the Corium. Or, at the very least, perhaps Lignum.

Ralph picked up his cup and made his way to the open window of the cluttered room, which offered a view of Kirkwood Forest. The sun hung low in the sky, and a warm breeze carried the scent of pine trees into the study. It was summer, but they had barely ventured beyond the Witch House's cramped wooden porch, where they drank their brew each morning. Although the weather outside was inviting, they'd both had their fill of the outdoors for the time being, having spent weeks journeying through the Edengar Mountains just two months ago.

'I think I've had enough today,' said Naldy, pouring herself a cup of brew.

The last rays of the sun glinted off Ralph's right ear, where a small emerald dangled on a delicate silver chain. Naldy's heart ached as the memory of Odorf surfaced. The old witch had guided them through the Edengar Mountains before Maverick had killed her and destroyed the Devante they had been trying to save. Now, only three remained: Aurum, Lignum, and the Corium. They knew where the Aurum resided—with Maverick—but had no clue where Lignum or the Corium were hidden.

'I'm certain they're not here,' Naldy muttered to herself.

'We've done twelve rooms,' said Ralph, turning

away from the window to face her. 'At the pace we're going, I think we can sort through the whole house in maybe one month.'

Naldy took a sip from her cup. She doubted they'd find any Devante at the Witch House, but Ralph had convinced her that searching every room was necessary. They'd started in the attic and worked their way from room to room, top to bottom.

'We've already found one valuable artefact,' said Ralph, taking a deep breath of the late-afternoon air. 'Your great-grandmother's Vase of Mon-gol-whatever-it's-called. I'm certain we'll find at least one Devante hidden here.'

So far, their hunt for the last surviving Devante had proven fruitless. The only valuable item they'd recovered from the neglected clutter was Naldy's great-great-grandmother's porcelain Vase of Mongonli, rumoured to have been stolen by Naldy's Aunt Geraldine and worth a small fortune.

'Ralph,' said Naldy, brushing her long black hair from her face. 'I know all this stuff gives the impression that my family might be the type to accidentally misplace a grand spellbook. But I know we won't find them here.'

'We found the vase, didn't we? That's valuable.'

'Yes, Ralph, but we're talking about the Devante. The most powerful spellbooks to ever exist. I think if my family had possessed one of those...'

Naldy hesitated. Her family *had* possessed one, called Rubrum, and it had been destroyed by Maverick, like most of the other Devante.

'If they'd possessed *another* one,' Naldy corrected herself, 'I think they would have taken care of it, like they did with Rubrum, and they wouldn't have let it disappear into an ocean of antiques.'

Something changed in Ralph's eyes. Was his hope diminishing?

Naldy felt a pang of guilt for dampening his spirits. Her own hope had waned long ago, but she'd tried not to let her lack of faith affect Ralph.

'I'll get dinner started,' said Naldy, side-stepping an old wooden trunk as she made her way to the door.

The truth was, Naldy knew that sorting through the hoard of junk brought Ralph some joy. It made him feel like they were taking small steps towards securing the future of magic for witches and wizards everywhere. But Naldy knew the chances of ever finding either Devante were slim. The grim reality was that the last two lost Devante—Lignum and the Corium—could be anywhere.

She prepared a hearty beef stew for dinner. Ralph spent most of the meal absentmindedly twiddling his spoon in the bowl.

'Ralph, I'm sorry if I upset you,' said Naldy, collecting his plate after he had finally finished. 'I just don't think we should get our hopes up so high.'

'You've given up, then?' asked Ralph pointedly. 'Admit it.'

'Given up?'

'Don't deny it. If we don't find these books here, will you stop looking?'

'Ralph,' said Naldy, but she stopped short, knowing there was some truth in what he was saying.

She turned her back on him and placed his plate on the cluttered kitchen benchtop before filling the sink with water to wash the dishes by hand. She feared Ralph might read the truth on her face if she faced him.

'And if we don't find either Devante here, what's your plan?' asked Naldy, scraping a few curls off the bar of dish soap.

'Then we keep searching,' replied Ralph firmly.

Naldy turned off the tap and made her way to the pantry. She retrieved an opened bottle of dark liquid, then collected two crystal glasses from the adjoining cabinet. She poured them both a small amount.

'What is this?' asked Ralph.

'An aged herbal concoction,' said Naldy. 'My aunt's recipe. No idea what is in it, but it's rumoured to be calming.'

'I don't need calming,' retorted Ralph.

'You need to accept reality,' said Naldy irritably, pouring more into Ralph's glass. 'Don't you see it's pointless to keep looking? We'll die before we find those other books.'

'What if we visit Oak?' suggested Ralph.

'Why would we visit Oak?' she asked.

'He had possession of a Devante,' said Ralph enthusiastically. 'He guarded Rubrum. The tree may have information that could help us. Besides, we still haven't warned him about the fortune teller's prediction—she said there would be a fire.'

'He already caught on fire,' said Naldy, rolling her eyes. 'He was lucky it was night-time, and I wasn't still cursed. The fortune teller was a crook, charging us for a prediction she'd already made.'

'We can't let Maverick win, Naldy.'

'He's already won,' said Naldy, downing the liquid in one go and topping up her glass again. 'Look, Ralph, the last three Devante have been on the list for months. We know Maverick has the Aurum. And Lignum must be hidden somewhere treacherous, since he can use the Aurum to locate it but still hasn't destroyed it. We know he can't see the location of the Corium. Let him try to find it! He'll likely die before he ever does. As for us, let's enjoy the rest of our lives in peace.'

Ralph lifted a hand to his ear, twiddling the dangling emerald earring. He had a habit of doing this when he was deep in thought.

'I'll help you finish sorting through the Witch House,' said Naldy into her glass. 'But if we don't find one here, you'll have to go searching on your own.'

'What about Betty?' asked Ralph slowly, taking a hesitant sip of the dark liquid before looking at her expectantly.

'Betty?' Naldy repeated, her tone questioning.

'She helped us the first time around. Maybe she can help us a second time?'

'I suppose if you insist on going traipsing after lost books,' said Naldy, agitated, 'visiting Betty at Heatherton might be a good place to start. But you'll have to do it on your own. I've had enough.'

'When did townsfolk begin to care more about saving magic than witches?'

'Until Maverick manages to find the Corium,' Naldy replied, 'we needn't worry. I should get some sleep, especially if I'm helping you tackle the second study tomorrow. It'll probably take most of the day to sort through.'

Naldy emptied her crystal glass and placed it on the bench beside the sink. She didn't feel any calmer as she sleepily made her way up the house's old, rickety staircase. After pulling on her pyjamas, she climbed into the warm sheets of her bed.

Before falling asleep, her thoughts drifted back to Odorf and the other witches in the commune. She remembered their wrinkled mouths crying out in anguish when they broke the news that Odorf had died in Edengar. A wave of hopelessness had rippled through the cave.

When Naldy awoke the following day, the sun was streaming through the window, warming her face. She assumed it must have been early, as Ralph usually woke her before nine by rapping on her bedroom door and calling, 'Sun shines, time to rise.'

After bathing and dressing, Naldy lazily made her way downstairs to the kitchen to prepare her morning brew. As she passed the old grandfather clock in the cramped hallway, she was surprised to see its hands pointing past midday.

Naldy wondered why Ralph had let her sleep in so late. He was usually eager to start sorting through boxes. Was Ralph less motivated to finish now that he knew Naldy wouldn't be joining him beyond the Witch House?

As she approached the kitchen, the scent of sweet baked pastry wafted into the hall, accompanied by the sound of clinking crockery and clanging cutlery.

Naldy entered and found Ralph clad in a floral apron, brandishing a wooden spoon. He had laid the table beautifully and was stirring something bubbling away on the hob.

The kitchen was usually cluttered, but a fresh stack of used cast-iron cookware towered beside the sink, adding to the everyday mess.

'Take a seat,' said Ralph, pointing to the wooden table. It had been dressed in a golden tablecloth— he must have fished it out from some cupboard. 'Brunch will be ready shortly.'

'Brunch?' said Naldy, sitting at one of the place settings, where a napkin had been folded into a dragon. 'What is all this? It's beautiful, Ralph, but what's it all for?'

'I've made sweet blueberry pastries, pancakes, boiled and poached eggs with a melted butter sauce, and a fresh batch of brew.'

'Yes,' said Naldy, picking up and inspecting an ornate fork she'd never seen before. 'But *what* is it all for? If you're trying to convince me...'

'I wanted to thank you,' he replied cheerfully, pouring pancake mixture into a sizzling pan. 'I went into town this morning and bought a few things.'

'Thank me?'

'I remember a time,' said Ralph, opening the door of the steaming oven. He carefully retrieved hot blueberry pastries with a kitchen towel. 'I remember when you wouldn't let me within a yard of this house. I just wanted to find a way to say thank you —for letting me search through it. And look, I found the most wonderful blueberries on the walk into town.'

'If it means you'll leave me in peace,' said Naldy, picking up the silver carafe, 'then I'm more than happy to rummage through every sock drawer and forgotten suitcase. But once we finish that, I go no further. I'd quite like to have my solitude again.'

'Of course,' said Ralph, picking up the pan's handle with the kitchen towel. He jerked the iron skillet, and the pancake flipped right out of the hot pan and onto the floor. 'Oops. That's my fifth attempt.'

'Come sit,' insisted Naldy, filling Ralph's glass with hot brew.

'But I still need to—'

'*Arcesso*,' said Naldy, waving a palm in the general direction of the benchtop. The pancake batter began pouring, and the blueberry pastries loaded themselves onto a silver tray before gliding gracefully over to the table.

'I wanted to do it for you,' said Ralph in a reprimanding tone. The butter sauce floated towards the table, but Ralph grabbed hold of it before it could complete its journey. 'I'm making your brunch, and I don't need your magic interfering.'

'Don't be stubborn, Ralph,' said Naldy as the pancake in the skillet flipped itself. 'Come and sit. You've done plenty.'

Ralph, somewhat reluctantly, took a seat opposite Naldy.

'Don't look so sulky,' she said, eyeing the excessive number of dirty pots and pans. 'I can leave you the washing up.'

Ralph unfolded his dragon-shaped napkin. 'I wanted to surprise you.'

'You went all the way to Frubry?'

'Surprise!' said Ralph, as they both helped themselves to food. 'And... yes, alright, I decided to let you sleep in... and... okay, I did get up early and make the trip into town because I wanted to convince you to come with me.'

'I'm not coming with you,' said Naldy as she generously poured thick butter sauce over her eggs. 'It's been so long since I've been left alone. I miss that.'

'But how can you just go back to living by yourself? Knowing that, somewhere out there, Maverick is actively hunting Lignum and the Corium. And you.'

'Me?'

'His floating ball of smoke—'

'Lied!'

'But it didn't lie, Naldy,' said Ralph, raising his voice as he cracked the shell of his boiled egg. 'The smoke was created by one of the Devante, and it said you know where the—'

'But I don't know, do I!' Naldy's voice rose above his. She was fed up. Ralph had broached this subject more than once since their return from Edengar, and every time, Naldy had told him the truth. 'I know Maverick's smoky-ball-lie-detector-thing said I know where the Corium is. But I really don't, Ralph. I have no idea why it said I do, because I don't.'

'Regardless,' said Ralph, helping himself to a serving of pancakes that had floated down to the table. 'Maverick knows he's got a better chance of finding you than finding another Devante.'

'What's that supposed to mean?'

'That it's likely he'll be looking for you,' said Ralph, a little too bluntly. 'If he believes the lie detector, he believes you know the Corium's location, even if you don't. It's a matter of time before he finds you here, and you'll be much safer on the move.'

'Let him come,' she said, meeting his blue eyes. 'I have my magic back, and I'll be ready for him.'

In the hope that Ralph would drop the subject, Naldy helped herself to a warm blueberry pastry and glanced out the kitchen window. Her black cat, Smookers, was curled comfortably on the exterior windowsill.

'I want to return to my quiet life,' Naldy said softly. A cloud shifted, and the warm sun streamed through the window, pleasantly catching on her face.

They finished their breakfast in silence. Naldy

could have used magic to help Ralph with the mound of dirty dishes, but instead, she left him in the kitchen to clean up and made her way upstairs to the second study.

She decided to start with a large cabinet—a maple bookcase with several creepy faces carved into sections of its lower wooden doors. The exposed shelves above were lined with dust-covered books and dark-coloured stones.

Naldy lifted the books down, flipped open their covers, and routinely checked the reverse side for the Devante's famed trademark: the embossed letter H.

She tossed each book aside, unsurprised they weren't Devante. By the time Ralph had finished washing up and entered the messy room, Naldy had inspected all the books on the shelf and started on the contents of the bookcase's lower cupboards.

'Nothing so far,' she said drearily, tossing an old sock aside.

'Naldy, I want to apologise,' said Ralph, pulling a nearby trunk closer and struggling to pry open its wooden lid. 'I'm sorry for what I said about Maverick looking for you. I don't want to do it all on my own, and the thought of you here by yourself does worry me.'

'You don't need to be concerned about me, Ralph.'

'I know you can take care of yourself,' he said, still working to open the trunk's lid. 'You aren't responsible for the survival of the Devante, and I shouldn't be holding you accountable.'

'Good, I'm glad you aren't,' said Naldy, directing her palms towards Ralph's trunk. '*Aperio.*'

The trunk flew open. Ralph peered into the chaos inside and began slowly sorting through it.

Soon Naldy had finished emptying the maple bookcase, except for a lone book resting on top. She stood on her tiptoes to reach it, but as she steadied herself with a hand on a lower shelf, she accidentally pulled the entire cabinet towards her. The book fell —hitting the floor with a slap—and Naldy lost her balance.

Her body slammed into the floorboards. As she glanced up, the tall bookcase was coming down after her.

'Naldy!'

Before she could utter a spell, the heavy cabinet stopped falling—hovering mid-air, inches from her body.

'I need you to move,' said Ralph in a strained voice, standing a few metres behind her.

Naldy turned her head to see Ralph's outstretched palm. He wasn't touching the cabinet.

'Move,' he said through clenched teeth. 'I can't hold it.'

Naldy rolled out of the way just in time as the entire cabinet thudded to the floor.

'Why didn't you use magic to get the book from the shelf?' said Ralph bitterly. 'You could have been squashed!'

Naldy clambered to her feet, gazing at him in shock. 'Ralph, do you know what you just did?'

He returned an exhausted stare. Dark circles had formed beneath his eyes, as if he had suddenly fallen ill.

'Why would you do that to me?' Ralph asked, annoyed.

'Do what to you?'

'You used me as some weird proxy thing,' said Ralph, sitting on a nearby chair with tattered green upholstery. 'Did you want me to suffer the pain of holding up the bookcase?'

'Ralph,' said Naldy, approaching him. 'I didn't use you as a proxy, and there's no such thing as lending your magic to other people.'

'Well, what happened then?' he asked uneasily. 'Whatever it was, I didn't like it.'

'*You* did the magic, Ralph.'

'Magic?' Ralph echoed in a doubtful tone. 'How is that possible?'

'I can't believe I didn't see it before,' said Naldy, placing her hands on Ralph's shoulders. 'The way you were able to fly a magic carpet so effortlessly —townsfolk can fly carpets, yes—but they usually only get them to go so far.'

Ralph opened his mouth to speak, then closed it again. He restlessly picked at the fabric of the chair's armrest.

'Naldy, I'm not in the mood for bad jokes.'

'It's not,' she insisted. 'I think you might be... a wizard.'

'A wizard? How could I be a wizard?' Ralph said, laughing. 'Townspeople have to train to be wizards, and I haven't trained. I'd need a magical object too, and I don't carry one of those around with—'

He stopped mid-sentence and lifted a hand to the emerald earring dangling from his ear.

'Of course,' said Naldy, her eyes widening with realisation. 'The earring, it chose you, Ralph. I should have seen it before. It only calls to you.'

He leant back in the chair as if she had just imparted some terrible news.

'I hate to admit it,' said Naldy, kneeling beside Ralph to emphasise her seriousness, 'the earring you found before we went to Edengar isn't a piece of junk. It's an Imporiom.'

'An Impor-what?'

'An Imporiom,' repeated Naldy, staring at the green jewel hanging from his ear. 'I thought you'd know this, aren't you a scholar?'

'Of witches, yes,' said Ralph, his voice cracking as if he were frightened. 'But I don't know anything about the art of wizardry.'

'You are right, Ralph, to become a wizard, you need skill and training. But most importantly, you also need—'

'A magical object, yes, I know that bit. A wizard cannot cast spells unless they have a magical object.'

'Well, the magical object a wizard carries is called an Imporiom,' said Naldy, smiling, pleased with herself for knowing something Ralph didn't. 'For example, Maverick's cane is an Imporiom.'

'You expect me to believe—'

'They are rare,' she continued, ignoring Ralph's

troubled look. 'But I'm certain it has to be the earring. Now that I think about it, maybe it helped guide us safely through Edengar more than we realised. An Imporiom, when united with its worthy owner, will usually create magic on its own, at least in the beginning. To get your attention. It's waiting for you to train, Ralph, to learn.'

'I'm not training to be a... a...' Ralph stood up and rummaged through his open trunk, pulling out feather quills, old parchment paper, and a silver candelabra. 'What nonsense. Let's finish this sorting.'

'It's not nonsense, Ralph. Wizards *are* created from simple townsfolk... like yourself.'

'But I never chose to be a wizard!'

'Nobody chooses to be a wizard. The earring has chosen you.'

Ralph was haphazardly tossing the trunk's contents aside, a stark contrast to his usual orderly and meticulous approach.

'What drew you to the Witch House?' asked Naldy, watching Ralph try to distract himself with the sorting. 'Before we knew each other, I mean. When you used to fly around on your magic carpet.'

'I'm a scholar, Naldy. I was studying witches, and I observed you so I could write about you.'

'Yes, but how did you find me here?'

'I don't know,' said Ralph irritably, 'one day, I got on my magic carpet and went searching for witches' homes, and I sort of passed by.'

'Passed by?' said Naldy thoughtfully. 'Oh, don't

you see, Ralph? The earring drew you to this house; you were always meant to find it. I had tried a few spells to get rid of you, remember? They always seemed to miss. That's why I went to see Oak, to find something stronger. Even though you weren't yet united with it, I think the earring might have been protecting you.'

'And what if I am what you say I am?' Ralph asked, abandoning the trunk and turning to face her.

'A wizard.'

'Yes. If I am a wizard, what then?'

'Then you study,' replied Naldy, smiling at him. 'I can teach you.'

—*Chapter Two*—

STUDENT

Their bottoms were sore, and their backs stiff. They'd been sitting at the round kitchen table for five hours. Ralph's frustration had peaked, while Naldy found herself surprisingly calm.

'These things take time,' Naldy said encouragingly. 'You can't expect to create flames from thin air after practising for less than a day.'

Ralph slumped further into his chair, crossing his arms childishly.

'Ralph, you just have to keep practising, okay?'

'Maybe I'm not a wizard,' he replied, defeated. 'Maybe you got it wrong. I can't manage a spark, let alone a flame.'

'It was you who stopped the bookcase from crushing me,' said Naldy as Smookers wound around her legs. 'We should take the rest of the day off.'

'Maybe the earring did it,' he muttered, reaching up to his right earlobe and unhooking it. 'It could have been the earring on its own. I think you've gotten it wrong, Naldy—I mean, *me*—a wizard?'

'Jewellery doesn't usually produce magic on its own,' said Naldy, holding out her hand. 'Here, give it to me.'

Ralph hesitated for a moment before handing over the delicate earring. Naldy placed it on the table, where the tiny emerald stone glinted in the afternoon sun streaming through the open window.

'There's a way to find out if it's an Imporiom,' she said, standing up. 'Ralph, I need you to stand by the sink.'

'What for?'

'Go on now.'

Ralph obligingly made his way to the kitchen sink. Smookers jumped onto the wooden table, sniffing at the glinting earring before flicking it with his paw.

'Off you go, Smookers,' said Naldy, picking up the cat and kissing his furry forehead. She passed him through the open window and gently placed him on the exterior windowsill, then closed it. 'I'd stay clear if I were you.'

'What are you doing, Naldy? Don't break it.'

'I'm more concerned about it breaking me,' said Naldy quietly. She held her palms over the earring. '*Prosterno!*'

What happened next occurred in a flash. A white light shot from Naldy's palms, aimed at the earring, but evaporated before it could reach the green gemstone. Then, a green light shot up from the jewel, colliding with Naldy's chest and sending her flying backwards, slamming her hard against the wall.

Ralph plugged his ears with his fingers as if trying to block out a painfully loud noise.

'Make it stop, Naldy!'

'Put the earring on,' said Naldy calmly from the floor. She couldn't hear any deafening sounds.

'What?'

'Put the earring on, Ralph!'

Ralph rushed to the wooden table, quickly picking up the earring.

'The noise, it's stopped,' he said in relief, holding the green emerald.

'Only you can hear it,' said Naldy, climbing to her feet. 'It calls to you, and you alone. It was warning you that danger was afoot.'

'Now we know I'm not a wizard, see,' said Ralph. 'I didn't *do* anything. The object did all that magic by itself—it must be evil or something, and there's our proof. It attacked you.'

'The earring didn't attack me, Ralph,' replied Naldy calmly, gingerly lowering herself into one of the dining chairs. 'You did.'

'But I didn't attack you. I was all the way over there by the kitchen sink, like you told me!'

'Objects like these aren't known to produce magic on their own,' said Naldy, stretching her sore back while sitting. 'But an Imporiom can produce magic if instructed by its rightful master.'

'But I didn't,' protested Ralph, already reattaching the piece of jewellery to his right ear.

'I know you didn't mean to,' said Naldy calmly.

'I'm not blaming you. You don't have control over your magic yet. There's a deep connection between you and your Imporiom, Ralph. Look, you've already returned the emerald to your ear.'

'I was standing by the sink,' Ralph objected firmly. 'I didn't do anything.'

'It is difficult to destroy a wizard's Imporiom,' said Naldy. 'Mostly because the master has a unique connection to it. The Imporiom is a living source of the wizard's power. You might not have been aware, Ralph, but something hidden within you instructed the emerald to protect itself. You ordered it to defend you. It is your Imporiom.'

Ralph slumped into the chair opposite Naldy. Smookers pawed at the window, wanting to be let back in.

'I'm sorry about your back. If it really was me that commanded the earring.'

'It's alright,' she said, sitting up to stretch again. 'We need to keep practising.'

Naldy picked up a nearby candle and placed it in front of Ralph.

'*Comburite,*' said Ralph, holding a palm over the candle. Nothing happened. '*Comburite.*'

The candle didn't so much as flicker. Naldy stood up to let Smookers back inside.

'Really, Naldy,' he said drearily. 'How can I, one moment, send you flying into the wall and the next fail to light a candle? At this rate, I'll manage a spark in a year or two—and what good will that do when it comes to facing Maverick?'

'Keep practising, Ralph,' said Naldy, petting Smookers' head. 'And I wouldn't worry. Mastering magic isn't about learning one spell at a time. It's more like learning how to read. First, you learn the alphabet, then you gradually get better at reading whole words. But once you know how to read, you can read almost anything. It's the same with spells. Once you nail the basics, you'll be able to do any spell you want.'

'Assuming they still exist,' said Ralph glumly. 'You seem to think Maverick wants to destroy everything magical—he might have destroyed all spells by the time I've mastered the basics.'

Naldy pushed the unlit candle closer to him.

They spent another hour at the kitchen table, but Ralph had no luck producing even a hint of magic. As darkness fell, Ralph grouchily lit the candle with a match.

Naldy started on dinner while Ralph disappeared upstairs.

Dinner was eaten in silence, and after clearing the plates, Naldy curled up comfortably on the sofa, with Smookers purring in her lap. Ralph sat sulking in a nearby armchair, muttering something under his breath. It took Naldy a moment to realise Ralph was whispering the words to the fire spell: *Comburite.*

When Naldy awoke the next morning, she was surprised it wasn't to the sound of Ralph repeatedly knocking on her bedroom door. She dressed and made her way into the kitchen, where she found him sitting at the table, bent over an unlit candle.

'It's after ten,' said Naldy, surprised. 'You didn't wake me. Are we continuing with our search today?'

'*Commm-buri-tay,   Combu-rit-tay,   Comburit-taaay*,' muttered Ralph, rubbing his temples. 'I've been trying out different inflections, like you said.'

'Your *inflections*,' said Naldy, pouring herself some lukewarm brew, 'sound more like miserable variations on being tired and fed up. Did you get any sleep?'

'I tried to sleep.'

'*Comburite*,' said Naldy as a flame flickered to life inside the wood stove. She placed another log into the grate. 'Have you eaten?'

'Not yet.'

'I'll make us some scrambled eggs,' Naldy offered, placing a cast-iron pan onto the hob. Ralph rubbed his eyes, looking crestfallen.

'Naldy, I wanted to ask you something?'

'Anything you like,' said Naldy, cracking five eggs into the pan.

'Would you mind if we took the day off and finished the second study tomorrow?' asked Ralph sheepishly. 'I'd really like to keep practising. I want to get the hang of it.'

'Of course, Ralph,' she replied, pleased they wouldn't have to spend the day sifting through junk. She picked up a large wooden spoon and stirred the eggs.

'Thank you,' said Ralph, returning to his spell practice.

When Naldy finished cooking, she placed a plate of scrambled eggs and toast beside Ralph and took a seat opposite him with her own plate.

'You need to sleep, Ralph. You look exhausted.'

'I couldn't sleep,' he said, picking up his fork and taking a bite of the eggs. 'I feel like I won't rest until I at least produce a spark. I don't quite believe it yet. A wizard!'

'Well, that's likely part of the problem. You doubt yourself, and doubt is to magic what water is to fire.'

Naldy put down her fork and made her way into the adjoining living room, searching for something. She scanned the small bookcase until she found a tattered green book. Its creased spine suggested it had been read many times.

'You should probably mix it up,' said Naldy, re-entering the kitchen. 'I can't listen to your *Comburites* any longer.'

She opened the green volume to a yellowed page. '*The Prosterno Spell*' was written at the top in elegant cursive. It was just one of the many spells in the book. Below that were three columns: the first contained the word *Prosterno;* the second and longest was filled with a string of foreign words stretching to the bottom of the page; the third column was half the length of the second.

'Do you recognise the language, Ralph?'

'I've never seen it before, no,' he said, staring curiously at the black ink.

'You have,' said Naldy, taking a sip of her now cold brew and giving him a moment to think. Ralph screwed up his tired face. 'You have a parchment in your pocket with this same language. You've translated it before, Ralph.'

'Olde Witchery?'

'Yes,' she said, smiling at him. 'It was you that translated Corium to mean leather and Lignum to mean wood.'

Ralph reached into his cloak pocket and withdrew a piece of parchment and a small black book with slanted gold lettering on the cover: *Translating Olde Witchery.* It was the book he had found when Maverick locked him in the reading room at Greenswood.

'But I thought spellbooks nowadays weren't written in Olde Witchery?' asked Ralph, staring at the mass of text waiting to be deciphered.

'There's no such thing as a *new* spellbook,' said Naldy, disappointed by how little he knew for someone who claimed to be a scholar of witches. 'Spellbooks haven't been made since The Great Witch Hunt. The Establishment banned most spells, remember, and ordered most spellbooks to be burnt. The Method was forgotten. The Devante are the last remaining hope of ever creating a new spell.'

Naldy was puzzled that Ralph hadn't let this crucial information sink in.

'All the more reason,' he began cheekily, 'for you to come with me to try and save them.'

'So long as they are lost,' she said, smiling back at him, 'they are safe.'

'You said you couldn't read Olde Witchery,'

replied Ralph curiously. 'I thought it was a language no longer practised or even taught?'

'I can't read it,' said Naldy, sounding agitated. 'And you're right—very few witches or wizards know the language, and most of it has been forgotten. Even most books on translating it, like the one you have there, tend not to be entirely accurate.'

'Then how do you perform the spells?'

'Because you only really need *one* of them,' Naldy explained, pointing to the singular word that made up the entirety of the first column. 'The first column is the spell.'

'But then what are the other two for?'

'The second,' said Naldy, pointing to the longest, 'gives instructions on positioning your body, especially your palms, while performing the magic. The third covers voice, tone, speed, breath, and inflection. But like I said, you don't need to know any of that to produce the magic.'

'Then why is it there?' asked Ralph insistently.

'Because it can help to—how do I put it?—*refine* the spell.'

'Refine?'

'Yes,' said Naldy, taking a sip of her brew. 'It's rumoured that you get better results if you manage all three. But trust me, the results are perfectly adequate if you only use the first part. Most witches don't bother with the second and third.'

Ralph ran his finger along the page of the green spellbook with newfound appreciation. From his expression, Naldy could tell he was thinking about translating all three columns.

'You might want to master the basics first,' said Naldy, draining her cup.

Ralph began flipping through his copy of *Translating Olde Witchery* as Naldy filled a cauldron with water to make a fresh batch of brew.

'*Prosterno* means—'

'To render someone physically weak,' Naldy interrupted.

'I thought you didn't know Olde Witchery?'

'I don't,' she said, adding chopped bark to the cauldron. 'Alright, I might know a few words— things my parents taught me when I was young —but barely anything. I can't read those longer paragraphs.'

'*Prosterno!*' said Ralph, holding up his palms towards Naldy. She played along, pretending to freeze like a statue. 'Very funny.'

Ralph spent the rest of the day poring over the fragile book. Naldy was quite glad he was content attempting to produce magic, which meant she had most of the day to herself. She passed the time in the overgrown garden out back. The flowers had long been overtaken by weeds, but the weeds themselves were attractive enough, with their pretty purple blooms. Smookers splayed out on the grass, enjoying the sun's warmth.

It was the first peaceful day Naldy could remember in a long time. She gazed out at the flat plains stretching ahead. She couldn't see the Edengar Mountains from where she stood, but she knew they were there, some distance away. Turning to face the Witch House's three wooden turrets and its aging, slanted roof, she noticed the tall pines of Kirkwood Forest looming eerily behind it. Naldy wondered if Ralph had been right about Maverick. Was he currently searching for her? Would he abandon his hunt for the Corium and come after her instead?

She lay in the grass beside Smookers, watching the puffy clouds drift across the baby-blue sky.

It was twilight when she stood and made her way back inside. Holding the door open for Smookers, she waited, but he was too busy licking the fur on his legs and enjoying the evening air.

'Suit yourself,' said Naldy, closing the back door and heading down the hallway.

When she entered the kitchen, she found Ralph bent over his books at the wooden kitchen table.

'Ralph, I'll make us a butternut pumpkin and potato pie,' said Naldy, thinking of how her mother used to make it when she was younger. It was an old family recipe she had made on occasion, though she had never quite mastered it the way her mother had.

'Yes, sounds good,' replied Ralph distractedly, his feather quill fervently scribbling.

Naldy went about preparing their evening meal. The last time she'd made the pie was before they'd set off for Edengar.

She was quietly glad Ralph was preoccupied with his books, as it left her with her own thoughts. While the pie baked, its sweet smell filled the house. Naldy set the table around Ralph, who was so immersed in his translations that he seemed startled when she scooped a generous helping of pie onto his plate.

'Books away.'

Ralph finished scribbling his sentence and tucked the feather quill into the old green spellbook to mark his page.

'This looks delicious,' said Ralph, stacking his translated parchment pages and pushing them to one side of the table.

Naldy picked up her fork, but before she could take a bite of the golden pie, a knock echoed from the front door.

'Who could that be?' she asked aloud. No sooner had the question left her lips than a troubling thought crossed her mind: *could it be Maverick?*

—*Chapter Three*—

THE VISITOR'S SECRET

'Ralph, we need to go!' Naldy said hurriedly. 'Let's slip out the back.'

'It's not Maverick,' replied Ralph sheepishly.

'How do you know it's not Maverick?'

'Please, don't be angry with me,' he said, standing with his palms outstretched in an attempt to calm her.

'Don't you raise your palms at me!' snapped Naldy.

'Sorry, I didn't mean to... look, Naldy, I don't want you to be upset. It's just—'

The knock came again, more impatiently this time.

'Naldy, because you said you could no longer help me with the Devante, and, well... I asked... umm...'

Naldy marched towards the front door, with Ralph following at a distance, lingering in the hallway.

'Who is it?' Naldy called warily as she reached the front door.

'She is cold and hungry,' came a familiar croaky

voice. 'Will you hurry up and let her in!'

'Betty?' asked Naldy, opening the door to find the old woman standing there, her unkempt grey hair wild atop her head, her kind, wrinkled face smiling back. Betty held a broomstick in one hand and Naldy's furry cat, Smookers, in the other.

'I found this little one outside,' said Betty, placing Smookers on the floor. 'Well, are you going to invite me in?'

'Come in, come in,' said Naldy, stepping aside to let Betty pass. 'I thought it might have been Maverick. But how did you find us here?'

'While we're on that subject,' the old woman said, looking past Naldy to stare down Ralph, who stood guiltily in the hallway.

'Hello, Betty,' he said, unable to contain his smile at the sight of her wrinkled face.

'Ralph contacted you,' Naldy guessed, taking the old woman's broomstick and leaning it against the stone wall alongside hers.

'I may have done,' said Ralph, his eyes averted. 'When I went into town the other day to fetch some things for cooking, I might have popped by the Tebellos and sent Betty a message.'

'You are lucky, boy,' said Betty scoldingly. 'Maverick could have intercepted your message sent from the Tebellos.'

Naldy, pleased to see Betty on her side, happily helped her remove her travelling cloak.

'You must be hungry,' said Naldy, hanging Betty's cloak on a nearby wall peg. 'I can't believe you've come from Heatherton at this hour. I've made my favourite—butternut pumpkin and potato pie. There's plenty.'

'I could smell it from the porch. It smells delicious.'

They entered the kitchen, and Naldy set another place at the table.

'I can't tell you how glad I am to have you here,' said Naldy. 'You must stay as long as you like, and hopefully, you can talk some sense into Ralph. He seems to think Maverick will be looking for me.'

'You needn't worry about Maverick,' said Betty, lowering herself into the comfortable kitchen chair. 'He's no longer concerned with either of you. I have it on good authority that he's busy seeking the remaining Devante far from here.'

Naldy was relieved to hear they were safe. She served a generous portion of pie onto Betty's plate, then placed the dish back in the warm oven before collecting three goblets from the overfilled cupboard.

'If he knows where the Devante are,' said Ralph, panicked, 'then we must go at once!'

'No, Ralph,' replied Betty calmly. 'Sit and enjoy your pie. There is no hurry because our journey ends here.'

'Ends here?'

'I know Edengar didn't go as planned, and the three Devante in the dragon caves were destroyed.'

Naldy's face flushed as she placed a fresh pot of brew in the centre of the table and took her seat, her posture rigid.

'Do not be saddened, Naldy. All three of us have done everything we could,' said Betty, picking up the pot and pouring the brew. 'It's time, I think, to leave the fate of the books to others.'

'Leave it to others?' said Ralph, outraged.

'You'll be pleased to hear,' Betty continued cheerfully, picking up her fork, 'that I've arranged for a skilled team of witches to follow Maverick. The remaining two Devante will be alright, and I believe the three of us have done enough.'

'See, I told you the books wouldn't be hidden here,' said Naldy, turning to face Betty. 'Ralph seems to think the Corium might be somewhere in the Witch House. I tried to tell him they wouldn't be.'

'Hidden here?' said Betty curiously. For a moment, Naldy noticed a flicker in the old woman's eyes as she seemed to retreat into her thoughts. 'Well, our quest has come to an end. Our part is done, and we should toast to that.'

'We can't give up,' said Ralph, impassioned. 'Not that easily, not after everything we've been through. Please, Betty, you must let me join the team of witches you've assembled to pursue Maverick.'

'It is over, my dear boy,' said Betty, taking a sip from her goblet. 'The team of witches is already trailing Maverick.'

'But I must join them. I didn't face dragons just to give up now.'

'It is up to others now,' said Betty, her stare firm. 'Though, it wouldn't hurt for us to continue searching the house. I doubt we'll find a Devante here, but precautions never go astray.'

'Continue the search?' asked Naldy, surprised.

'Maverick may be looking in the wrong direction, and if he finds nothing where he's headed, your house, Naldy, could be the next place he tries.'

'But where is he going now?' probed Ralph.

'That does not concern you, boy.'

Naldy felt a weight settle on her mind. Would Maverick really seek her out if his current journey turned out to be fruitless?

'Do not trouble yourself,' said Betty kindly, reaching across the table to place a warm hand on Naldy's arm. 'We will finish searching the Witch House together, and I'll ensure Maverick learns there are no Devante here. I doubt he'll bother coming if he hears we've ended up empty-handed. Now, let's eat and drink. I'm eager to hear all about your travels in Edengar.'

They regaled Betty with an in-depth account of their journey through the mountains. The sweet and salty pie, paired with the spiced brew, eased them into a relaxed state as the hours slipped by peacefully.

'Oh, and Ralph is a wizard,' added Naldy, almost forgetting.

'A wizard?' said Betty, intrigued.

'Apparently,' remarked Ralph, a little bitterly. Naldy knew he was still sour about his inability to produce any magic.

'I think your visit calls for dessert, Betty,' said

Naldy, raising a palm. '*Arcesso.*'

The pantry door opened, and a tin of shortbread cookies glided across the room. Betty caught the tin mid-flight and happily removed the lid, her wrinkled cheeks stretching into a smile as she bit into one of the biscuits.

'You have quite the talent with food, Naldy,' said Betty, already picking out a second cookie before finishing her first.

'I don't think I'll ever get the hang of being a wizard,' said Ralph, picking up his goblet. 'I haven't managed to do any magic at all.'

'Except knocking me into the wall when I tried to stun your Imporiom.'

'But not any magic I've had *control* over,' said Ralph, glancing briefly at Naldy. 'Maybe you could help me with it, Betty?'

'Of course,' replied Betty kindly, reaching into the tin again. 'There'll be plenty of time for training. I think I might be able to help you, Ralph. But first, we should focus on finishing the search through this house.'

'Who have you sent to follow Maverick?' asked Ralph, trying his luck again now that Betty had consumed a few shortbreads.

'I won't give you their names,' said Betty, her glassy eyes widening with seriousness. 'You must trust me. They are exceptional witches, and they will not let Maverick destroy any more Devante.'

Naldy's chest tightened as she noticed Ralph staring remorsefully into his brew. They had failed to protect the Devante.

'Well, we'll get through the rest of the rooms quickly enough,' said Naldy, trying to inject some lightness back into the conversation. 'Especially with three of us. I'm glad you're here, Betty, and that you've found someone more… appropriate… to finish the search.'

Naldy had spent countless hours longing for their quest to be over, and now that the end seemed near, a sense of calm washed over her.

'I'll go and have one of the spare rooms set up for you,' said Naldy, collecting their empty plates and carrying them to the sink.

'I'm glad you're here too,' Ralph added warmly. 'Even if it does mean the end of our quest.'

The next few days were hot, and even with all the windows thrown open, the house remained stuffy. They spent most of their time cooped up in the humid, cluttered rooms, sorting through mountains of disordered junk.

Naldy suspected that Ralph was deliberately working slower than usual, hoping to delay the inevitable end of their hunt for the Devante. His mood soured with each passing day, and it didn't help that both Naldy and Betty could use magic to sift through the chaos, while Ralph had yet to produce a spark.

In the evenings, when the weather cooled, Naldy and Betty spent their time happily chatting, sipping brew, or preparing dinner together. Meanwhile, Ralph remained hunched over the round table, poring over a spellbook. He spent hours translating Olde Witchery, despite both Naldy's and Betty's insistence that it wasn't necessary. Ralph would stack his notes into a neat pile during dinner, only to spread them out again as soon as the plates were cleared. He often practised well into the night.

'You're trying to cram an entire childhood of learning into a few days,' Naldy remarked one evening during dinner.

'I don't want to waste time,' replied Ralph, dunking a chunk of freshly baked bread into his pot of gravy. 'I want to master it. Betty, you said you might be able to help me?'

'I will, yes,' said Betty, smiling at her dinner plate. 'There'll be plenty of time to master your magic, Ralph. But first, we should finish our treasure hunt.'

Two weeks quickly passed since Betty's arrival. The weather turned cold, with grey clouds blanketing the sky. They moved from room to room, shutting windows and drawing curtains to keep the warmth in. The Witch House was no cleaner—if anything, the clutter seemed more disorderly than ever. Trunks had been turned inside out, and the junk merely shifted from one side to the other.

The kitchen was their final room. Naldy was confident they wouldn't find any Devante hidden amongst the kitchenware, but Betty insisted on finishing the job properly.

Ralph had never looked more downcast now that they had reached their last day of searching.

'Don't be sad, Ralph,' said Naldy once night had

fallen, making a weak attempt to cheer him up. They'd reached the final cupboard in the kitchen. 'I told you from the start we wouldn't find it here.'

While Betty and Naldy shifted things around in the pantry, Ralph absentmindedly flipped through a pile of old, yellowing cooking spellbooks.

'It's not the Devante that's weighing on me,' said Ralph.

'Then what is it?'

'It's been weeks now,' he replied, tossing aside the spellbook he was holding. 'I haven't managed to shift even the thinnest parchment.'

'Oh, Ralph,' said Naldy, walking over to him. 'You don't need to worry about whether you can do it— it's just a matter of time.'

Before Ralph could reply, a knock echoed from the front door.

'I'm not expecting anyone,' said Naldy, as Betty glanced around nervously from the pantry.

The front door creaked open, and someone had managed to let themselves into the Witch House.

'Who is it?' Naldy called out, her eyes fixed warily on the open arch leading to the hall. She didn't dare move closer to see who the intruder was. Like Ralph and Betty, she froze, waiting.

Then came the sound of footsteps—but there was another sound, making the hairs on Naldy's neck prickle: the dull clunk of wood on wood.

Naldy instinctively raised her palms, outstretched and ready. Their newest guest rounded the corner calmly, stepping into the kitchen's archway.

'Maverick?' Ralph gasped, his voice thin with fear.

Naldy tried to speak, but no words came out. It wasn't for lack of effort—she wanted to cast a spell to stun him, but her voice had abandoned her. Maverick must have hexed her in some way.

'Here we are all together again,' Maverick said softly, leaning casually on his black cane.

It wasn't just Naldy's mouth that wouldn't move. Her feet were stuck to the ground as well. She could tilt her head and sway her arms, but she knew that would not defend her against the wizard.

Maverick's pale face came into the light of a flickering candle, his cold black eyes narrowing as he stared unflinchingly at her. Then, breaking their shared glower, he turned his attention to Betty, who stood nearby.

'You have carried out your work wonderfully, Barbra.'

'Barbra?' Ralph managed to say. Unlike Naldy, he could still speak, though his limbs were clearly immobilised.

Naldy's mind was making quick work of deciphering the moment. The old, innocent-looking woman standing beside the pantry wasn't Betty—it was her twin sister, Barbra. Had she been sent to carry out Maverick's plan, to search Naldy's home in the hope of seizing another Devante?

'You're early,' said Barbra warmly, smiling at Maverick. 'Regardless, neither book is hidden here, Maverick. The place has been turned inside out.'

'How could you betray us!' snapped Ralph. 'You lying witch!'

'The boy is a wizard,' remarked Barbra calmly, her attention fixed on her accomplice.

'A wizard?' Maverick repeated, his curiosity piqued.

'An untrained wizard. He couldn't float a feather if his life depended on it, so you needn't worry.'

'You let us go,' spat Ralph, struggling against the immobilising spell. 'You let us go now!'

'Precautions never go astray,' said Maverick, tapping his cane ominously.

Ralph fell silent, and Naldy surmised that Maverick had hit him with the same silencing spell she was under.

Unlike her, Barbra and Maverick were Effangales and could simply think the words of a spell to produce magic without uttering a sound. Naldy knew they had little chance of escaping.

'You are quite right, girl,' said Maverick, as if reading her thoughts, seating himself casually at her table. 'You have no chance of escaping, even if you could speak. Do come and join me at the table.'

Naldy's body moved towards the table of its own accord, her limbs betraying her will. No matter how hard she tried, she couldn't stop them. Ralph, too, was moving to sit at the table, his face a mixture of confusion and wonder.

Naldy had never seen magic like this before, and it only took her a moment to realise that it must have been the work of the Aurum. A thought crossed her mind—had Barbra's betrayal not been her own decision? Was she merely carrying out Maverick's orders under the Aurum's influence?

'She acted of her own accord,' said Maverick, as if plucking the question from Naldy's mind. Barbra made her way over to the pantry.

'You can read my thoughts?' Naldy said aloud, surprised to find her voice had returned. She tried to lift her palms, but they wouldn't move.

'It is of no use trying to obstruct me,' said Maverick as he placed his black cane—his Imporiom —on the kitchen table. 'The Aurum has been in my possession for some time now, and as the second-highest-ranking Devante, it is proving to be quite... co-operative. They say first, second, and third are the most coveted.'

'Please, let us go,' said Ralph quietly. 'We don't have any of the Devante.'

'You see,' continued Maverick coolly as Barbra returned from the pantry carrying the tin of shortbread biscuits. 'You may speak and move freely, but only if your intention is not to harm me. And while the Devante will not allow me to take control of your thoughts directly—'

'Pity,' added Barbra, as shortbread crumbs fell onto her cloak.

'It has allowed me to access them while I am in the room with you, and I can hear exactly what you are thinking.'

'Barbra, please,' said Ralph desperately. 'He destroyed your book, and you mustn't help him.'

'You silly boy,' said Barbra, glaring at Ralph. 'You forget it was I who intercepted your message. My sister's and my messages are often delivered to each other by accident, a common error experienced amongst twins. I took your message directly to Maverick myself.'

'But why would you do that?' said Ralph, reaching into his pocket and placing the list of the Devante onto the kitchen table between them. 'There's proof! He destroyed your book Metallum! Look! It is gone, and *he* did it.'

Naldy stared at the parchment resting beside Maverick's cane. Only two Devante were listed: the Aurum, which she knew Maverick possessed, and the Corium. Another Devante was missing. Naldy's heart sank. They had foolishly not checked the list since Barbra's arrival because the old woman had convinced them that a team of witches was trailing Maverick. She felt silly for ever believing it.

'It's gone,' said Naldy numbly.

'You destroyed Lignum?' asked Ralph, horrified.

'Me?' Maverick replied, aghast. 'I did no such thing! It was the two of you that destroyed it.'

'We're trying to protect them,' said Naldy, taken aback. She turned urgently to face Barbra. 'He's lying to you. We didn't destroy—'

'You did!' said Barbra, sharply cutting across Naldy. 'I've seen how desperate you both are, particularly the untrained wizard, wanting to find the Devante. Hungry for them! I know you persuaded my sister, Betty, to tell you where her books and mine were. Then you went after them and destroyed them.'

Naldy wanted to tell Barbra the truth—that Maverick was a liar and had destroyed the Devante— but her mouth betrayed her once more and wouldn't open. She knew Maverick's spell was preventing her from saying anything more.

'They are on a mission,' said Maverick gravely, 'to destroy the Devante. But now that you have searched the house with them, Barbra, we know there are no Devante here.'

'I've done my part,' said Barbra, her tone clipped as she addressed Maverick. 'You will keep your word, won't you?'

'I wouldn't dare break it,' replied Maverick convincingly. 'The Aurum is yours, as promised.'

There was an intense pause. Barbra was waiting for Maverick to relinquish the Aurum.

'But before...' said Maverick, turning away from Barbra to meet Naldy and Ralph with his black eyes. 'Let's make this quick and painless, shall we? Tell me where the Corium is.'

I don't know, thought Naldy.

Maverick curled his lip into a sneer as he scrutinised her.

I really don't know where it is, thought Naldy again.

'It seems I'll have to force it from you,' he said, picking up his cane. 'And I will not be so lenient this time.'

Before Maverick could inflict any pain, Barbra

interjected.

'I won't wait, Maverick,' insisted Barbra restlessly. 'I have played my part dutifully, and I expect you to hold to your word. Pass over the Aurum. I do not like to be kept waiting.'

Maverick surveyed Barbra's wrinkled face. She didn't flinch under his gaze but stared doggedly back with her piercing grey eyes.

The chaos that ensued began suddenly. Both witch and wizard were Effangales, so green and black light shot across the room without the usual forewarning of a spell being uttered.

Barbra and Maverick leapt out of the line of fire, while Naldy tried to move but couldn't. Maverick's spell had forced her and Ralph to remain dangerously perched in their seats.

Spells shot around the room, narrowly missing their hot-headed targets and colliding with Naldy's pots and pans, creating ear-splitting clangs.

'You think you can beat me?' shouted Barbra, throwing her old body out of the way of an oncoming green flash.

'Oh, I've been playing nice because you're an old woman,' spat Maverick bitterly, sending a red jet of light speeding towards Barbra. It collided instead with the door of Naldy's pantry, sending splinters of wood flying.

'I should never have trusted you,' snapped Barbra. Her black spell rebounded off a small cauldron and hurtled towards the window, shattering the glass. 'You made me believe you were protecting them, and now you'll pay the price for your betrayal.'

Naldy and Ralph could only swivel their heads; it was a miracle none of the spells had touched them.

'My plans are nearly complete,' said Maverick, gracefully dodging a rich blue ball of whizzing light. 'There is one Devante left to find, and mark my words, I will find it, and I will'—he deflected another of Barbra's spells—'change the world as we know it.'

Maverick skilfully sent a black spell rocketing towards Barbra. She was too slow, and it collided with her chest. The old witch fell to the kitchen floor with a thud and lay motionless.

'Nobody should have access to this much power,' uttered Maverick scornfully, standing over Barbra's body as he ran a hand through his greasy black hair.

Surprisingly, the list of Devante still rested in the centre of the kitchen table. It caught Naldy's eye amongst the broken furniture and shattered kitchenware because it had burst into flames. Maverick seemed unaware, which was understandable considering the state of Naldy's kitchen—it was far worse than any of the messy rooms they'd spent months rummaging through.

Ralph was staring at the flames now licking the wood of the kitchen table, but he didn't appear worried—in fact, he seemed overjoyed.

'You're an Effangale wizard,' said Maverick curiously, finally noticing the burning parchment. 'But unless you tell me where the Corium is located, sadly, you won't live long enough to master your skills.'

Ralph had obviously tried to cast a fireball at Maverick, but had only managed to set the parchment alight instead.

Maverick pointed his black cane at the round wooden table, and it was instantly engulfed in large, red-hot flames.

'Tell me where it is,' called Maverick over the roar of the fire. 'And I'll put it out.'

'We don't know,' said Naldy desperately, her voice returning.

'I shall leave you both here to burn. Tell me.'

'Please, we don't know,' she pleaded. 'We really don't!'

The flames were dancing alarmingly close to their bodies now, and Naldy could feel the hot air from the fire stinging her skin. Breathing was becoming difficult as thick smoke filled the kitchen.

But I really don't know, thought Naldy, struggling to take in air.

'So, you've always been telling the truth,' said Maverick, sneering as he turned to leave the kitchen. 'If you don't know, I have no use for either of you.'

'Wait!' Ralph shouted after him, his voice thin from the smoke in his lungs. 'Don't leave us.'

Maverick was gone. The roaring flames spread along the wooden floor as Naldy heard the front door close behind him.

'I can't move,' said Naldy, struggling to speak. 'You'll have to... undo...'

'I don't know how,' said Ralph as a large flame

leapt from the table, beginning to consume the pantry. Barbra lay unconscious nearby, dangerously close to the disintegrating shelves.

'Ralph,' said Naldy impatiently, 'you lit the fire without moving your palms or using your voice... If Maverick... is right... you are an Effangale.' She paused, gasping for breath as smoke swirled around the room. 'You don't need... your palms. Try *Exstinguere.*'

'*Exstinguere,*' said Ralph aloud, but nothing happened. Neither Ralph nor Naldy could move from their kitchen chairs. The fire was now creeping up the walls.

Smookers rushed into the room, meowing frantically, as if ordering her to move. He paced helplessly.

'Try *Turbatus Venti.*'

'*Turbatus Venti,*' cried Ralph, but still, nothing happened. '*Turbatus Venti... Exstinguere.*'

Smookers' meows grew louder and more urgent as the vivid orange flames danced through the thickening smoke.

'Yes, I know, Smookers,' said Naldy before being overcome by a fit of coughing.

Smookers stopped pacing and raised one paw, distressed. His ears drooped sadly as he turned and fled from the house.

'*Exstinguere,*' said Ralph hoarsely. 'I can't....'

Naldy felt lightheaded as the fire rapidly engulfed the room. The red flames burned through the kitchen ceiling, and the smoke became so thick that

Naldy could no longer draw air into her lungs. She couldn't speak or breathe. Maverick had left them to die.

Then, she felt herself lift into the air. She was gliding above the flickering red and roaring orange, through the fire and smoke.

Everything went dark.

—*Chapter Four*—

FOLLOWING FIRE

Naldy heard the sound of rain on water. Though her hearing had returned, her sight had not. She wondered whether she was sitting beside a river or a lake. The pit-pattering was soothing, and it relaxed her.

She could feel the wood of the kitchen chair beneath her, and although Naldy could hear the rain, she couldn't feel it on her skin. Her body felt warm—hot, even—and she wondered if the sun was shining.

'Naldy?' she heard a voice say. When the voice spoke again, she recognised it as Ralph's. 'You're awake.'

When Naldy opened her eyes, she realised she wasn't sitting beside a lake or a river, it wasn't raining, and the sun wasn't shining.

She was perched beneath the trees at the edge of the Kirkwood Forest, still sitting on her kitchen chair. It was night-time, and the pit-pattering sound she had heard was the crackle of the enormous fire consuming the Witch House.

'I'm so sorry,' said Ralph, standing beside her, fiddling apprehensively with the sleeve of his cloak as he took in the sight before them. The fire was reflected in his emerald earring. 'I tried several spells to put it out, but I couldn't manage it.'

Naldy stood, keeping a hand on the kitchen chair to steady herself. Her limbs felt weak. The building was beyond saving, and the fire looked like it had been burning for some time. Even from this distance, the heat pressed against her skin. She wanted to cry, but the shock of seeing her family home engulfed in flames seemed to stunt any expression of grief.

'I'm so sorry, Naldy,' said Ralph gently.

Naldy couldn't find the energy to speak. She noticed Smookers sitting beside Ralph's feet, unmoving, watching the fire consume the two-storey building. The three of them stood like this for some time, black smoke billowing upwards, stretching high over the tall pines of the forest. The fire roared as the junk-filled rooms continually fed it. Occasionally, a loud popping noise came from deep within the blaze.

It felt almost dreamlike to Naldy. Some time passed before she spoke.

'Where's Barbra?' she asked softly.

'I couldn't go back for her,' Ralph replied quietly. 'It was too late.'

Though Naldy knew Barbra had betrayed them, she still felt sad to learn she had perished in the fire.

'Who saved us?' asked Naldy weakly.

'I did,' said Ralph, as Smookers wound fondly around his legs. 'I think the intensity of the situation forced the magic to work. I used it to carry you. But once we were out, I couldn't do anything more. I tried to whip up dust to extinguish the fire, but I couldn't even move a leaf.'

'I knew you would manage it eventually. You'll be able to do magic again. You probably just need to rest.'

'I don't know where Maverick went,' said Ralph, running his fingers over the emerald earring. 'I think he finally believes us, that we don't know where the Corium is located. I'm not sure what made him believe us in the end, but I don't think we need to worry about him anymore. Judging by the trail of that smoke, he probably thinks we're both dead.'

'He penetrated my thoughts,' said Naldy. 'I think Maverick knew I couldn't lie to myself. We're lucky to be alive.'

'I'm sorry I contacted Betty,' Ralph said, his voice tense with self-reproach. 'I didn't realise the message would be intercepted by Barbra. I mean, I know Betty said not to—oh, Naldy—I was so stupid. I'm sorry.'

Tears trickled down Naldy's face. A deep sadness washed over her, weighing heavily.

'I've really messed things up, Naldy.'

'It's okay, Ralph,' she said feebly. She knelt and picked Smookers up from the ground. 'What's done is done. Let's make our way into town and find somewhere to sleep. I'm exhausted.'

Naldy turned her back on the heat of the burning house, walking beneath the tall pine trees where the air was cool. Ralph trailed behind her, but he kept his distance. Naldy was glad of this, as she didn't feel like talking.

They followed the dirt road, zigzagging through the forest. Tears continued to drip down Naldy's cheeks as she walked, her legs numb.

The forest was unusually dark, and when Naldy looked up at the sky, she saw a thick cloud of black smoke shrouding the moon. Anxiety gripped her, and her heart ached as she watched the smoke swirl across the night sky.

The Witch House had been in her family for centuries. But it wasn't just the many years of hoarded relics, passed down through generations, that Naldy was mourning—she was grieving the loss of her parents. Naldy had been twelve years old when her mum and dad left one evening and never returned. She had always thought they might come home one day, but now there was no home for them to return to.

'Wait, Naldy! There!'

She turned to see Ralph pointing at the dirt road ahead, where a small, contained fire flickered.

'It's probably some burning debris that floated across on the wind,' said Naldy impatiently.

'What if it's Maverick?' Ralph remarked tensely. 'I doubt debris would have floated this far, Naldy. It looks more like a campfire to me.'

'You think Maverick is camping out?' said Naldy flatly. 'It doesn't seem like his style.'

Naldy turned away from Ralph, and continued

along the narrow road, unafraid. She hoped the small fire was unattended, as she wasn't in the mood for small talk with travellers.

As they neared the fire, the smell of burning flesh assaulted their nostrils.

'Oh my,' said Ralph, horror spreading across his face. 'What is that?'

As she approached, Naldy realised it was some kind of large animal burning. The bitter scent of searing meat mingled with the putrid stench of charring skin, bones, and entrails.

'What is it?' asked Ralph.

'I'm not sure,' she replied.

Smookers hissed at the nearby trees.

'Look,' Ralph said, pointing into the thicket.

An animal slightly larger than a hog stood watching them sadly from the trees. The beast had a large udder, its skin a hairless, thick grey leather. Its elongated, almost mouse-like face was pointed downward, tears glistening in its eyes.

'It's a leagon,' Naldy said. 'They often travel in pairs.'

She was shocked someone had killed its companion. People usually tried to capture them for their milk, which was sugary and sweet—a delicacy. But the hog-like beasts were quick. Some towns kept herds of leagons for their supply of syrupy milk. Their meat, however, was tough and as leathery as their skin, making it unsuitable for eating—so why had this beast been slain?

'Who would do such a thing?' asked Ralph.

The animal had not been dead long. Its companion grunted in distress, pressing its hooves into the dirt. The leagon didn't dare approach any closer, remaining in the shadows of the trees.

'Can we please keep going? I can't stand the smell,' Ralph said, holding his nose.

'Do you think Maverick did it?' asked Naldy, staring into the fire. 'It was done by some wizard or witch. Those are not ordinary flames—magic is involved.'

'Let's keep going,' he said nervously. 'I don't want to stay on this road any longer than we have to, and I've seen enough fire for one day.'

Ralph and Smookers continued along the road, but Naldy lingered, her gaze fixed on the leagon. She wondered why anyone would do such a terrible thing to such a beautiful creature.

An hour later, they reached the town of Frubry and checked into one of the dwellings, *The Lichen*. Naldy was relieved to climb between the warm sheets, with Smookers curled up at the foot of her bed. She tried to sleep, but the image of the burning leagon remained vividly etched in her mind, keeping her awake.

Early the following day, they made their way to the dwelling's bar for breakfast. Naldy wiped her sore, sleepy eyes as she sipped her brew. The dwelling was a cosy place—clean, warm, and welcoming.

'How'd you sleep?' asked Ralph, taking a bite of his toast.

Naldy ignored him. She had spent part of the night crying into her pillow, trying her best not to wake him. Now, she wondered if she had kept him awake.

'You should eat something,' said Ralph tenderly.

'I'm not hungry,' she replied truthfully. Her appetite had abandoned her.

'Naldy, I know it won't make up for what I've done,' began Ralph delicately. 'I know it's my fault Maverick found us, and I started the fire—'

'Ralph, please,' she said in a tired voice. 'I don't feel like talking.'

'But I just want to say that I will help you rebuild. I feel horrible. I want to make it up to you. I know it won't fix everything, but—'

'I should take some food up to Smookers,' Naldy interrupted, collecting some fried fish from the breakfast board and placing it onto her empty plate.

'Wait, Naldy, I want to say—'

'I'm not in the mood, Ralph,' Naldy snapped sharply, picking up her plate and leaving the table.

She made her way to the room they were lodging in. It was spacious, with two identical twin beds and a large window letting in ample sunlight. Her cat, Smookers, was curled comfortably on the edge of Ralph's bed. As Naldy entered, Smookers lifted his small head curiously before jumping down excitedly at the smell of fried fish.

She placed the plate on the floor, and Smookers eagerly licked at the fish, clearly delighted. Naldy climbed onto her bed, resting on the cool sheets.

Her head felt heavy as it settled on the pillow—her emotions still raw from the events of the previous night.

She knew Ralph wasn't entirely to blame; eventually, Maverick would probably have found the Witch House regardless of whether Ralph's message had been intercepted. She appreciated his offer to help rebuild her family home—it was a kind gesture. Still, Naldy understood that rebuilding wouldn't be the same. It wouldn't bring back the house where she had grown up, where she had created so many fond memories.

'What are we going to do now, Smookers?' asked Naldy quietly. Smookers, too busy enjoying his breakfast, paid her no attention.

When Naldy closed her eyes, she found herself sitting by a large white window sill. A small leather book was propped on her lap, and sunlight streamed pleasantly through the open window. She could see a stretch of slightly overgrown green grass leading to the edge of Kirkwood Forest.

'Naldy, put the book away. It's time for us to go.'

Naldy turned to see a tall woman with angular features and black hair reaching her lower back. At thirty-six, Naldy's mother, Tarren, still had a kind, youthful face.

'I don't want to go, mum,' said twelve-year-old Naldy, her voice sulky. 'I don't like him. He scares me.'

'Oak is not scary,' replied Naldy's mother, bending to pluck the spellbook from her lap. 'It's a glorious day outside. Let's not spend it cooped up indoors.'

Naldy begrudgingly followed her mother to the wooden front door of the Witch House, where she fished out her favourite flying boots from the crowded shoe rack. Most of the shoes had been abandoned, collecting dust and cobwebs.

'Why do you have two?' asked Naldy as her mother retrieved two old brooms from the broomstick holder.

'Because today I thought you could lead the way,' her mother said kindly.

'Me?'

'I've seen you practising your flying, and you are getting quite good, Naldy.'

'Yes, but I don't think I could fly over Kirkwood Forest by myself.'

Naldy finished fastening her flying boots, and then her mother handed her one of the old broomsticks. They stepped outside, and the sun warmed their skin.

'I'm not sure I really remember the way,' said Naldy nervously.

'I'm sure it'll come to you,' her mother reassured her, mounting her own broomstick. 'I'll be right behind you, darling.'

Naldy had flown the route they were to take many times. She had always enjoyed whizzing over the Kirkwood Forest, but she'd always been perched safely on her mother's broom.

'I don't want to fly by myself,' said Naldy

anxiously. 'Why can't I come with you, like I usually do?'

'One day,' said Tarren gently. 'You might need to visit Oak by yourself.'

'I'll never visit Oak by myself. I hate that lump of wood! You go. I'll stay here and read my spellbook.'

'Naldy,' said Tarren, in a tone she knew meant she wouldn't be allowed to stay behind.

'You'll be right behind me?'

Naldy's mother smiled tenderly. Naldy mounted her broomstick, lifting her leg over. She gripped the handle and hovered in the air for a moment, giving her mother one last pleading look, trying to convey her insecurity. Tarren simply smiled back encouragingly.

Twelve-year-old Naldy kicked off the ground, shooting upwards. Her broomstick rose above the tall pine trees. The brilliant blue sky and the round yellow sun drew nearer, easing her worries. She felt a sense of autonomy she had never experienced—at least not like this, not this unencumbered, this free. Peering down in search of a familiar landmark, Naldy was surprised she could recognise the clustered towns below. She spotted the roof of an old house and the distinctive pattern of a cobbled street. Confident she was flying in the right direction, her heart leapt with joy, and instinctively, she steered her broom to the left.

The air on her face was comforting as they flew over narrow dirt roads embedded amongst the green pine trees below. Naldy felt disappointed when the small clearing where Oak was situated came into view—she wished the flight had been longer.

Glancing behind to ensure her mother was still close, Naldy pointed the tip of her broom towards the clearing.

Oak's enormous grey boughs stretched upwards, reaching for the sun. His branches were bare, and his soot-coloured bark stood out starkly against the backdrop of green pines.

Naldy touched down smoothly, and her mother landed softly beside her.

Oak always slept during the daytime. His moss-green eyes and bird's-hollow mouth were closed. He could have passed for an ordinary oak tree, if not for the enormous red spellbook lodged high up in his finger-like branches. The book belonged to Naldy's family.

'We shouldn't wake him up,' whispered Naldy to her mother. 'I've proven I can find the tree. Let's fly home now and let him sleep.'

Tarren placed a warm hand on Naldy's shoulder before turning to face the tree.

'Oak,' Naldy's mother called loudly. At once, the tree opened his bird-hollow mouth in a wide yawn. Two thick branches lowered themselves— one holding the spellbook, the other stretching. Moments ago, the tree's eyes had seemed like mere jutting twists in the wood, but now they flicked open, fixing on them from above.

'Tarren,' the tree said in his drum-like voice,

peering down his long, slanted wooden nose. 'I wasn't expecting you for at least another half hour.'

'She surpassed my expectations,' replied Tarren, squeezing Naldy's shoulder.

'And how are you, Naldy?' asked the oak tree.

'Fine,' said Naldy, positioning herself partly behind her mother. She didn't want to get too close, but she didn't want to appear cowardly either.

'It is never too early to begin these lessons,' said the tree to Tarren. 'If you want my opinion, you've left it quite late. You should be training her in advanced magic.'

'Oak, let's take one step at a time.'

'She will need to be prepared.'

'She's twelve years old, Oak,' said Tarren sternly. 'Let's celebrate her achievement in successfully navigating her way here. There will be plenty of time for other lessons. We'll take them steadily.'

'You don't want to leave these things too late,' remarked Oak warningly.

Naldy was unsettled by their conversation. As much as she had enjoyed leading the way to Oak, she didn't feel ready to take on advanced magic.

'I think I've done enough for one day,' said Naldy confidently as she stepped out from behind her mother.

A little surprised, the oak tree lowered his moss-green eyes as his bark lips stretched into a slight smile.

'You have, yes,' said Oak kindly. 'Because you've done such a wonderful job flying here, Naldy, I think it's only fair you should have a reward. You can pick a spell from your family's book.'

'We've already got spellbooks at home,' said Naldy indifferently.

'Well, yes,' said Oak with a chuckle. 'But if you think of something, you can always fly here and ask me, alright?'

Naldy noticed a white bird with grey wings flying down from the sky. It landed in Oak's higher branches, its yellow beak pointed in their direction. It took Naldy a moment to recognise the bird as a seagull. She found it strange, being so far from the seaside. Oak didn't seem to mind, or perhaps he hadn't noticed the seabird resting atop his branches.

Naldy drew in a deep breath. She was lying on the cotton sheets of a twin bed. She must have fallen asleep, still fully clothed. The room was dark, but she could hear Ralph's soft, snoring breaths. Moonlight cast a dim glow across the room, and Naldy could just make out the shadowy shape of Smookers curled up by Ralph's feet.

Her thoughts churned over the dream—*but had it really been a dream? No, surely it had been a memory, one she had forgotten until now.*

Her parents had left when she was twelve years old, so the memory must have been from before their unexpected disappearance. The only dreamlike aspect was the presence of the seagull—Naldy couldn't recall ever seeing a seabird in Kirkwood Forest.

She shut her eyes, wanting to forget the Witch

House had burnt to the ground and that there was no home to return to. She tried to clear her mind, but after sleeping through the entire day, she no longer felt tired.

Naldy climbed out of bed, pulled on her travelling cloak and made her way to the main bar of the dwelling. It was dark and deserted. The dwellingtend had long since closed the bar and retired for the evening.

She crossed the empty bar and stepped outside, hoping the cool night air would make her sleepy again. Naldy strolled along the large cobbled street. The lamplights, spaced at intervals along the road, were burning low. Some hadn't survived the cold air and had long since been extinguished.

The streets were empty, and the moon hung high in the sky. It must have been quite late. The wooden cottages lining the road were submerged in darkness. Naldy was glad to be alone. She sauntered along until the houses gave way to open pastures, and the cobbled street became a dusty dirt road. The tall forest trees loomed like great, imposing shadows in the night. She had reached the last open pasture on the edge of town, flanked by towering pines.

Naldy turned to head back—but stopped when she noticed several dark spots scattered across the nearby grassland. A lone wooden cottage stood in the centre of the pasture. There must have been at least fifteen, maybe even twenty, of these strange black patches dotted around the field. Curious, Naldy approached the fence to investigate more closely. The dark blotches were the charred remains of small fires. She climbed over the wooden fence and approached the nearest black pit. Squinting, she saw large, blackened bones resting in the centre of the scorched grass.

'Leagons,' whispered Naldy to herself, feeling sickened.

She wondered if the farmer had killed them. Had the leagons fallen ill with some terrible disease? Maybe the farmer had been left with no choice.

Naldy also wondered if it was the same farmer responsible for the burning leagon she and Ralph had seen the previous night.

The sight churned her stomach. She climbed back over the fence and hurried along the road towards the town's dwelling.

Later, when Naldy settled back into her comfortable bed, all she could think about were the skeletons of the leagons. Her thoughts kept her awake well into the night. Who would do such a horrendous thing? Why had the leagons been murdered in such a horrible way?

When morning finally came, it brought a warm sun, which was at odds with how Naldy felt inside. She felt cold and unsettled, disturbed by what she had seen in the field the night before and by the memory of the Witch House burning down.

'It's such a beautiful day,' said Ralph as they ate breakfast in the dwelling's bar.

'How is your magic coming along?' asked Naldy, wanting to distract herself from her thoughts.

Ralph scrunched his face up.

'I really am sorry, Naldy,' he said, chewing his food more slowly than usual. 'I wish I could have done more to save the Witch House.'

'It's okay, Ralph,' said Naldy, buttering her toast. 'We have our lives, and that's what's most important. Have you been practising?'

'A little. I've been thinking we should return to the edge of Kirkwood today and start building a new house for you.'

'There'll be time for that,' said Naldy softly. 'But there are some things we need to take care of first.'

'If it's about the Devante...'

Neither had mentioned the Devante since they arrived in Frubry.

'I've been thinking a lot,' said Naldy earnestly.

'Well, there's something I want you to know,' said Ralph delicately. 'I've decided to give up the quest. You've been right all along. It was foolish of me to want to keep searching for the books. It's caused heartache and trouble.'

'Give up the quest?' repeated Naldy, putting down her buttered toast. A wrinkled woman at a nearby table caught her attention—she was dressed in a grubby skirt that reached her ankles and was sipping a glass of syrupy milk. Naldy knew from its thick consistency that it was leagon milk. She tried not to think about the pockmarked field.

'Yes, Naldy,' said Ralph, noticing he didn't have her full attention. 'Looking for the Devante has brought nothing but grief, and I think the destruction of your family home was the last straw. There's only the Corium left now, and we know Maverick has no idea where it's hidden. He wouldn't have sent Barbra to snoop around if he knew where it was, and I'm convinced he'll never find it.'

'It's not the *only* Devante left,' said Naldy, leaning back in her chair.

'What do you mean?'

'There's still the Aurum. Maverick still has that.'

'Yes,' said Ralph dismissively, 'but it ranks lower than the Corium, and Maverick can't use the Aurum to find the Corium.'

'He's not going to stop hunting them,' said Naldy, brushing the crumbs from her fingers. 'And I know this might come as a surprise because I wanted to abandon our search, but I've changed my mind. We shouldn't give up the hunt.'

'You and I have proven we're no match for Maverick,' said Ralph, leaning forward in his chair. 'I think you were right to abandon the hunt. Someone else will have to finish the job.'

'I don't want your help rebuilding the Witch House, Ralph. I need your help with the Devante,' said Naldy, crossing her arms. The woman in the grubby skirt finished her glass of milk and tottered out of the dwelling. 'I won't give up. I can't. Not now, after losing so much because of it.'

'We don't have any real chance of finding the Corium,' said Ralph.

'But we do know where the Aurum is.'

'You want to steal the Aurum from Maverick?'

asked Ralph, glancing nervously around the bar. Though there were only a few other patrons, he lowered his voice. 'Have you lost your mind, Naldy? A day ago, you were ready to walk away, and now you want to steal the Aurum from Maverick?'

'Will you help me or not?'

'Don't you see, Naldy, we're both free.'

'Free?'

'Maverick finally believes you don't know where the Corium is located,' said Ralph, nodding. 'He probably thinks we perished in the fire, so we're both free to walk away without the looming threat of Maverick coming after us.'

'I don't want to walk away,' said Naldy, watching as the dwellingtend collected the empty glass of milk. 'I've changed my mind. I want to finish what we started. I want to stop him, Ralph. Are you going to help me or not?'

Ralph hesitated, and Naldy worried he had lost his enthusiasm for the quest.

'I'll continue on myself,' said Naldy.

'Of course, I'll help you,' said Ralph quickly, a nervous excitement in his voice. 'So, we'll track Maverick down and take the Aurum from him?'

'Yes. But before we go looking for Maverick, there are some things we need to do first.'

'What things?'

'We need to pay Betty a visit.'

Chapter Five

THE BANNED SPELLS

After visiting the local Treasury to refill their drawstring pouches with currents, they purchased new black travelling cloaks, a sturdy broom, and a few other supplies in Frubry before setting off. The sky was bruised a purplish pink when they landed the broomstick outside Betty's house in Heatherton.

It had been a pleasant flight, and both Naldy and Ralph were filled with anticipation and joy at the thought of seeing Betty.

Smookers had been curled comfortably on the broom's end behind Ralph, asleep for most of the journey. Once they landed, he jumped off and stretched, arching his back sleepily.

'It is nice being in Heatherton again,' said Ralph, using his fingers to tidy his windswept hair.

'You seem more at ease on the back of a broom now,' Naldy commented as they walked up the path of Betty's well-kept front garden.

'I still miss that old carpet of mine,' said Ralph. 'I wonder if Maverick still has it.'

Before knocking on the door, Naldy glanced up

the wide cobblestone street. From Betty's doorstep, she could see Barbra's decrepit house at the far end. Unlike Betty's well-kept home, with its neatly trimmed garden and immaculately maintained exterior, Barbra's looked abandoned, held together by little more than flaking paint and rusted nails. The front garden was choked with unchecked weeds.

Ralph shuddered, and Naldy knew he must have been thinking of the time he had eaten Barbra's poisoned scones.

'Hello there, Smookers,' said Ralph, as the cat wrapped himself fondly around his legs.

Turning back to Betty's front door, Naldy gently knocked, and a wave of jitters rose inside her. The excitement of being in Heatherton had almost made her forget they were bringing bad news. At some point, they'd have to tell Betty that her sister had perished in the fire and that they'd failed to save the Devante in Edengar. They heard footsteps approaching down the hall.

For a brief moment, Naldy considered diving into the bushes beside the house. But it was too late.

'My goodness,' said Betty upon seeing them. 'Come in, come in. Oh, my dears, what a surprise. Such a pleasant surprise.'

Betty ushered them inside, taking their travelling cloaks and hanging them on the cloak rack. Smookers sauntered down the hallway, making himself comfortable.

'I'm so glad to see you both alive,' said Betty,

clasping their shoulders warmly.

Naldy had always known Betty and Barbra were identical in appearance, but she'd forgotten how different their demeanours were. Betty was courteous and welcoming, with kindness in her eyes. Naldy wondered how they had ever allowed themselves to believe Barbra was Betty.

'I've been so worried about you both. It's so good to see you. You've come in time for dinner. I've made a stew, and there's plenty.'

'We have to tell you some things,' said Ralph, lowering his head.

'There'll be plenty of time to talk, but first, come in. I'll serve dinner while it's hot. Let's discuss these things on full stomachs. Follow your cat along the hall—he's got the right idea.'

Naldy couldn't shake her unease. She hoped Ralph would take the lead in delivering the heavy burden of bad news.

The modestly sized kitchen lay at the far end of the hall. Naldy and Ralph had been in this room once before, only briefly, as they rushed through to escape Maverick. The large windows overlooked the small, lovingly nurtured garden they had once flown from in haste.

'Is that Rupert?' asked Ralph in surprise, staring out the kitchen window.

Naldy was stunned to see the tall, handsome man with strawberry-blonde hair pruning a bushy purple flower in the fading light. Betty made her way to the door and called out to him.

'Rupert, dear! We have visitors.'

Rupert raised his chin, then beamed at them.

'Took you both long enough,' said Rupert with a toothy smile as he approached. When he reached the door, he took off his muddy gardening boots. 'Well, tell us, did you save the books?'

'Give them a chance to settle in, Rupert,' said Betty, gently reprimanding him as she made her way to the stove to ladle stew into clean ceramic bowls. 'Come in and close the door. It's getting chilly. Wash your hands, and then give them both a hug.'

'I didn't think you'd be here,' said Naldy as Rupert embraced her fondly. 'I thought you'd be off on your travels.'

'Well, I'm part of the Society now,' said Rupert cheerily, turning to welcome his cousin. 'Aren't you happy to see me?'

'I'm surprised to see you,' Ralph admitted.

'*I'm* surprised to see you,' Rupert echoed with a grin. 'But glad. Extremely glad to see you both alive and looking well.'

'Come on,' Betty said firmly, 'wash your hands and fetch the spoons.'

'What's this Society?' asked Naldy, taking a seat at the rectangular table in the corner.

'The cutlery, please, Rupert,' said Betty as she carried over two bowls and placed them on the table. The sweet, earthy aroma of tomato stew filled the kitchen. After washing his hands, Rupert laid out the silverware, then struck a match and lit the tapered candles.

'I've never seen you so domesticated, Cousin Rupert.'

'Betty kept telling me you'd both likely be dead,' replied Rupert cheekily. 'But I didn't believe a word of it. I knew you'd be alive. You're made of stronger stuff than she gives you credit for.'

He ducked into the pantry and emerged carrying crystal goblets. Betty brought over two more bowls of stew and a carafe of amber brew.

'I won't wait until after we've finished eating,' said Rupert, settling into the seat opposite Naldy. 'You'll have to tell us everything while we eat.'

'We failed,' said Naldy, unable to contain the miserable truth. 'Maverick destroyed Metallum, Rosea, and the Caeruleum—and we failed. He has possession of the Aurum. And there's something more—something worse.'

Betty seemed neither upset nor angry upon hearing the books had been destroyed. She calmly took her seat next to Rupert. Naldy paused, the words lodged in her throat, unsure how to continue. Ralph picked up the conversation.

'Maverick found us because I tried to contact you, Betty,' he admitted, avoiding everyone's gaze. 'I know I shouldn't have. You warned us not to send messages through the Tebellos, and you were right. The message was intercepted by your sister, and... I'm so sorry, but she's gone. There was a fire, and I couldn't save her. She's gone.'

At first, Naldy felt a weight lift now that they'd relayed the horrible news, but a pang of guilt soon set in. Betty picked up her spoon and began to eat her stew. Rupert's smile had faded. The wrinkled woman's expression was difficult to interpret, and a bitter moment passed.

'You should eat while it's hot,' Betty said calmly.

Naldy and Ralph exchanged bewildered looks.

'Eat before it gets cold,' repeated Betty kindly. 'I'm glad to see you both alive. You've been through quite the ordeal, and I'm curious to hear about your travels in more detail. But there's no need for such glum faces. It was a quest that was always bound to fail.'

'But your sister, there was a fire and—'

'She is still alive,' Betty interrupted, reaching down the neck of her woollen jumper and retrieving a white pearl pendant hanging from a thin gold chain. 'This is how I know. Years ago, when I had possession of my Devante, I used it to create this pearl. The pearl will turn black when my sister leaves this world.'

'But she was unconscious,' said Ralph in disbelief. 'The fire ravaged everything, and it was too violent to go back for her. There's no way someone could have survived those flames. We barely saved ourselves.'

'It appears she made it out,' said Betty calmly. 'Come now, eat and drink. It is good to be together again after all these months.'

As Rupert poured the brew, Naldy and Ralph eagerly tucked into the delicious stew. Naldy felt relieved that Betty didn't seem angry or disappointed with them.

Rupert soon asked a barrage of questions, prompting Naldy and Ralph to recount their journey through Edengar and their search of the Witch House. Betty became stony-faced when Naldy reached the part where Barbra had impersonated her.

By the time they finished their retelling, it was dark outside and the candles had burned low. Betty cleared the bowls and gave Smookers some leftover meat on a small plate. She then brought a freshly boiled pot of brew to the table.

'Are you joking about being a wizard, though?' asked Rupert, shaking his head. 'Because I didn't fall for it.'

'It's no joke,' said Ralph seriously.

'Prove it, then,' said Rupert, blowing out the nearest candle. 'You set the Witch House on fire. This should be a cinch.'

Ralph bit his lip, leaving the candle untouched.

'He's still in training,' said Naldy, 'but it won't be long before he masters it.'

'If you really are a wizard, Cousin, does that mean I could be a wizard too?'

'That's not how wizards work,' said Naldy, laughing. 'It's not hereditary like being a witch. To be a wizard, an Imporiom has to choose you.'

'Well, how do I find one of these important Imporioms?'

'You don't,' said Ralph smugly, lifting his goblet from the table. 'It finds you.'

'We've talked and talked,' said Naldy, smiling at Betty. 'We want to know what you've been up to?'

'Yes,' said Ralph, smirking at his cousin. 'Have you been staying with Betty this whole time? It's unlike you to stay put in one place.'

'You might be a wizard, Ralph,' said Rupert with a priggish grin, 'but I am a part of the Seagull Society. A great honour.'

'The what?'

'You've never heard of the Seagull Society?' asked Rupert, pointing proudly to his chest, where a small silver brooch of a seagull rested. 'Are you sure you're a wizard?'

'It's nonsense, don't listen to him,' said Betty, pouring herself another brew. 'I've tried to tell him, but he wears the little pin like a fool.'

'But what is this Seagull Society?' asked Naldy, wondering if she was less of a witch for never having heard of it.

'It's an ancient club—' began Rupert.

'Of old fools,' Betty interjected.

'Of protectors of magic,' continued Rupert, unperturbed. 'Betty was once invited to join.'

'And I sensibly rejected the invitation,' remarked Betty with a smile. 'And on more than one occasion. It is a group of old academic fools who award silver seagull pins to those who commit themselves to protecting magic forever.'

'I'm shocked to hear you know nothing of them,' said Rupert, eyeing Naldy and Ralph. 'Didn't you study witches, Cousin?'

'Exactly,' said Ralph, relighting the candle Rupert had blown out by using one of the other burning candles. 'I studied witches, not secret societies.'

'Traditionally,' Betty said, 'the Society has only welcomed magical folk as members. It appears they've recently diversified and extended an invitation to Rupert here.'

'For my achievements in exploring magical terrain,' said Rupert, sitting up proudly in his chair. 'I've been to Edengar—not quite as far as you two, mind you—but I spent some time with the commune there. It's considered an impressive feat just to set foot in Edengar. I've journeyed through the Mortous Woods, stayed with the Boat Builder on the east coast, and travelled the plains west and south.'

'I've seen that brooch before,' said Naldy curiously as the candlelight reflected off Rupert's seagull pin. 'I think I recognise it.'

'It's an honour to be invited as the first non-magical member,' said Rupert boastfully. 'Few receive such esteemed recognition in their lifetime.'

'Protecting magic will take more than pinning silver seagulls to people's chests,' Betty scoffed before draining the rest of her goblet and standing. 'It is getting on, and we should all get to bed. I will have the spare room made up.'

'The witch commune,' Ralph blurted out. 'That's where we've seen the brooch, Naldy. Odorf had one pinned to her chest.'

Rupert peered sadly into his goblet. Long ago,

he, too, had spent time with Odorf at the witch commune on the borders of Edengar.

'We must get some sleep now,' said Betty softly, making her way to the kitchen bench.

'I couldn't sleep even if I wanted to,' said Naldy, watching Betty place her empty goblet by the sink. 'There's still so much to discuss, and we have many questions.'

'Yes,' added Ralph, 'like what sorts of things Rupert and this Society are up to.'

'I'm quite a new member,' said Rupert sheepishly. 'I'm yet to be trusted with the Society's secrets, but I will be with time.'

'Do let us have another carafe?' asked Ralph, his big blue eyes pleading. 'We can sleep in tomorrow.'

'Oh, alright,' said Betty as the carafe lifted from the table and floated towards her. She refilled it with more brew from a large cauldron. 'Just the one more, and then to bed with us.'

'I won't be able to sleep until I've told you about our plans anyway,' said Naldy, as Ralph shifted uncomfortably in his seat.

'A plan, you say?' said Betty curiously, returning to the table with the carafe and generously topping up their goblets.

'We know Maverick has the Aurum,' said Naldy, 'and we think we should go after him.'

'Go after him?' Betty exclaimed, spilling the brew as she topped up Rupert's goblet. 'Go after a wizard in possession of a Devante! Edengar *has* driven you mad.'

'It is our one chance of saving any of the Devante,' said Naldy.

'Not our only chance,' said Rupert, standing to fetch a cloth to wipe up Betty's spilt brew. 'We've been busy while you've been in Edengar. We've spent the past few months tracking down Lignum, and we think we're close. Very close. It's somewhere southwest of here, in Kirkwood Forest.'

Naldy realised that in all the excitement of seeing Rupert and Betty, she had forgotten to mention that Lignum had been destroyed. A lump formed in her throat.

'What is it?' asked Betty, eyeing her seriously.

'It's gone,' said Naldy quietly, wishing she could disappear into her goblet. 'Lignum had vanished from the list before Ralph set it on fire.'

'Are you certain?' asked Betty, straightening her back.

'Yes,' said Ralph gently. 'We know it's gone. I'd show you the proof, but the list we had... well, it perished in the fire.'

'It is over, then,' said Betty, her eyes narrowing with quiet dread. 'We could storm Maverick with a hundred highly skilled witches and wizards, and he'd still win the fight. There is no hope for us without a Devante.'

'That's what you said about us finding the books in Edengar,' said Ralph cheekily.

'You got lucky,' Betty replied, pursing her lips. 'But we can't rely on luck, and we certainly can't defeat a wizard in possession of a Devante with luck alone.'

'We needed Lignum,' said Rupert sadly, turning to stare out the window at the darkened garden, where a soft breeze made the flowers sway eerily. The flickering candlelight accentuated his jawline, his lips curving downward in disappointment.

'If Maverick can use the Aurum to do *anything*,' said Naldy, 'then why hasn't he been using its power? We believe he might be trying to destroy magic—but why hasn't he done exactly that?'

'Because of the *Banned Spells*,' said Betty, sighing. 'I've touched on this with you before. But it is late, and these conversations are best had in the light of day.'

'If he can do almost anything, then why is Maverick wasting his opportunity?' asked Ralph, baffled.

'All the more reason for us to be worried,' Betty said, as one of the candles flickered out in its hot wax.

'Can a Devante really produce *any* magic, though?' Rupert asked dubiously.

'Except for the *Banned Spells,* the imagination is the limit,' responded Betty quietly. 'I think he must want to remain unseen, at least for the present. Maverick must have a darker plan in store.'

'How many *Banned Spells* are there?' asked Ralph.

'You seem overly interested,' said Betty, her forehead creasing with reproach. 'Finish your goblets, and then to bed with us. These things are best left unknown.'

'We can't let Maverick destroy all magic,' said Ralph animatedly. 'I won't allow it—not before I've fully learnt to master magic myself. Will you tell us about the *Banned Spells?*'

They looked at the grey-haired witch with hopeful eyes. Even Rupert seemed eager to learn more about the powers of the Devante.

'I will tell you a little,' said Betty, the dim candlelight dancing across her wrinkled face. 'I suppose you've earned it after all you've been through in service of the books. But let's have more light—I don't like speaking of such things in the darkness of night.'

A nearby drawer opened, and a dozen small pillar candles glided out, joining them at the table. Their wicks flickered to life with dancing yellow flames, brightening the room considerably.

'There are three *Banned Spells,*' said Betty. '*Time, Death* and *Knowledge.*'

'*Knowledge?*' repeated Naldy, puzzled. 'That seems like a significant limitation.'

'You cannot use the Devante to make oneself smarter,' continued Betty, as the others hung on her every word. 'You can't gift your neighbours with increased intelligence. Nor can you extract answers to questions you do not already know the answer to.'

'But Maverick used the Aurum,' said Ralph bluntly, 'to extract information from Naldy and me.'

'It is possible to use the Devante to aid in seeking answers,' explained Betty. 'For example, the truth spell Maverick used against you in Edengar.

He could not simply ask the Devante to reveal the information. He needed a way to force you to relinquish it.'

'I'm not quite following,' said Rupert, as Smookers came over and jumped into his lap.

'The simplest way to explain it,' said Betty, as the candles crackled softly, 'is this: the Devante can tie your shoelaces for you, but it won't reveal *how* it tied them. It will give you a spell to do the job, but it will never divulge its inner workings.'

'Well, Maverick's ball of smoke got it wrong anyway,' said Naldy flatly. 'It accused me of knowing where the Corium was—yet I have no idea.'

Betty hesitated before continuing, and Naldy sensed that the old witch believed Maverick's orb.

'Under the umbrella of *Knowledge*,' said Betty, 'you cannot use the Devante to discover someone's or something's location. With the sole exception, of course, of a higher-ranking Devante being able to locate a lower-ranking one.'

'That sounds like a lot of restrictions,' said Rupert, displeased. 'And we're only on the first *Banned Spell*.'

'The great gift of magic,' said Betty level-headedly, 'is that one doesn't need to know how it works. One simply needs to know the spell. And you see, someone with a skilled enough imagination can always find creative ways to bypass the *Banned Spell of Knowledge* without breaking it. Maverick did this when he read your thoughts, Naldy. He could access them while in the room with you, but he couldn't force you to answer. You answered willingly, and you're lucky that he believed you.'

'Sounds overly complicated to me,' said Naldy, stifling a yawn. She wondered if Betty had been right —perhaps these conversations were better reserved for daylight hours.

'What about *Death?*' asked Ralph, his blue eyes narrowing in curiosity. 'Maverick used a spell to murder Odorf, didn't he? And that wasn't any ordinary spell.'

'Despite the *Banned Spell* being called *Death,*' said Betty, her lips tightening into a frown, 'it doesn't mean one cannot kill.'

'What does it mean?' Ralph leant forward. 'Can you bring people back from death? Or is that what the ban is?'

Betty seemed reluctant to answer, almost scowling at Ralph for having asked the question.

'The course of history is altered when such spells are brought into play,' the wrinkled woman replied uneasily. 'One *can* use any Devante to bring people back into this world. It is not a *Banned Spell* —although I wouldn't advise interfering with the natural order of things.'

'We've no Devante,' returned Naldy restlessly, 'so you needn't worry about us altering the course of history.'

'What else could *Death* consist of, then?' wondered Rupert, his brow wrinkling. 'If it isn't the limitation of killing or bringing someone back from the dead.'

Betty hesitated. The candles glinted ominously. The others stared at her expectantly.

'The *Banned Spell of Death* is this,' said Betty cautiously. 'You cannot kill a person or thing *unless* you are within sight of them—or unless you truly know them.'

'What do you mean?' asked Rupert.

'You cannot simply end the life of someone many miles away, nor can you take the life of someone you've never known. But if the ban is broken, life and death can be dealt to anyone, anywhere.'

'Without being near them?' said Ralph, horrified. 'And Maverick knows us—does that mean he could cast a spell and we could drop dead at any moment?'

'You are acquainted with Maverick,' replied Betty. 'But the wizard does not truly know you. However, if the ban were broken—he could give and take life without restriction.'

'And what about bringing someone back to life?' asked Naldy, thinking of her parents. She believed them to still be alive, but if the worst had happened, she might be able to use a Devante to bring them back.

'To give life,' said Betty uneasily, looking pained as she spoke, 'you must have known the person.'

'And if the *Banned Spell* is broken?' asked Rupert.

'Of course, if the *Banned Spell of Death* is broken, one could bring back everyone who has ever walked this earth, whether you were acquainted or not. Such magic is dark—no good can come from it, mark my words. Even if intentions mean well.'

'It's difficult to believe such magic exists,' said Rupert, leaning back to stretch out his long body. Smookers, annoyed by the movement, tapped his paws before resettling in his lap.

'Let us be thankful,' said Betty, 'that only the Corium can break the three *Banned Spells,* and Maverick does not possess that.'

'Just before,' said Naldy, 'you mentioned *thing.*'

'Yes, because the rules apply not only to people but to animals, objects, and other things.'

'Other things?'

'Other things, like magic,' murmured Betty gravely.

'Do you think Maverick is seeking the Corium to undo the *Banned Spells?*' asked Naldy, shuddering at the thought. 'So our inkling is right and he wants to... what? Kill all magic?'

'I believe so, yes,' said Betty. 'But we cannot be sure. Maverick currently has possession of a Devante, so he can take away someone's ability to perform magic if he is looking directly at them, or if he truly knows them. From what you've told us about the wizard showing up at your family home, I believe he already accomplished this using Aurum, because he was near you. Your friend Oak also used a spell from Rubrum on you, Naldy—the curse that temporarily took your magic away by daylight. Of course, Oak has known you since you were a child, so the tree didn't need to break a *Banned Spell* to cast the curse.'

'But why does Maverick need the Corium,' said

Ralph, 'if he can already strip people of their magic?'

'That is why I believe he has bigger plans. He is seeking to undo the *Banned Spell of Death* so he can end all magic, everywhere, for everyone. Only the highest-ranking Devante would have the power to reverse it. Maverick would be unstoppable. It is a theory of mine, but all signs point towards that bitter end.'

'And it will be as simple as uttering a spell?' asked Ralph, his face troubled.

'Breaking the *Banned Spells* is not easy,' said Betty, staring into the nearest candle's flame with narrowed eyes. 'I fear Maverick is skilled enough to achieve it if he desires. There are two possible reasons he would seek the Corium so passionately: to protect it or to undo the *Banned Spells*. He already possesses the other powers the Devante offers.'

'We have sufficient evidence,' said Ralph stroppily, 'to assume he has no intention of protecting the Corium.'

'We need to stop him,' said Rupert intensely.

'What's the third?' asked Naldy.

'Oh yes, the third is *Time*. You cannot use the Devante to go back in time, forward in time, or to stop time.' Betty began clearing the kitchen table of their empty goblets. 'And now we really must go to bed.'

'How do you know so much about these *Banned Spells*, Betty?' asked Rupert, lifting Smookers from his lap.

'I have had an interest in them for some time,' she

replied, turning on the tap and filling the sink, 'ever since my mother left her Devante to me. Look, we all have dark circles around our eyes.'

'I am sorry we failed to save your Devante from Edengar,' said Naldy quietly.

Betty placed their empty goblets into the hot water. Naldy wondered whether she had heard her apology.

'And how do you break the *Banned Spells?*' asked Ralph.

Betty dropped the bar of dish soap she was holding. 'You don't,' she said firmly, spinning to face Ralph with a stern expression.

'But Maverick is going to try and—'

'Maverick is a fool,' said Betty resolutely. She returned to the table, blowing out the candles and leaving the dishes to wash themselves.

'So, you'll help us retrieve the Aurum from Maverick?' asked Naldy as they followed Betty along the darkened hall.

'Retrieving the Aurum is not the priority, my dear. Now that Lignum has been destroyed, we have no option but to search for the Corium.'

'How are we supposed to do that?' asked Ralph, strolling sleepily behind.

Naldy could have sworn the old woman's gaze lingered on her briefly before she opened the door to the spare room.

'You'll be in here, Naldy,' said Betty in the dim light. The room's candles ignited, and the spare bed began to dress itself in clean linen. 'Ralph, you'll have to take the sofa in the sitting room as Rupert is in the other spare room. We can discuss further plans tomorrow.'

Chapter Six

ASHES

T he rose-pink curtains blocked out most of the dull morning light. Throughout the night, Naldy had drifted in and out of sleep, and as dawn approached, she lay watching the seeping light illuminate the edges of the frayed curtains.

She climbed out of the soft bed and made her way into the empty hallway. Long shadows were cast across the walls as she plodded towards the kitchen to make herself a pot of brew. On the way, she passed the lounge, where she found Ralph perched on the sofa, a feather quill scratching away at a leather journal. The blankets and pillows he'd slept in had been neatly folded and rested on the sofa's armrest.

'Where'd you get a new journal?' asked Naldy.

'When we were in Frubry,' said Ralph, pointing to a bronze tray laden with delicate ceramic cups and a fresh pot. 'A scholar must have his paper and brew.'

'Couldn't sleep either?' asked Naldy, sitting in the armchair and helping herself to the brew.

'Watch this,' said Ralph, facing an unlit candle resting on the small table beside him—it ignited with a dancing yellow flame. 'I've been practising whenever I get the chance. I just have to imagine the palm movements and think of the spell's words.'

'We haven't really spoken about you being an Effangale.'

'We've had more pressing matters,' remarked Ralph, closing his leather journal and setting it aside. The lone candle flickered pleasantly in the dim grey light.

'Did you see how Betty looked at me last night?' asked Naldy softly. 'I can't help but believe she thinks I know the location of the Corium. The way she kept glancing at me.'

'It doesn't matter what Betty thinks,' replied Ralph kindly. 'If you don't know, then you don't know. Betty believes searching for the Corium is wise, but I disagree. I think our plan to go after Maverick is the only plausible path. Finding Maverick will be easier than finding the Corium.'

A silver plate carrying a small dish of raspberry jam and hot toast glided into the room.

'You are getting the hang of it,' said Naldy, grabbing the silver tray as it wobbled. She helped herself to a slice of toast.

'There's still a lot for me to learn,' said Ralph. 'I'm no good under pressure—but I'm finally mastering the basics.'

Naldy sipped her brew and waited for Ralph to speak again.

'There's something I've been meaning to tell you, Naldy. You see, there is something I managed to save from the Witch House. I should have told you earlier, but I didn't want you to take it from me.'

'What is it?'

'The small spellbook you lent me. It's the only thing that survived—apart from the chair I carried you out on—and I know I should give it back to you, but you cannot have it back. I won't part with it until I've committed it to memory.'

Naldy smiled at him affectionately.

'I keep thinking about all the different spells we could create,' said Ralph, smiling back. 'Imagine what we could do if we got our hands on the Aurum. Just imagine.'

Naldy thought of her parents, and a longing weighed on her heart.

'Any suggestions on where we might find Maverick?' asked Naldy, wanting to push the thought of her parents from her mind.

'Well, we know he's on the board for the Bleckdale Witchery Museum.'

'We'll be locked up if we set foot anywhere near The Great City,' said Naldy, recalling their last disastrous visit to the museum when Ralph was imprisoned.

'We know Maverick is the mayor of three nearby towns, too,' added Ralph.

'Are you thinking of dragging me to another of those horrid town fairs?'

'I find them quite enjoyable,' said Ralph, 'and it is tradition for the town's mayor to officially open the fair.'

'It's autumn,' said Naldy, shaking her head. 'The next town fair will likely be months away.'

They sipped their brew in silence, stumped on how they might find Maverick. The lounge filled with golden shafts of light as the sun continued its rise.

Betty was the next to wake. Wrapped in a purple dressing gown, she entered the lounge, cleared their trays, and then pottered around the kitchen until Rupert woke. By nine o'clock, they were all seated around the kitchen table. Betty served them bowls of yoghurt topped with fresh berries. Naldy tried to broach the subject of hunting Maverick. This put Betty in a sour mood, and her manner became more like Barbra's as the conversation progressed.

'But what you're suggesting could take years—centuries, even,' Naldy complained. 'Looking for the Corium is a waste of our time.'

'No more,' said Betty sternly. 'We've spoken about this already. Now finish your yoghurt.'

'*You* can look for the Corium, but I'm going after Maverick,' snapped Naldy. She had tried to say it calmly, but her frustration proved impossible to quell.

'Go marching after Maverick, and you'll get yourself killed,' hollered Betty before lowering her voice to soften it. 'Naldy, dear, I know you want this to be over. We all do. But there is no quick fix to ensuring the Devante are protected. Rupert and I have been working hard these last few months to find the remaining books.'

'Lignum has been destroyed,' said Naldy irritably. 'And we already *know* where another Devante is—in Maverick's cloak pocket!'

'We came close,' said Rupert feebly. He wasn't his usual chipper self. 'There were rumours Lignum was somewhere southwest of here, and Betty and I found various sources that confirmed it. I think we might be able to find the Corium if we work together.'

'And how long, Rupert,' interjected Ralph crossly, joining ranks with Naldy, 'how long will it take for you to get bored?'

All eyes anchored on Ralph, surprised by his hostility towards his cousin.

'Well, don't deny it,' said Ralph sourly. 'It's your pattern. You become overly invested in things, and then, quick as the wind, you're bored, and you bail.'

'I've been helping hunt these books ever since you told me about them,' said Rupert defensively. 'Don't think you're the only one who's been working to save magic.'

'I think you're taking respite from your travels,' mumbled Ralph, almost under his breath. 'That's what I think. Before you up-and-go again.'

Rupert stood and, placing his palms on the table, calmly leant closer to Ralph—not in a menacing way but in an affectionate manner.

'I know you wish this to be quick and easy, Cousin,' said Rupert gently. 'But rushing it will get us all killed.'

Rupert turned and headed out through the back door into the garden.

'That's settled then,' said Betty, sighing. 'We take the path that leads to the Corium.'

Betty picked up her bowl of half-finished yoghurt and followed Rupert out into the back garden. Ralph and Naldy were left alone, feeling deflated and irritable. Through the kitchen window, Naldy saw Rupert pulling on his gardening gloves and beginning to tend to Betty's flowers.

'They're wrong,' said Ralph, staring into his yoghurt.

'Maybe,' said Naldy, slumping her elbows on the table. 'But what if they're right? Betty does know a lot about the Devante, and undoubtedly more than we do.'

'They have no sense of urgency,' said Ralph, spooning yoghurt into his mouth. 'I wish there was someone else we could consult about these Devante. Betty is overly cautious, and time is a luxury we don't have on our side.'

'But that's it, Ralph!'

'What's it?'

'There is someone else we can ask,' said Naldy, suddenly enlivened. 'You've suggested it before. We can ask Oak. He used to possess Rubrum. At the very least, he knew how to use it. He cursed me with it, and I'll wager he knows more than Betty.'

'I like this plan,' said Ralph, rubbing his hands together. 'Let's hope he confides in us about what he knows. Though, I must say, I have some doubts. He did keep Rubrum a secret from you until it was stolen.'

'He sleeps during the day,' said Naldy. 'I think he will help us if he can, and he isn't far from here. We can visit him this evening and ask for his advice.'

'Let's not tell the others,' Ralph remarked, glancing at the garden where Betty was chatting to Rupert, who was pruning a leafy plant. 'It'll offend them that we're seeking a second opinion.'

'I think you might be right.'

Once they'd finished eating, Ralph returned to practising spells while Naldy lay sleepily on the sofa, watching him. He was picking up the craft faster than she had expected.

By lunchtime, the tension that had surfaced during breakfast had dissolved. They sat comfortably around Betty's table, enjoying good food and pleasant conversation—swapping notes on their survival tips for tackling Edengar. The Devante weren't mentioned.

Rupert spent the afternoon in the back garden again, watering plants and pruning more bushes. Betty settled herself on the garden's stone bench, and the two were deep in conversation.

'What do you think they're talking about?' asked Ralph curiously.

'Don't worry about it,' said Naldy. 'They can talk all day, but it won't help them find the Corium. I'm sure Oak will be more reasonable.'

Ralph and Naldy decided to slip out through the front door as the sun was setting.

'I've left a note,' said Naldy as Smookers snuck out with them, winding fondly around Ralph's feet. 'I've written that we've gone out for a flying lesson before dinner.'

'You'll need to stay here,' said Ralph, picking Smookers up, kissing his forehead, and gently placing him back inside the house. Smookers meowed at the closed door, displeased to be left behind.

'Quiet now, Smookers, or they'll come asking questions,' said Naldy. 'We'll be back soon enough.'

'I may as well have a go at flying,' suggested Ralph, 'now that I'm getting the hang of spells. It's been so long since I had my carpet and I'd quite like to steer.'

Smookers had stopped meowing, and through the door's frosted glass windows, Naldy could see him slinking away down the hall.

'I suppose we're not really in any hurry,' said Naldy, reluctantly passing the broom to him.

Ralph settled himself at the front, gesturing happily for Naldy to climb on behind him. She lifted her leg over the broomstick and gripped Ralph's shoulders.

'Are you sure you want'—But before Naldy could finish her question, Ralph kicked off hard from the ground, and Naldy toppled backwards, landing in one of the neatly trimmed bushes with pretty golden buds. She sat up to see Ralph shooting upwards, almost vertically, higher and higher, zigzagging wildly as if the broom had become possessed.

The front door opened, and Betty peered out to

see what was making all the noise. She saw Ralph hollering for help, then glimpsed Naldy lying in the bush. She shook her head.

'Point it forward, boy! Hold it straight!' Betty shouted, but it was no good—Ralph was too preoccupied trying to grip the broomstick for dear life and wasn't listening.

Smookers slunk out of the open door and cocked his head to the side, following the broom's chaotic movements with his eyes as if tracking the flight pattern of a fly.

'Calm, boy! Be calm! Just sit upright and hold it still, Ralph!'

Rupert came sauntering down the hallway, lifting Betty's broomstick from its holder near the door.

'I could see him from the garden,' said Rupert, passing the broomstick to Betty. He still had his gardening gloves on.

Betty effortlessly hopped onto the broom and zoomed up into the purple sky. She commandingly took hold of Ralph's broomstick and guided it towards the ground. Ralph tumbled off the broom, clutching his stomach, and landed in the same bush Naldy had.

'Not my Grehgangles,' moaned Rupert, 'I've been tending those for weeks.'

'I thought he'd flown before?' said Betty, passing the broomstick to Naldy.

'Magic carpets,' replied Ralph, pulling himself out of Rupert's beloved bushes. His face was pale.

Betty nodded, giving him an understanding look as she brushed the leaves from Ralph's cloak.

'Thanks for saving me,' said Ralph.

'Lesson one,' said Betty. 'You must remain calm. If your energy is all stressed, the broom won't know which way you want it to go, will it? That's the first lesson of flying, although I have a feeling maybe this wasn't a flying lesson.'

Naldy studied the ground, trying to hide her guilt, while Ralph busied himself pretending to salvage Rupert's Grehgangles.

'I don't know what you are both up to,' said Betty in a motherly tone, 'but you'd best let Naldy steer, boy. And be back in two hours, or dinner will be served cold.'

Betty pursed her lips before making her way back inside the house. Naldy found it odd that Betty didn't press them to find out where they were going. Did she already know they were sneaking off to visit Oak?

'Are you ready, Ralph?'

'I think we might need to try tomorrow, Naldy,' said Ralph. 'I'll be sick if I take to the skies again.'

'If you like,' said Rupert, removing his gardening gloves, 'I'll come with you. Wherever you're sneaking off to.'

'We're not sneaking off,' muttered Naldy, fidgeting with the handle of the broomstick.

Ralph took his cousin's gardening gloves, approving of the idea, before lowering himself onto the front doorstep. He gripped the corners of the step as if afraid he might suddenly shoot up flying again.

'Alright,' said Naldy, climbing onto the broomstick. 'Get on and hold tight, Rupert.'

Once Rupert's hands were around her waist, Naldy waved at Ralph and kicked off the ground. The sky was turning grey as the sun slowly disappeared.

The pine-scented air felt refreshing on their faces as they soared over the tops of cottages and winding roads.

'A beautiful night for flying,' said Rupert cheerily from behind. Naldy knew Rupert was pleased to be travelling—unlike Ralph, flying seemed to enliven him.

'Yes, the air is wonderful,' said Naldy, 'but if you look ahead, dark clouds are forming in the distance.'

'Are you going to tell me where we're going, then?' asked Rupert.

'We're visiting an old friend,' she replied. 'We think he might be able to tell us more about the Devante.'

'Splendid,' said Rupert.

By the time they approached their destination, night had fallen, and a large moon shone brightly through a break in the clouds that had gathered above. Naldy's stomach twisted as she peered down at the clearing.

'I must have taken a wrong turn,' said Naldy, pulling the broom to a stop mid-air.

Oak—usually standing tall in the centre of the clearing below—was nowhere to be seen.

'This can't be the right place,' said Naldy, peering at the stretch of pine forest, searching for another clearing. 'I must have gotten confused coming from the east.'

'Everything alright?' asked Rupert from behind her.

'I think I've miscalculated,' said Naldy. 'I can't remember where the clearing is.'

'There's a clearing there,' said Rupert, pointing at the only noticeable one.

Naldy's stomach felt like it was tying itself in knots. Deep in her heart, she knew the clearing below was the right one, where Oak usually stood tall. But there was no sign of him.

'Hold tight, I'm going to land.'

The broom began its descent. As they landed on the hard ground, Naldy dropped the broomstick and raised her palms.

'Naldy, what is it?' asked Rupert, worried.

She lowered her hands as the moonlight illuminated a large blackened stump surrounded by cold, charred earth stretching across the clearing. Naldy's legs gave way, and she fell to her knees.

'Naldy,' called Rupert, hurrying to place a comforting arm around her shoulders.

'He's gone, Rupert, someone… someone has…'

Naldy couldn't finish her sentence, but Rupert didn't need her to. The evidence in front of them was clear—Oak had been burnt to ashes. Naldy's fingers touched the cold soot on the ground.

She raised her head and, through tear-filled eyes,

saw that Oak had been gone for a long time, as there was no smoke. Naldy's soul felt as if it had burst apart as she looked upon the clearing's harrowing centrepiece—the blackened, jagged, lifeless stump.

'I'm sorry, Naldy,' said Rupert softly. His cheeks were stained with tears.

'I should have warned him,' said Naldy, her voice weak.

'How could you have known this would happen?' said Rupert, as Naldy leant into his arm.

'Diamone predicted it,' she replied softly. 'Before we left for Edengar, she warned us that an oak tree would be on fire. But I was too busy chasing after these darned books. I could have warned him, Rupert.'

Naldy sobbed into Rupert's shoulder, and they stayed on the ground together for some time, Rupert's warm arms embracing her. Eventually, Naldy stood, breaking free of his hug. She took a few deep breaths, stumbling closer to the charred trunk protruding eerily from the ground. She half expected it to move, but it was devoid of life.

'Who would do such a thing?' asked Rupert, staring sadly at the ash-covered clearing.

'Maverick,' said Naldy painfully. 'Who else? He knows about Oak and has tried to set him on fire once before. He probably came back for the same reason we did—to get information about the Devante. We're caught up in a fight we can't win.'

'I'm so sorry, Naldy,' mumbled Rupert, his forehead creased with pity. 'I'll let you have a moment alone.'

'No,' she said firmly. 'Let's fly home. There's nothing here, and I don't want to stay.'

Naldy walked over to her broomstick, breathing deeply, trying to press her feelings down as she swung a leg over. Rupert climbed on behind her, and they rose into the cold night air as more clouds gathered nearby.

Rupert didn't speak the whole flight back, and Naldy was thankful for his silence. She didn't want to talk about the pain surging within her.

They whooshed over the tops of the pine trees, occasionally passing the twinkling lights of secluded towns nestled in the forest below.

Naldy felt numb, and her eyes soon felt raw and dry. The night air was cold against her skin, but she wished it were colder still. She wanted to turn to ice, to freeze, to stop thinking altogether.

When they landed on the road outside Betty's house, warm, welcoming lights glittered through the curtained windows—but Naldy wished nobody was inside. She couldn't face telling Ralph and Betty that Oak was gone.

'It's horrible,' said Rupert, his expression strained. 'I'm so sorry.'

'Look at that,' said Naldy, pointing up the darkened road towards the ramshackle building at the end of the street. Candles were flickering in its windows. 'Someone's inside Barbra's house.'

'Yes,' said Rupert, turning away. 'It's probably Barbra. Betty is convinced she didn't perish in the fire.'

Naldy began walking up the road, holding her broomstick, her black cloak billowing behind her.

'Naldy!' cried Rupert, hurrying to catch up. 'Naldy, you've had a shock. I don't think now is the best time to confront Barbra.'

'She'll know where Maverick is,' replied Naldy, quickening her pace and fixing her gaze on the dishevelled house.

'Does she?' asked Rupert. 'Because from what you've told me, it sounded like Maverick tricked her.'

'Then she'll want to hurt Maverick as much as I do,' said Naldy, lifting the broomstick and jumping on. She glided away from Rupert towards Barbra's home. The clouds overhead obscured the moon.

Chapter Seven

THE EGG'S MESSAGE

Naldy landed in a garden bed beneath one of Barbra's windows on the side of the house. Slowly, she lifted her head to peek inside. She recognised the room where she'd once been served a purple brew made from Kineleek tree bark, supposedly meant to help build immunity to the tree's poison. The well-worn antique furnishings, including the sagging floral sofa where Ralph had once unknowingly eaten Barbra's poisoned scones, were bathed in muted candlelight.

Barbra entered the room, and Naldy lowered her head slightly. The old woman shuffled over to a small table burdened with a large pile of books. Barbra picked up one, opened it, and tossed it aside.

'Where did I put it?' Barbra muttered to herself, throwing another book at the wall. 'Dear me, dear me. I misplace everything, I do.'

The candlelight briefly caught Barbra's face. Naldy saw that her left cheek had been scorched by flame, the skin melted against the bone. Her left eye was swollen, red, and blistered.

'Are you going to knock?' whispered Rupert,

catching his breath as he joined Naldy in the garden bed.

'You scared me,' said Naldy, lowering herself below the windowsill to face him.

'Or is your plan to spy on Barbra through the window?'

'Something's not right,' said Naldy quietly. 'How did she escape the fire? It doesn't make sense. She's in there now, looking for something. Maybe she managed to steal the Aurum from Maverick?'

'Naldy, I'm not sure this is the right time to confront Barbra. You're still in shock, and I think we should wait until tomorrow. Perhaps Betty will come with us.'

'I need you to go and knock, Rupert,' said Naldy, flicking her long black hair out of her face.

'Knock?'

'Yes,' whispered Naldy seriously. She gestured at the rickety porch where most of the wood had been eaten by termites. 'I need you to keep her distracted, only for a few minutes.'

'Distract her?' said Rupert, his teeth disappearing behind a look of concern. 'Why? What are you planning?'

'Tell her you adore her books or something, that you're here for an autograph,' insisted Naldy, pushing him out of the garden bed. 'I need to know what she's looking for, and I think it might be important.'

Rupert's mouth dropped open, and Naldy could see him trying to think up some way to talk her out of her impulsive plan.

'I thought,' she continued before Rupert could reply, 'you were the adventurous traveller.'

'Okay, Naldy, I'll do it,' said Rupert, slightly offended. 'But promise to be quick. If she catches you, I hate to think what she'll do.'

'I just need a few minutes.'

The death of Oak was fuelling her adrenaline, and Naldy couldn't bear the thought of returning to Betty's house to sit around and grieve. She felt restless.

Rupert, frowning, straightened his green cloak and made his way to the porch. Naldy heard his gentle knock, followed by the sound of Barbra hobbling out of the sitting room. Brushing the leaves from her cloak, Naldy stood and tried to pry open the sitting room window, but it was locked.

'*Aperio,*' whispered Naldy, and with a soft click, the window released.

As the front door creaked open, Naldy cautiously lifted the window. She hoisted herself onto the wooden ledge of the windowsill. The rotting wood flaked under her grip, and she nearly slipped, but she managed to steady herself before pulling her body into Barbra's sitting room.

'What do you want?' Barbra's shrill voice drifted from the hall.

'Hello,' came Rupert's nervous reply, a poor attempt at sounding cheerful. 'I'm sorry to disturb you at such a late hour, Miss Hexogg.'

'Yes, boy, you will be sorry if you don't hurry and

get to the point of why you're disturbing me.'

'I've come because I was passing through Heatherton, and I'm a huge fan of your work. Just adore it, I do, Miss Hexogg.'

'I see, yes,' said Barbra, sounding delighted. 'I'll go and get a quill for signing.'

'No,' Rupert said quickly. 'I can't stay long.'

Naldy rushed to the table of books Barbra had been eagerly searching through. She ran her hands over the spines of the stack. None bore the brilliant gold cover of the Aurum. Frustrated, she flipped open the nearest spellbook. No 'H' was imprinted inside; it wasn't a Devante or anything special—just an ordinary spellbook. Quietly, she set it aside and picked up another.

'Why don't you come inside?' Barbra's voice rang out from the hallway. 'There'll be rain any moment. I can brew us something while I sign a few of my prized works. I'm sure your other engagements can wait.'

'I really cannot stay,' said Rupert. 'I only wanted to tell you how much I admire you.'

Naldy opened another book. No indented 'H'. She opened another. And another.

'Do you have a favourite written work of mine, then? I'm sure I'll have a spare. It will take but a moment to sign.'

'Well, erm,' said Rupert tensely, 'I love them all. I don't think I could choose a favourite.'

'Oh, yes,' Barbra chuckled. 'A true fan.'

What had Barbra been looking for? None of

the books appeared exceptional. Naldy opened another and then another—tossing them aside in frustration.

'I'm working on a new best-seller, *Charmed and Cheapened*,' continued Barbra. 'You'll be pleased to hear, I'm sure. It explores the dark side of magic being peddled at town fairs. I've no doubt it will be well received.'

Naldy was running out of time. She glanced frantically at Barbra's books scattered across the floor before hurriedly trying to set everything back in its place.

'Forgive me,' came Barbra's voice from the hallway, 'but you do not dress like a witch. Are you a wizard?'

'No, I'm neither.'

'Neither you say,' Barbra mused. 'Yes, well, I think you best be going.'

Naldy heard the door slam shut. Time was up— and she hadn't returned everything to its original state.

She tossed the book she was holding onto the sofa, but two loose pages slipped out. There was no time to pick them up as the sound of Barbra tottering down the hallway reached her ears.

'Townspeople reading my work,' muttered Barbra to herself. 'How strange the world is becoming.'

Naldy was about to swing her leg over the window when she noticed the parchment that had slipped from the book was strangely familiar—

embossed with a decorative pattern of baby dragons. She bent and picked up the two pages. They were the same size and shade as the parchment she and Ralph had once found inside Harmony Esterfield's dragon egg. The only difference was that these two aged scrolls had been unravelled and flattened inside the book.

Naldy shoved the scrolls into her cloak pocket before diving through the open window, landing hard in the garden bed below.

She didn't close the window—Barbra's footsteps had already reached the sitting room.

Naldy scampered towards the darkened road where Rupert was anxiously waiting.

'Well, I hope that was worth it,' said Rupert angrily. Naldy had never seen his cheeks flushed so red. 'I haven't read any Barbra Hexogg, and I'm sorry, but I couldn't distract her any longer.'

'Never mind that,' replied Naldy, holding out the broomstick. 'Let's get back to Betty's as fast as we can. Climb on.'

Rupert swung his leg over Naldy's broom, and they glided up the darkened street. Droplets of water were beginning to fall from the sky.

'If you've never read any Barbra Hexogg,' Naldy said as they landed outside Betty's house, 'why did you once gift Ralph and me one of her books? I remember the note you left: *A step in any direction is better than no step at all.*'

'The woman is notorious for her mad scribblings,' said Rupert, glancing nervously up the street to make sure the old witch hadn't followed them. 'Once in a while, someone's madness proves useful. But after meeting her, I doubt that's truthful in this case.'

When they first entered the kitchen, Betty scolded them for being late, but she quickly realised something was wrong. The moment Rupert told her about Oak, her rebuke vanished, and she pulled them into tight hugs. She offered comforting words and served them generous portions of roasted meats with extra pan juices. Naldy wasn't hungry, spending most of the meal quietly holding back her emotions.

'After dinner, you take yourself straight to bed,' said Betty in a soothing tone. 'Get cosy, and I'll bring you a hot water bottle.'

Once they'd finished eating, Rupert confessed that Naldy had broken into Barbra's home. Betty's expression grew tense, her eyes filled with unease.

'Ralph and I have seen these scrolls before,' said Naldy, the rain pattering against the window. 'They belonged to a witch named Harmony Esterfield. She was part of the witch commune on the edge of Edengar. Before she went missing—presumed dead —she sold dragon eggs at Maverick's town fair. This proves Barbra must know something about it.'

'Regardless,' said Betty irritably, 'we'll have to return them right away, and you'll need to apologise at some point. But for now, you should take yourself to bed.'

'Apologise?' Naldy scrunched her nose. 'I don't

see why we should do that, not after all she's done to us.'

'I believe she also owes you an apology,' replied Betty calmly. 'But stealing her scrolls won't help us, or our quest. We don't want my sister as an enemy while we're trying to find the Corium.'

Once the plates were cleared, Betty sent Barbra a lucurn candle. They sat awkwardly around the table, sipping fresh cups of brew by candlelight, waiting for Barbra's response.

'Maybe she's already gone to bed,' Ralph suggested hopefully.

'It would be most unlike her,' replied Betty as the rain drummed on the roof. 'My sister is a night owl. She usually stays up late, writing or reading. Naldy, my dear, you've been through an awful lot tonight. You needn't stay up. I'll make sure the scrolls are returned safely to my sister, and I'll pass on your regrets.'

'I couldn't sleep now even if I wanted to,' said Naldy. 'I'd like to ask her how she came to possess them.'

'I don't want any duels in my kitchen,' said Betty sternly.

Lightning flashed, illuminating the two pressed scrolls lying in the centre of Betty's rectangular wooden table.

'I don't see why we have to give them back,' said Naldy. 'I doubt Barbra came upon them by fair means. I think we should keep them and use them ourselves. The scrolls could help us find the Corium's location.'

'They won't do that,' said Ralph, as thunder clapped in the distance. 'Remember, the scrolls reveal their message to the one who cracks the egg. They won't help us.'

There was a knock at the door, and Betty rose from her chair.

'Wait here,' she said flatly, leaving them in suspense at the table.

'She might help us,' said Naldy. 'She must be as angry at Maverick as we are.'

'It's worth a try,' said Rupert meekly, though it was clear he didn't believe his own words.

The sound of the front door opening was followed by a brief, muffled conversation between the twins in the hallway. Soon, footsteps approached. When the sisters entered the kitchen, they were dressed so similarly in black that Naldy could only tell them apart by the burnt flesh on Barbra's face. Her travelling cloak was speckled with raindrops.

'Take a seat, Barb,' said Betty kindly. 'I'll make us all a fresh batch of brew.'

'I don't want to sit,' replied Barbra sharply, eyeing Naldy and Ralph. 'I see you two escaped the fire. Unscathed. Both without any damage, it seems.'

'I'm sorry I pinched your scrolls,' said Naldy softly, readying her hands beneath the table in case Barbra engaged her in a duel. To her surprise, Barbra changed her mind and slid calmly into the seat beside Ralph.

'Yes, a fresh batch of brew sounds delightful, Sister,' said Barbra.

A small cauldron beside the sink filled itself with water from the tap before floating over to the wood-fired stove.

'Thank you, Ralph,' said Betty kindly, nodding towards him, acknowledging that he had set the brew-making into action. Betty took a seat at the end of the table.

'The wizard's a fast learner,' remarked Barbra, suspiciously eyeing Ralph. 'So, what do you call yourselves? You all claim to want to protect magic, yet you've roasted more spellbooks than I've had hot frog stews.'

Naldy wanted to remind Barbra that Maverick had been the one to destroy the Devante, but she held her tongue.

'We have your scrolls here,' said Betty, gesturing towards the centre of the table. 'Barb, you must know by now that Maverick is no longer your friend. He was never a friend to you.'

'I've always been too trusting with my fans,' said Barbra, wrinkling her forehead. 'I'll admit that. Maverick had read my entire collection of works, even my blacklisted early essay collection on the superiority of witch-to-witch unions. Unlike this young chap here'—she sneered at Rupert—'who was sent as a distraction so that you could rob me.'

Rupert coughed awkwardly, his ears turning pink.

'You needn't worry,' continued Barbra. 'Maverick

will never find the Corium. Nobody ever will. I'm sure Hannah Hale hid it well. She was, after all, one of the greatest witches to have ever lived, or so some will tell you.'

'Barb, dearest,' said Betty, shifting in her seat. 'I hate asking you for it—'

'But you need my help,' Barbra interjected, finishing her sister's sentence.

'Yes, we do need your help. Ralph has told me these magical scrolls only work for the one who cracked the egg.'

'Give me one good reason,' said Barbra, laughing amusedly, 'why I should use *my* scrolls to help you?'

'They aren't your scrolls,' said Naldy waspishly. 'They belonged to Harmony.'

'What we are doing,' said Betty, 'is critical work.'

'Chasing after the king of the Devante,' scoffed Barbra.

Ralph slumped back in his chair.

'Besides,' Barbra continued, the candlelight flickering over the wounds on her face, 'these little scrolls won't help you find any Devante. If they could, Maverick would have done so already. He has betrayed me, and I want my revenge. I will help you find him.'

Barbra reached into the centre of the table and picked up one of the pressed scrolls. She stared intensely at the paper, and Naldy knew a message was forming, though from where she was seated, she couldn't read the black ink.

The scroll burst into flames in Barbra's hands,

then vanished in a curl of black smoke.

Barbra's melted face began to repair itself. Her skin became waxy, shifting until her features perfectly resembled Betty's, down to every last wrinkle.

'Why did you waste it on your looks?' snapped Betty, shaking her head in disappointment. 'Maverick has already used the Devante to create a spell to heal wounds. We could have done it for you, instead of you wasting a precious scroll.'

'They are my scrolls, and I'll do with them whatever I please,' said Barbra, using a hand to tease up her wiry grey hair as she checked her reflection in the back of a silver spoon. 'I don't want any of you testing new spells on my face.'

'Miss Hexogg?' asked Naldy as the small cauldron on the stove began to boil.

'What is it, child?' Betty and Barbra asked in unison. They looked so alike now that Naldy had to remind herself who was sitting where.

'Do you mind me asking,' said Naldy, locking eyes with Barbra, 'how these scrolls came into your possession?'

'It was at the Valingfield town fair, where they were gifted to me,' said Barbra, smiling slightly. 'Maverick had arranged a charming stall for me to sign books—it was very kind of him. He also gave me three large eggs as a gift. Inside were these three little magical scrolls.'

'But what about Harmony Esterfield?' asked Ralph. 'What did he do with her?'

'I do not know her,' said Barbra, her tone sincere.

'Did you say Maverick gave you all three eggs?' probed Naldy. 'But I only found two scrolls in your book.'

'What nosey beaks you have,' responded Barbra, as the cauldron poured hot water into the brewpot. 'I always carried one of the scrolls with me, and this third scroll you speak of spared me from the fire. The irony is, it was Maverick's gift that saved me. I left the other two safely hidden in a spellbook at home, as Naldy here well knows.'

'So, Maverick used dragon eggs to win your affection,' said Betty, piecing it together while the brewpot glided over to the table and filled their cups with an earthy-smelling brew.

'I admit I have a weakness for rare magic,' said Barbra, as her sister sighed. 'I followed Maverick's plan because it served me well—or it should have. Keep power close when you can, they say. Maverick is on the board for The Bleckdale Witchery Museum and is highly influential amongst the elite.'

Barbra sipped her brew, her face twisting with distaste. 'You may have learnt the spell, Ralph, but you've over-brewed it.'

'Wait,' cried Betty as Barbra's hand reached for the final scroll. 'You must hear us out before you waste another on something frivolous.'

'I will do as I please,' said Barbra tensely, but she still listened to Betty, crossing her hands over her chest and leaving the scroll in the centre of the table.

'Maverick has the Aurum, Sister,' replied Betty

calmly.

'A fact I am well aware of,' snapped Barbra. 'It was promised to me, and I intend to go and prise it from Maverick myself.'

'You will not beat him in a fight without a Devante,' said Betty dryly. 'Trying to find Maverick will not help you.'

Barbra leant back in her chair, knowing her sister was right—she had lost a duel with the wizard before.

'Is someone here going to offer a better solution?' asked Barbra impatiently. 'Or will we sit here all night sipping burnt brew and die contemplating?'

'These scrolls,' said Betty thoughtfully, 'are most curious. I have not seen magic like this before, apart from the Devante.'

'You are quite right,' replied Barbra with a grin. 'Maverick used my book, Metallum, to create the eggs. The scrolls are pages torn from the book, gifted a life outside of the Devante at the sacrifice of a baby dragon. But, alas, they survive for one-time use.'

'And only the one who breaks the egg can retrieve the scroll's message,' added Ralph, sharing a look with Naldy. Many months ago, they had escaped from the confines of a bird cage using one of these magical scrolls.

'No, no,' said Barbra, her brow furrowing.

'What do you mean "no"?' asked Betty.

'Were you not listening?' said Barbra, sighing heavily. 'These aren't messages at all. Whatever you were told is wrong. These scrolls are simply pages from the Devante. They don't deliver any message.'

'But that can't be true,' said Ralph, leaning forward. 'When Naldy and I were locked in the Greenswood prison, I tried to use the scroll to set us free, but nothing happened. It only worked for Naldy, who had broken the egg. It revealed a key to her.'

'It did not work for you, Ralph,' began Betty, but Naldy interrupted—

'Because you weren't yet a wizard. You hadn't been united with your Imporiom.'

'Only witches and wizards can use the magic of a spellbook,' said Barbra. 'Even the magic within a Devante is reserved for the magical.'

'You think these are, what, pages from a Devante?' asked Ralph, staring at the yellow parchment with wonder.

'But why would Maverick keep Harmony Esterfield alive?' asked Naldy, as the rain outside intensified. 'Why set her up with a stall at his town fair, selling pages of a Devante trapped inside dragon eggs? Anybody could have bought them! Why not just kill her?'

'He did something far worse than kill,' said Barbra. There was fear in her voice.

'So you do know Harmony then,' said Rupert.

'I didn't know her,' corrected Barbra sharply. 'But I heard what happened. Maverick drove Harmony slowly mad. Killing her would've drawn attention— something he couldn't risk.'

'You know more than you are letting on,' said

Betty curiously. 'We are on the same side, Barb.'

Barbra reached for the parchment in the centre of the table.

'Please,' said Betty calmy. Barbra's hand faltered, leaving the scroll untouched. A flash of lightning illuminated the room. 'Tell us what you know about Harmony Esterfield.'

The sisters locked eyes for a moment. Their gaze was tense, but there was also a friendliness in the look they shared.

'Maverick told me the old woman showed up at the museum with the four eggs, and Getergrin declared them to be fake.'

'Why would he do that?' Betty probed. 'Why not let the museum have the eggs?'

'Because by this stage Maverick had used my book, Metallum, to discover that Rosea and Caeruleum were not lost, as you had made me believe, Sister. They'd been hidden in Edengar, inside the dragon cave.'

'I was protecting the books,' said Betty defensively, pouring herself more brew.

'Protecting,' snapped Barbra. A boom of thunder cracked nearby. 'All *my* books have now been destroyed. But not your precious Aurum.'

'Maverick is the one who destroyed them,' said Betty. 'Not anyone at this table.'

'Maverick,' continued Barbra, ignoring her sister's comment, 'demanded Getergrin declare the eggs as fakes because he couldn't risk the museum publicly announcing dragons still existed. Not until he had time to collect the books himself.'

'But why not announce dragons still exist?' asked Rupert, as another flash of lightning lit up the kitchen.

'If people knew dragons were alive,' said Barbra croakily, 'I personally know many travellers who would risk their skin to scour the mountains. Dragon properties are worth a fortune, and their obscene value saw them hunted and killed for decades. Maverick could not risk people exploring Edengar before securing the books.'

'Yes, but he didn't secure them,' said Ralph irritably. 'He destroyed them.'

'That still doesn't answer an important question,' said Rupert, glancing outside at Betty's garden with concern for his plants exposed to the intensifying storm. 'Why did Maverick bother turning Harmony's eggs into magical scrolls?'

'I could do with some water to wash away this bitter taste,' said Barbra, pushing her cup of brew aside. A glass of water floated towards her, and she took a sip before continuing. 'Maverick could not risk Harmony returning to the witch commune, for they might return with more proof of the dragons. He thought it best not to take chances. He needed to destroy the evidence.'

'The unborn dragons,' said Rupert sadly.

'But he couldn't help himself,' continued Barbra. 'Such potent magic in his possession—dragon eggs and a Devante—so he placed a page of Metallum inside each egg. Then, he sent Harmony slowly mad, for that was wiser than having her killed.'

'It explains why Harmony was so different from the rest of the commune,' said Ralph. 'There was something strange about her. Maverick had sent her mad. The way she screeched "thieves"… I'll never forget it.'

'Maverick knew nobody would buy something so expensive,' said Barbra, 'not from a town fair. He knew townsfolk wouldn't believe they were real. So he hid the eggs in plain sight. Foolish, if you ask me.'

'No wonder he locked us up,' said Ralph.

'I wanted to go with him,' Barbra added, a glint in her eye. 'To Edengar. It was my book waiting there, after all. But Maverick refused to let me go. He said it would be too dangerous because of you two'—she glared at Ralph and Naldy—'said you were on a mission to destroy them. So, he gave me the eggs as a sign of good faith and promised to recover the books and protect them.'

'We didn't destroy your Devante,' said Naldy.

'I know that now. Maverick returned from Edengar with only the Aurum. I demanded that he give it to me, for it was my sisters—he had failed to save the other Devante, and I no longer trusted him. He had failed to protect Metallum as he had promised. I decided I'd find someone else to keep the book safe. But Maverick refused to give me Aurum.'

'Is that when you made the deal?' asked Naldy. 'To pretend to be Betty?'

'When Ralph's message to my sister was mistakenly delivered to me, I chose to take the information to Maverick. Yes, I struck a deal with him. If I searched the house, he would relinquish the Aurum. When I arrived, I was relieved to find you both already searching the Witch House. Alas, I suppose it was foolish to trust the wizard a second time.'

While Barbra had been talking, a thought struck Naldy—if these really were pages from Metallum, the magic should work for her. All she had to do was reach out and take hold of the parchment resting in the centre of the table.

'You always put your trust in the wrong people,' said Betty, glaring at her sister.

Naldy wondered how the Devante worked. Did she simply need to think of the magic she wanted to create? If they could find the Corium, it might help her find her missing parents.

'Do not lecture me on trust,' said Barbra grumpily. 'I won't have it, especially not from the person who stole my Devante and carted it off to Edengar.'

In one swift movement, Naldy reached out and grabbed the scroll. She closed her eyes, focusing all her energy on the whereabouts of the Corium, hoping it would lead her to her parents—but she had never seen the Corium before, and she struggled to imagine it. The parchment was snatched from her hands.

'How dare you!' said Barbra hotly. 'I was right not to trust any of you.'

The parchment, now in Barbra's hands, remained

blank.

'I'm pleased to see you've failed,' said Barbra, standing and peering down at them in contempt. 'And what exactly were you hoping to waste my last precious page of Devante on?'

'I was thinking of the Corium,' said Naldy, trying to glimpse the scroll again, hoping a message had revealed itself.

Barbra laughed—a sound that was almost a cackle.

'A lower-ranking Devante,' Betty said kindly to Naldy, 'can't reveal the location of a higher-ranking one.'

'What's the use?' spat Naldy irritably. 'It won't let us find Maverick's location because that is a *Banned Spell,* and even if we manage to find him some other way, one little scroll is no match for a wizard with a whole Devante.'

Barbra's mouth fell open as splotches of black ink emerged on the parchment in her wrinkled hand.

'But that can't be—'

They all watched as the ink slowly shaped itself into cursive letters:

Ask Audry

'Who's Audry?' wondered Rupert aloud.

Before anyone could reply, the enchanted scroll burst into flames, which were quickly extinguished in a puff of dark smoke.

'There,' said Barbra testily. 'Now you have wasted our last chance of beating Maverick.'

'I don't know anyone named Audry,' said Naldy, squinting as she searched her memory.

'It appears no one here has heard of anyone by that name,' said Betty, glancing around at their confused faces.

'The foolish girl tried to break a *Banned Spell*,' grumbled Barbra, making her way to the hallway entrance. 'It spat out gobbledygook and went up in flames.'

'I didn't mean to destroy it,' said Naldy, tears welling in her eyes.

'Well, that's that,' said Barbra, wrapping her black cloak tightly around her body. 'Another chance gone.'

Barbra offered her sister a strained smile before departing the kitchen, huffing as she marched down the hallway. The front door opened and slammed shut.

Nobody said anything. They listened to the heavy rain as disappointment hung in the air.

'I'm sorry,' said Naldy weakly. 'I should have given it more thought. I forgot about the *Banned Spells*.'

'Do you think we confused it?' asked Rupert.

'No,' said Betty slowly. 'I think it's given us a clue.'

'A clue to finding the Corium?' asked Ralph excitedly.

'Perhaps,' said Betty, though her face looked troubled. 'I might be mistaken, but it seems Naldy has broken through the *Banned Spell of Knowledge*.'

'But if I've broken it,' said Naldy desperately, 'won't Maverick be able to see the location of the

Corium too?'

'If he tries using Aurum, I fear he may receive the same clue,' said Betty anxiously. 'I am not entirely sure what has happened, Naldy, but the *Banned Spells* are difficult to break, and it's rumoured it can only be done using the Corium.'

'But I wasn't trying to break it. I was thinking about... well, about...'

'It may not have been your doing, my dear,' said Betty, standing and carrying their empty cups to the sink. She seemed distracted, lost in thought. 'Maverick may have unintentionally weakened the *Banned Spell* when he tore out the pages and sacrificed the unborn dragons. Dragon properties are potent, and mixing such magic was foolish. One thing is certain: the parchment has given us a clue, and we must try to find Audry as quickly as possible.'

'Let me wash up,' said Rupert, making his way to the sink.

'Magic will do it,' said Betty, picking up one of the low-burning candles. The dishes began washing themselves. 'Let's get to bed. We need rest. Tomorrow, we begin our search for Audry.'

—*Chapter Eight*—

AUDRY

When Naldy entered the kitchen the following day, the early morning sun shone brilliantly onto the plants in Betty's back garden. The rain clouds had dispersed.

'Have you started a book club?' asked Naldy from the doorway.

Betty, Ralph, and Rupert were all sitting around the kitchen table, which was covered in stacks of dusty books.

'Come, have some brew,' said Betty sympathetically. 'You need time to process what you've been through, dear. Ralph tells me Oak was somewhat like a family member.'

'I'd rather the distraction,' replied Naldy, shifting a stack of books from the chair onto the table so she could sit.

'I'll make you some eggs,' offered Rupert, closing the book he'd been staring at. He seemed happy for the excuse to put it down.

'What is all this, then?' asked Naldy.

'We're searching for Audry,' said Ralph casually, turning the page of his large volume.

'In *The Rise and Fall of Witchcraft?*' said Naldy, reading the title of Ralph's book. 'I don't see how it'll help if we find a reference to an Audry who's no longer living.'

Betty rubbed her sore eyes in frustration, as though she'd been reading for a long time.

'The Devante,' said Betty, 'seems to have a pattern of being bequeathed through families. Rubrum was given to you, Naldy, and my family's Devante was passed to me through the Hexogg line. The Corium might also have been passed down through a family, and we might be able to find information on who that family is.'

'We think Audry could be a family name,' explained Ralph.

'Personally, I don't think books are the way to go about this,' remarked Rupert, cracking three eggs into a hot pan. 'We should ask the Seagull Society. I'm sure they'd be more than happy to help us.'

'The Seagull Society cannot be relied upon,' said Betty, pursing her lips. 'And I wouldn't trust them so willingly. Not all their members have good intentions.'

'I loathe reading,' Rupert muttered, adding chopped mushrooms and mashed garden turnips to his pan. 'We can't be certain it's a family name.'

'But you must agree,' said Ralph, putting his book aside, 'it's likely the scroll referred to an Audry who existed at the time the Devante were first created.'

'It seems,' said Naldy, 'we'll have as much luck finding Audry as we will finding the actual Corium.'

Ralph returned to his book while Betty stared out the window. When Rupert finished cooking, he brought Naldy's plate over and set it on a small pile of books, since there was no free space on the table.

'Maybe Barbra was right,' said Rupert. 'If Hannah was one of the cleverest witches to have ever lived, as everyone claims, then I imagine she was perfectly capable of hiding the Corium. We're wasting our energy trying to look for it.'

'If you aren't going to be helpful,' said Ralph tetchily, 'you ought not to bother helping. All you've done all morning is complain.'

'I'll be out in the garden,' replied Rupert, making his way to the back door. 'The plants need tending after last night's storm.'

He picked up his gardening gloves and stepped out into the sunshine.

'There must be loads of Audrys,' Naldy said glumly, eating breakfast carefully to avoid toppling the plate from the stack of books.

'I don't think reading will help us,' said Betty, squinting in thought. Ralph's expression deflated, but Betty quickly added, 'But I think Ralph is on the right track. I believe we're looking for an Audry— whether it be a first or last name—from the time of The Great Witch Hunt, when the Devante were created. There's one place we can find a trove of information from that time.'

'It's too dangerous,' said Ralph flatly.

'What's too dangerous?' asked Naldy, watching Rupert through the window as he replanted some uprooted flowers that had been battered by the storm. She felt disheartened that he was no longer participating.

'It has the largest collection of witch history,' said Betty. 'And not just books. We'd be bound to find something useful.'

'The Bleckdale Witchery Museum?' guessed Naldy. 'But it's huge. We'd need months to search the entire museum, and thousands of years if we planned on reading all the history books they have.'

'Not to mention,' added Ralph, with a hint of fear in his eyes, 'the last time we showed our faces there… have you forgotten? We've been warned not to return by Sallandra herself, the head of The Establishment and chairman of the board for the museum.'

'Yes,' said Betty, ignoring Ralph's hesitation, 'but it's the obvious place to search for Audrys from that period.'

'Is it?' said Naldy through a mouthful of mash. 'If we find a reference, how do we know it's the right Audry?'

'We can't be certain,' said Betty. 'But we can gather all references to Audry and then trace each lineage.'

'I suppose we could go in disguise,' suggested Ralph, his fear giving way to excitement at the prospect of exploring the vast museum again. 'No other place holds so much history—especially about witches!'

Betty drummed her fingers on the book she held,

her wrinkled face deep in thought.

'You can't both be serious,' said Naldy, looking from Betty to Ralph. 'We can't search The Bleckdale Witchery Museum. Have you both gone mad?'

'We'll need decent disguises,' said Betty calmly. 'They'll need to be very good if they are to protect us. I know just the person who can help with that.'

Betty stood and made her way to the window. She knocked on the glass, and Rupert glanced up curiously from the garden. Betty beckoned him to come inside.

'It will take us years,' said Naldy, frustrated.

Rupert entered, holding a bunch of purple flower clippings in his gloved hand.

'Rupert, how are your Pezileons coming along?'

'They're fully matured,' replied Rupert, removing his gloves. 'You need disguises?'

'We're paying The Bleckdale Witchery Museum what they would call an unwelcome visit.'

'I'll help with the disguises,' replied Rupert, sighing heavily, his expression tense. 'Though I'm not coming along with you. I think searching the museum is a mistake, and you'll be wasting your time.'

Rupert went about arranging his purple clippings into a vase. Betty squinted at him curiously, considering his words.

'The plan *is* madness,' agreed Naldy, setting down her knife and fork.

'But we haven't got another,' said Ralph.

When Rupert finished with the flowers, he placed

the vase on top of one of the books scattered across the table and returned to the garden.

'Madness it may be,' said Betty, turning to face them, 'but it's a risk worth taking. If we can trace Audry's family, we might have a real chance of finding the Corium.'

Once Ralph had reluctantly cleared most of the books from the table at Betty's insistence, Rupert returned from the garden, carrying three large white pods with green, string-like stalks attached at each end.

'Everybody pick one,' said Rupert, placing the pods on the table and sliding into a seat.

'What are they?' asked Naldy, reaching for a pod. Its outer skin had a slight furriness to it.

'Place your fingers in the top like this,' said Rupert. 'And pull the stalk to tear it open.'

Naldy tore open her pod and jumped with fright —there was a hairy blonde creature living inside! Rupert laughed, and Naldy realised the hair wasn't moving or, thankfully, attached to anything alive.

'It's not a creature,' explained Rupert, opening his plant's casing, which was filled with long red strands. 'It's hair, almost like the stuff on our heads, see?'

'Why do we need hair?' asked Ralph, squeamishly poking at the inside of his pod, which was filled with platinum-blonde strands.

'For your disguises,' said Rupert, taking Betty's pod from her to help remove the insides. Naldy watched as Rupert delicately pulled the strands in bunches until he held a large clump that looked as if it had been freshly clipped from a human's head.

'You need to be careful not to break them,' said Rupert. 'It's a little more delicate than human hair.'

Rupert made the hair extraction seem far more straightforward than it was. Naldy kept pulling out tangled clumps, unable to unknot them without snapping the strands. She was relieved to see Betty and Ralph struggling too. Rupert was patient, moving from one to the other, guiding their technique until they each held a head's worth of hair.

'It's so pretty and soft,' said Naldy, holding the blonde hair up to her own.

'I'll get the sewing kit,' said Betty, draping her red strands over the back of her chair.

By nightfall, they had each fashioned a realistic wig, thanks to Betty's knowledge of needlework spells. Bathed in flickering candlelight, they stood in the kitchen, laughing at how unrecognisable they looked.

'Ralph,' giggled Naldy, eyeing the platinum blonde strands that seemed firmly attached to his head. 'You are quite trendy with your long locks.'

'It might need more trimming,' said Ralph, brushing the long blonde fringe away from his eyes.

'No,' said Betty, holding the scissors away from him. 'You need to look unlike yourself. Keep it this length.'

Naldy's wig was shorter than Ralph's, barely covering her ears. Betty seemed years younger with her long red locks, much straighter than her usual wiry hairdo.

They remained in good spirits for the rest of the evening, and after dinner, Naldy climbed into bed feeling light and hopeful. She drifted off to sleep peacefully.

Her comfort didn't last long. She woke in the middle of the night, anxious and sweaty. As she lay restless in the darkened room, her hope slowly soured. Although making the disguises had been fun, she didn't like the idea of searching the museum. Naldy thought Rupert was right: finding a reference to Audry wouldn't help them. Were Betty and Ralph simply holding onto false hope?

Naldy wished she could ask Oak for his advice. He had always been wise on such matters. But Oak was gone. There was nobody left in Naldy's life whom she could truly trust and depend upon. A day of good company could never replace the bond of someone who had known her since birth—someone who had watched her grow and change over the years.

Naldy pulled the covers tight around her body, feeling acutely aware of her loneliness. She couldn't shake the image of Oak's lifeless, blackened stump. The dim room felt cold around her as she turned and sobbed into her pillow.

The next day brought more sun, and Naldy found Betty in the kitchen, instructing several sewing needles to fashion brightly coloured cloaks for them.

'We're trying *not* to draw attention,' said Ralph as

Betty passed him a bright purple cloak.

'We're trying to become other people,' replied Betty, handing Naldy a multicoloured floral cloak and reaching for the small needle, which was still busy securing the final thread.

'You should all change before you set out,' said Rupert wisely, waving a spatula. He was busy cooking breakfast by the stove.

'Rupert is right,' said Betty, wrapping her own cloak around her body. It was patterned with illustrations of blue trumpet flowers. 'We must put on our cloaks and wigs before we leave.'

'How do I look?' asked Ralph as Naldy straightened his platinum-blonde wig.

'Frightful,' said Rupert, smiling.

'Are you sure you don't want to come with us?' asked Naldy hopefully.

'I find museums dull,' replied Rupert, bringing the frypan over to fill their plates.

After breakfast, they made their way out into the garden. They couldn't help but smile at each other, dressed in their disguises.

'I wish you were coming with us,' said Betty sadly, turning to Rupert.

'You all look wonderful,' said Rupert, standing on the lawn and petting Smookers. 'I'll be fine here. Someone has to tend to the garden and keep Smookers company. I'd rather not spend days searching through old books and reading plaques in a stuffy museum.'

'We best be off,' said Betty, climbing onto her

broomstick. 'The day is getting on.'

Naldy mounted her own broom, with Ralph climbing on behind her. She was struck by how different the old witch looked, wrapped in her floral-print cloak, the breeze catching her long red hair. Ralph, too, appeared unlike his usual self, dressed in purple, with his blonde locks reflecting the sunshine.

'We will see you—hopefully soon,' said Ralph to his cousin as he gave Smookers one last pat.

Waving goodbye to Rupert, they kicked off the ground and shot upwards. Naldy wasn't nervous about returning to the museum and felt confident in their disguises. She also reminded herself that Maverick, who was on the museum's board, likely believed she and Ralph had perished in the fire.

The flight was serene. The sky was a brilliant blue with a few fluffy clouds and a gentle wind. Before long, Naldy could see the Great City's stone buildings jutting out above the tops of the Kirkwood Forest's pines. They descended, landing on one of the bustling streets. The main road hummed with horses pulling carts, bicycles, and people darting in and out of the many stone storefronts.

They weren't sure how long it'd take to find mentions of Audry at the museum, but Betty had arranged for them to stay nearby in one of The Great City's dwellings for a few weeks. They planned to visit the museum daily until they collected as many Audrys as possible. From there, they hoped to trace each Audry's lineage.

'This way,' said Betty, leading them away from the main road and along a narrow side street. They passed cafés and restaurants full of people joyfully drinking brew and eating scrumptious-looking meals.

They blended in with the rest of the city folk, draped in their patterned prints.

The cobblestone alley opened onto a wide street. Naldy saw the grand stone steps ascending to the tallest building—The Bleckdale Witchery Museum.

'We're just down here,' said Betty, guiding them past the familiar bistro, *The Mortismor,* where they had once traded fake artefacts for Ralph's freedom.

They stopped at the adjacent building. A sleek sign above the entrance read *The Golden Opulent.* Betty held the door open for them to enter.

Inside, the dwelling was the most extravagant Naldy had ever seen. It was a luxurious affair, with the staff all dressed in matching red cloaks lined with gold trim. When their porter led them up the varnished wooden staircase and opened the door to their shared suite, Naldy and Ralph audibly gasped at its elegance.

The suite was spacious, complete with a beautiful sofa and a grand fireplace. A clean marble bench separated the sitting room from the kitchenette, and a round, ornate dining table made of rosewood sat beneath a metal chandelier.

Floor-to-ceiling windows, framed by thick green velvet curtains, overlooked the museum. Through the glass, Naldy could see people across the wide road climbing the museum's many steps and entering through its enormous wooden doors.

'This is lovely,' marvelled Ralph, running his hands over the burgundy fabric of one of the lounge chairs.

'We need somewhere comfortable to return to at the end of each day,' said Betty. She tipped the porter and locked the door after he departed. 'Now, we must be careful not to leave the dwelling without wigs and cloaks.'

'I want to see the bedrooms,' said Ralph excitedly, darting down the gold-carpeted hallway that led to three comfortable bedrooms, each with its own spacious lavatory.

'I'd like to start immediately if we can,' said Betty, once Naldy and Ralph had finished exploring the suite. 'We're already dressed, and the museum won't close for a few hours yet.'

'Alright,' said Ralph hesitantly. 'But before we go, we must eat something. I'm so hungry after our flight.'

'I'll serve us lunch and tell you our cover story.'

'A cover story?'

'We are to be historians,' said Betty, 'researching for our new compendium. We don't want our many visits to draw suspicion.'

'Splendid,' said Ralph, though his voice betrayed a hint of nervousness.

Betty unpacked the food she'd brought in her rucksack and served them plates of buttered bread and dips. Naldy ate quickly, eager to make her way to the museum.

By the time they crossed the street, the afternoon sun was already low, casting long shadows across the buildings. They darted past two large horses pulling a carriage filled with several jovial male witches before making their way up the magnificent steps.

A guard greeted them with a friendly nod as they passed through the first set of grand wooden doors and approached the security checkpoint.

After emptying their pockets, the guard waved them through the second set of inner doors, which opened into an expansive entrance hall. Above them, a monstrous display of dragon bones hung from the ceiling, arranged to resemble a dragon in mid-flight.

'It's not quite as impressive as I remember,' said Ralph, staring up at the rib cage as they passed underneath, crossing the foyer. 'Not after being chased by the actual beast in Edengar.'

Glancing around, Naldy noticed how many stone corridors led out from this one room. Memories of the building's vastness flooded back. They had tasked themselves with the impossible, and Naldy wondered again if Rupert had been right—were they wasting their time trying to find references to Audry?

Betty led them along a corridor to the left, and they passed cabinets displaying ancient hand-woven rugs.

'Ooh, look,' said Ralph, delighted, 'magic carpets.'

'No, no,' said Betty, continuing on. 'These are regular floor carpets. The flying carpets, I believe, are three stories down.'

'Shouldn't we read the plaques?' Naldy asked, noticing that each rug had a metal plate beside it engraved with text. 'Perhaps one belonged to an Audry?'

'We could spend eternity in this museum,' said Betty, turning down a domed corridor. 'We must be strategic. Floor rugs are not a good place to start. We need to think about magical things invented around the same time Hannah Hale created the Devante. Then we'll move on to history books.'

Betty stopped when they reached a dimly lit room filled with glass cabinets exhibiting what appeared to be an extensive collection of dead insects.

'Is that a hairclip?' asked Ralph, unimpressed.

'It's not very imaginative, I admit,' said Betty, touching her red Pezileon hair. 'But they were invented during Hannah's era. I'll start on this side here, and you both inspect the plaques over there.'

Naldy strolled over to one of the displays featuring hairclips shaped like bright butterflies. She read the plaque:

The Insect Identification, Date Unknown
During The Great Witch Hunt, insect-shaped adornments symbolised defiance amongst witches and wizards rebelling against The Establishment. These disruptors often wore insect-shaped clips or brooches

in their hair or cloaks to identify themselves as part
of the rebellion. Butterflies were especially favoured
by witches living on the eastern side of the Kirkwood
Forest. The Establishment soon became aware of the
symbol and used it to capture those who sought to
violate its rules.

Naldy took a moment to observe the various hairclips, with their exquisite colours and patterns, before moving on to a cabinet filled with brown moth pins.

'I'm starting to doubt our plan will pay off,' said Ralph, coming to join her. 'We've allowed hope to get the better of us.'

'This is only our first room,' said Naldy, trying to remain optimistic. 'Let's give it some time, Ralph. We might find a mention of Audry yet.'

'I'm not convinced this is the best room to start with,' said Ralph, side-glancing Betty across the room. 'As pretty as the dragonfly buckles are, this room seems like a waste of precious time.'

'Let's give it a chance,' said Naldy. 'It seems these were quite popular during The Great Witch Hunt.'

'Yes, but the engravings weren't around then. I don't think reading all these plaques will help us. I think we ought to start with the history books.'

Naldy had read what felt like hundreds of plaques when a polite guard approached to inform them the museum would be closing. She had a headache from all the historical facts her brain had endured. Exhausted and disappointed, they trudged towards the exit.

The street was quiet when they emerged from the museum, and the sun had long since disappeared. A bright quarter moon hung low in the night sky.

'It's only our first day,' said Betty as they descended the museum's steps. 'We must give it time.'

'I think we should begin with the books tomorrow,' said Ralph, resolute.

'The museum has millions of books,' said Betty. 'I think our best option is the artefacts.'

Three-quarters of the way down the stairs, Naldy halted, hearing a strange noise drifting on the night air.

'Does anybody hear that?' asked Naldy. Ralph and Betty both stopped to listen.

The sound was faint but chilling, and it was coming closer with each passing moment. It was repetitive—a tormented, deep bellow followed by a high, reverberating squeal—growing louder and louder.

'It sounds like some sort of animal,' whispered Ralph, watching the street.

Whatever was producing the spine-tingling noise was moving in their direction. Its quick clops on the cobblestones echoing as it approached the main road. Betty took her hands out of her pockets, readying them—Naldy followed suit.

The stone buildings flanking the street reflected a dazzling orange light. A leagon, engulfed in flames, bolted down the centre of the main road. The beast appeared to be in intense pain, surrounded by unforgiving fire wrapping around its torso. The leagon's disturbing cries sent a chill through them. The few people walking the streets jumped out of the way in horror as the leagon passed.

'Can't we do something?' shrieked Ralph, but there was no water or dust nearby to use magic to extinguish the fire, and Naldy felt it was too late to save the creature.

The animal charged blindly along the road, stumbling slightly before disappearing from sight as it struggled into a side street. Soon, its squeals for help ceased altogether, and the street fell silent once more. They stood frozen on the museum's steps.

'I think I'm going to be sick,' muttered Ralph, holding his stomach, his face pale.

'Who would do such a thing?' asked Betty, her cheeks stained with tears.

Naldy couldn't speak. Her mouth felt dry.

'Someone without a heart,' said Ralph.

They walked sombrely across the road, not speaking as they entered the dwelling and climbed the staircase to their luxurious suite.

The image of the burning leagon seemed etched at the forefront of Naldy's mind. She wanted to push it out of her thoughts but couldn't. Betty poured them large glasses of apple cider, and they sat in the burgundy lounge chairs in silence. Naldy took off her wig and stared out the window at the street lamps, feeling drained and exhausted.

'Maybe we should take tomorrow off?' suggested Betty delicately.

'No,' said Ralph and Naldy in unison.

'The poor beast,' said Betty quietly.

'I've seen too many burnt leagons of late for it to be an accident,' said Naldy softly.

'But what would anybody gain by killing the leagon, and in such a brutal way?' asked Ralph, clutching his apple cider.

'I don't know,' replied Naldy, 'but I don't like it.'

'Let's get some dinner and then to bed with us,' said Betty. 'We can continue our search tomorrow— if you insist. Perhaps we'll have more luck finding Audry.'

While finishing their apple cider, Betty prepared them a large chickpea salad to share. A tension hung in the air while they ate their meal, and Naldy knew they were all thinking about the leagon, unable to shake the horrible image from their minds.

The next morning, when Betty knocked gently on Naldy's bedroom door, she felt groggy and tired. Despite the comfort of the bed, Naldy had barely slept and didn't feel like going to the museum. As she sleepily pulled on her cloak and pinned her wig, she wished she'd never agreed to return to The Great City.

That day, they had no luck finding any mention of Audrys. They had no luck the following day, nor the day after that. Hours were spent wandering down stone corridors and reading metal plaques. They read about strange magical items—

ancient cloaks, old scrolls, magical kitchen utensils, retired traditions, broomsticks, flying chairs, crystal balls, enchanted mirrors—the list of artefacts went on and on. However, none of the brass plates mentioned or hinted at a witch or wizard named Audry.

A week rolled by, then two, and they finished each day more exhausted than the last. During peak times, the museum was busy, and the noise from the excited patrons gave Naldy a headache. Luckily, the museum was large enough for them to move to a quieter chamber. Even there, however, Naldy often found her head still ached. She soon realised it wasn't the noisy chatter from the other visitors causing it, but rather the result of reading too many engraved panels.

Their brains were cloudy from all the new historical facts. Each evening, when they tossed their disguises aside, they felt deflated and barely had the energy left for conversation. They ate dinner, usually in silence, and then went to bed early.

One frosty morning, as they walked up the museum's steps, Naldy was surprised when Betty informed them it was their twenty-fifth day of searching. The guards at the museum entrance now waved and smiled at them fondly as they passed through the large wooden doors. They would ask how the research for their compendium was coming along, and the three of them would return forced smiles.

'This will take us longer than we're able to live,' said Ralph, skimming a plaque in a room full of poisonous swords.

'Should we go down to the books?' suggested Betty, rubbing her bloodshot eyes.

'I couldn't,' said Ralph, yawning. 'Not today. Let's do the next room and then call it a day.'

They lumbered along the stone corridor. Naldy scratched at her blonde wig, which had become unbearably itchy—Rupert had warned them washing the wigs would weaken the Pezileon fibres.

When they entered the next chamber, they were met by the sight of many aged tapestries hanging from the stone walls.

'Of course,' said Betty excitedly, 'how could I have forgotten!'

'Forgotten what?' asked Ralph.

'The family tree tapestries,' said Betty. 'This room might provide the answers we need.'

'We've spent weeks looking at knick-knacks,' said Ralph irritably, 'and meanwhile, there's an entire room dedicated to family trees.'

'While you were in Edengar, I turned ninety-eight, boy,' said Betty, the skin around her lips wrinkling as she pursed them. 'You cannot expect me to remember everything. Start on the wall over there.'

Naldy eagerly made her way to the far end of the chamber to begin along the left wall.

She wasn't interested in the artistry of the tapestry, and her eyes moved mechanically to the small metal plate:

Remains of Family Tapestry, 16th century
Before The Great Witch Hunt, decorative tapestries were a popular tradition in ancient magical families, primarily those of witches, though wizards later adopted the practice. The tapestries were often wrapped around the bodies of magical folk before they were burnt at the stake. Not surprisingly, the tapestries that survived the fire are only a portion of what these great artworks once were.

Naldy felt irritated at the mention of fire, and the image of the burning leagon pierced her thoughts again. She thought of Oak and the Witch House. She had lost a lot to the viciousness of fire.

Naldy stared at the tapestry—only a portion had survived, and its fabric was charred at the top. The entire bottom half was missing.

She wondered if her parents had ever owned a family tapestry like this one. She hadn't found one when they'd searched her family home for the Corium.

The delicate fabric was intricately woven, and all the names on the tapestry were embroidered in a gold cursive font. Dark green threads were twisted to resemble plants and flowers, enshrouding each word and connecting the names. The family name had been written boldly at the top, but only the last two letters had survived: L and E. Below this, there must have been at least fifty witches listed on the tapestry.

'Audry,' read Naldy aloud. 'It says Audry. I found one. Oh my, I can't believe it—quickly, come look! Near the bottom, there... Audry!'

Betty and Ralph rushed over, expressions of disbelief on their faces. They were lucky no museum guards were around, for they could hardly contain their excitement.

'Look near the bottom,' said Naldy, pointing at the golden lettering. 'The fabric is all black, but you can just make it out, and it's connected to somebody called'—Naldy gasped.

The name Audry was connected by a green thread to the name Hannah.

'Do you think it could be *the* Hannah?' asked Ralph with hopeful eyes.

'Hannah Hale, you mean,' said Betty, squinting thoughtfully at the tapestry. 'It is a possibility, yes. But only a slight one, I think.'

'But look,' said Ralph, pointing to the top of the tapestry. 'The family name ends in L-E—you can't deny it could be the Hannah Hale.'

'Hannah Hale is believed to have never married or had any offspring. This Hannah, however, is wedded to Audry, and together they had two children, though we cannot make out their names.'

Ralph shuffled his feet irritably, squinting at the two green threads stretching to where the tapestry ended, frayed and black.

'It is not as legend tells it,' remarked Betty. Noticing Ralph's deflated shoulders, she quickly added, 'But I suppose legends can be wrong.'

'It doesn't matter anyway,' said Naldy, her enthusiasm waning. 'There is no discernible last name, and the two children's names have been lost to the fire.'

'We should have listened to Rupert,' mumbled Ralph. 'We've wasted all this time searching for a name, and now that we've found one, it's proven to be a dead end.'

'Let's get back, and I'll make us some food,' said Betty, fidgeting with her floral-patterned cloak, and trying to sound encouraging. 'We will come back tomorrow, and we will keep going. There's bound to be other Audrys hiding in this enormous museum.'

'I don't want to keep looking tomorrow,' snapped Ralph, his voice echoing off the stone walls. 'We might have to accept it's useless. We should go home.'

'We don't have any other choice,' said Naldy gently. 'If this is the Audry we've been searching for, it's not enough information to track down any ancestors.'

'Come,' said Betty, 'I'll make us a comforting meal once we return to *The Golden Opulent*.'

They trudged after Betty back to the main entrance, dragging their feet stroppily. Betty took hold of their hands as they passed under the dragon bones.

'Stay calm,' she whispered, squeezing their fingers firmly. 'Just keep walking, and don't panic.'

'Panic?' said Ralph. 'Why would we panic?'

Naldy glanced up to see two familiar faces

conversing in the foyer beside the exit: a tall, pointy-nosed wizard—Sallandra—and, next to her, a spindly man with a black cane... Maverick.

Chapter Nine

MORTOUS

N aldy instinctively wanted to send a hex towards Maverick—not that it would have done any good if she had tried, as magic couldn't be used inside the museum without one of the guards' access stones. The wizard's presence stirred a deep hatred within her.

Betty calmly led them across the large entrance foyer, approaching Maverick and Sallandra, who were talking near the exit. Betty sidestepped patrons marvelling at the dragon bones dangling from the ceiling. Naldy felt heat rise within her as they drew closer to Maverick. Her mind flashed back to the cold black ash that Oak had become, and something in her knew it was Maverick who had killed the wise old tree. They were now within earshot, and Naldy slowed her pace, listening intently.

'And you're certain, my friend?' said Sallandra. She was as tall as Maverick, and her black hair reached her waist. She smoothed the delicate black fabric on the sides of her satin-lined cloak. 'It will be sad to see you depart. You have done much for the museum.'

'I am sad to be resigning from the board,' replied Maverick. His eyes were fixed on Sallandra's long nose as he leant on his black cane, his Imporiom. 'It feels like the right time, I think, to pass on my responsibilities to someone else.'

'You are too young to retire, Maverick.'

'Ralph,' muttered Betty under her breath, 'stop walking like someone is about to curse you.'

Ralph moved as though each step caused him pain. His disguise was good, and Naldy felt confident Maverick wouldn't recognise him clad in his platinum-blonde wig and purple cloak.

'I hear you plan on spending some time by the coast?' said Sallandra, tilting her head as if the idea struck her as out of character.

'Yes, I think some sea air will do me good,' replied Maverick. 'I also have some personal business I need to attend to.'

Naldy wished Betty would slow her pace. She wanted to hear what business Maverick would be attending to—had he located the Corium?

Betty was already halfway out the door, leaving Naldy little choice but to slip out after her, not wanting to attract attention. The museum guard smiled as they passed through the wooden doors.

They walked down the museum's steps and crossed the sunlit street, which was bustling with horse-drawn carriages and people going about their business.

By the time they unburdened themselves of their wigs and cloaks and slumped into the suite's cosy lounge chairs, Naldy had convinced herself Maverick had discovered the location of the Corium.

'I should have stayed and listened,' said Naldy, vexed with herself for not stopping to eavesdrop. She turned her head and noticed the late afternoon sun poking over the top of the museum across the road.

'There would have been no point in lingering,' said Ralph, with tired eyes, defeated from the long day spent reading historical facts. 'Even if he has found it, Maverick wouldn't have told Sallandra where it was.'

A tray floated over with fresh brew for them.

'I'm glad you didn't linger,' said Betty, helping herself to the brew. 'If they'd recognised you, we'd all be sitting behind bars. You don't need to be disappointed, though. We can keep looking tomorrow.'

'Not be disappointed,' repeated Naldy in a weary voice. 'We're no closer after all these weeks, and Maverick is off to the coast! We should change our plan. Now that we know where Maverick is, we could ambush him—or at least follow him. I've heard the northern beaches are divine.'

'It may not be the northern coast he's going to,' said Ralph.

'It'd be foolish,' said Betty sternly, 'to attack Maverick without the protection of a Devante. Tracking him would be just as risky.'

'I'm not sure we should give up on the tapestry,' replied Ralph gently. 'It's the only Audry we've found.'

'There wasn't enough information,' said Naldy.

'For argument's sake,' replied Ralph, thinking aloud, 'let's assume she was married, and it was *the* Hannah Hale. Surely somebody out there must know something about her relationship with Audry.'

Betty pursed her lips, leaning back in her chair. Naldy sensed the old witch's doubt.

'We're going to lose,' said Naldy sadly, glancing at the window where the sun had dipped below the stone blocks of the museum. It would be dark within the hour. 'We don't have time to trace Audry's ancestors. Maverick was talking about going to the sea—he's found the location of the Corium. I just know it.'

'Our best chance,' said Ralph, 'is the Audry from the tapestry.'

'I know a great deal about Hannah Hale,' began Betty, 'and let me tell you this, as history tells it: Hannah didn't have any children or spouse, and you won't find anyone from here to Arkus Day who believes she did.'

Naldy stood abruptly, causing Betty and Ralph to flinch in fright, their brews spilling everywhere— she had finally understood the scroll's message!

'We're not looking for any Audry,' said Naldy excitedly.

'Why'd you go and jump like that?' said Ralph, dabbing at the spilt brew with the sleeve of his cloak, trying to salvage the expensive chair.

'Don't you see?' said Naldy, unable to stop herself from smiling. 'We were never meant to be looking for Audry. The scroll has told us exactly where the Corium is. Ask Audry is not a person.'

'If Audry's not a person,' said Ralph irritably, 'then *what* is Audry?'

'It's a place.'

Both Betty and Ralph stared at Naldy with befuddled expressions.

'I don't know any places called Audry,' said Ralph, still blotting the chair with his sleeve.

'There is no Audry,' said Naldy, her heart racing. 'Ask Audry is an anagram—it's so obvious now that I see it. It's an anagram for Arkus Day. It came to me when Betty said the words. The egg's scroll told us exactly where we needed to go. It just jumbled the letters, and if you rearrange them, you get "Arkus Day".'

'Yes, so you do,' said Betty sombrely—she didn't seem to share the same excitement Naldy had.

'Do you think I'm wrong about it?' asked Naldy. 'It's along the coast, and I bet you that's where Maverick is going.'

'The problem, Naldy,' said Betty, waving her palms. A sponge from the small suite's kitchenette floated over to assist Ralph in cleaning up the spilt brew. 'The problem is that I believe you are quite right.'

'Then why aren't you as enthusiastic as I am?' said Naldy.

'Arkus Day,' remarked Ralph gloomily. 'That's

why we aren't excited.'

'We've travelled through Edengar, Ralph.'

'Yes, but Arkus Day is something else entirely.'

'Arkus Day,' said Betty quietly, 'is a place you would be unlikely to ever return from—if you were even lucky enough to make it there in the first place.'

'The journey to the east coast alone,' said Ralph, grimacing, 'requires navigating the Mortous Woods. Rupert's tales have put me off ever wanting to go there.'

'Then six months, at least, with the Boat Builder while you construct a ship,' added Betty. 'Then you have to face the sea, and if, after all that, you managed to make it to Arkus Day, you would still have to search for the Corium in the endless sand.'

'Maverick is talking about visiting the sea,' said Naldy, beginning to pace in frustration. 'If we don't race him there, he'll find the Corium and use it to eradicate all magic. We don't have a choice.'

'Perhaps you got it wrong, and we should spend some more time seeking another Audry,' said Ralph, trying to shift the conversation away from the idea of journeying to Arkus Day. 'Besides, maybe Maverick is just going on a sea holiday.'

'The only possible reason,' said Naldy, placing her hands on her hips, 'Maverick would resign all his positions with The Establishment is to go and fetch himself the Corium.'

'But how did he find out it was in Arkus Day?'

'Barbra,' answered Betty softly. 'She must have solved the anagram the night the scroll presented it to us, and she tipped off Maverick.'

'But why would she go and do that after Maverick betrayed her?'

'She is weak when it comes to promises of grandeur,' said Betty, rubbing her temples as if a headache had surfaced. 'I should have seen this coming.'

Betty perched on the edge of her seat. Though the sun had not fully set, a man outside was already lighting the streetlights in preparation for the approaching darkness. She beckoned Naldy to sit, and Naldy slid into the chair closest to the large window.

'What is it?' asked Naldy, concerned by Betty's seriousness.

'I fear we are too late,' said Betty thoughtfully. Ralph and Naldy leant forward, hanging on Betty's every word. 'This quest has always had little prospect of triumph. There has always been little hope. But now our hope has diminished further, it seems, nearly to the point of extinction. I ask you both to consider this and take a moment to reflect. Few have ever journeyed to Arkus Day, and fewer have returned.'

Betty paused, her expression tightening as if some pain bothered her.

'My sister is too old to journey to Arkus Day, and I believe that's why she reached out to Maverick. She wanted him to do her bidding, no doubt. But Maverick will not honour his agreement with her, whatever the agreement may be. My sister is perpetually the fool.'

'You're not coming with us?' said Naldy softly.

'It's not that I do not want to,' said Betty, tears in her eyes. 'But I, like my sister, am too old for such expeditions.'

'Too old?' said Ralph grumpily. 'Odorf was two hundred and fifteen, and she was always ahead of us in Edengar.'

'Odorf,' replied Betty snappily, 'may have been centuries old, but she was part of the Seagull Society and drank Veserum, which kept her youthful in body and spirit. I do not plan on going on forever. I do not think it wise.'

'But we cannot do it without you,' said Ralph bluntly.

'Do not feel obligated to do it at all,' said Betty, hardening her voice to emphasise her seriousness. 'It's a quest with the odds stacked against you, and I don't want either of you to feel it's your burden to carry—especially when it is likely to fail.'

'I won't speak for Ralph,' said Naldy, watching the lamplighter move on to another streetlight, 'but I plan on seeing this journey through to the end, whatever that may be.'

'Me too,' said Ralph, lifting his chin in Betty's direction. 'Even if we have to do it without your help.'

'Although I won't be able to travel with you,' said Betty, glancing out the window at the sky, now a dull navy blue, 'I do plan to do all I can to help from afar. Maverick will waste no time, and neither should we.

In the morning, we must head to Heatherton and then make for the Mortous Woods.'

'Cousin Rupert has tackled The Mortous Woods before,' added Ralph. He seemed glad they at least knew someone familiar with part of the journey. 'He also built a small ship under the Boat Builder's guidance.'

'Assuming he still wants to help us,' said Naldy, rising and crossing to the large window. Rupert had been right—they had wasted so many days studying ancient trinkets.

The museum steps were quiet, and Naldy was happy they no longer had to spend their days walking the long, stuffy corridors.

Naldy caught Betty's reflection in the glass as the old woman cast a spell to light the candles.

'I'll get dinner started for us,' said Betty, making her way to the small kitchenette. 'Ralph, would you go down and let the dwelling staff know this will be our last night? We'll be leaving first thing tomorrow.'

Morning brought a cold mist, and as they ate breakfast for the last time in the luxurious suite, the museum couldn't be seen across the road through the white haze.

'We'll need to put our wigs and cloaks on one last time,' said Betty, wrapping her pink dressing gown tightly around herself. 'We can take them off once we are far away from The Great City.'

Once they were dressed and Betty had settled their bill with the head dwellingtend, they stepped out into the thick fog and mounted their broomsticks. Rising above the white mist into the sunshine, they had a clear view of the Kirkwood Forest trees emerging from the fog. In The Great City only the Bleckdale Witchery Museum stood tall enough to poke through the haze.

The flight back to Heatherton was enjoyable, with the sun's warmth, fresh air, and wide open space. It was a welcome change after spending weeks crammed inside the museum's passageways, where the air had been stagnant. The mist cleared as they approached Betty's home.

Rupert was busy labouring in the back garden when they dismounted, and he beamed happily upon seeing them.

'It's been lonesome without all of you here,' he said, removing his leather gardening gloves and hurrying to embrace them in tight hugs. 'It's so good to see you all safe. Your hairpieces look well-worn. Come inside, and I'll make us some brew.'

Betty leant their broomsticks up against the house. Smookers came over to greet them, meowing happily, and they all made their way inside through the back door. Rupert had done a fine job caring for Betty's house while they'd been away. The wooden table had been freshly polished, and the windows were streak-free. They removed their disguises.

'I'm glad the Pezileon pods kept you out of trouble,' said Rupert, scooping dried bark and leaves into the cauldron. 'Tell me, were there any Audrys hiding at the museum?'

'There was one,' said Betty, standing by the kitchen bench, cutting thick slices of bread for them. 'But it wasn't helpful to us.'

'"Ask Audry" was an anagram,' explained Ralph.

'For "Arkus Day,"' added Betty, observing Rupert's reaction with curiosity.

Naldy, too, found herself gazing at Rupert, trying to decipher his thoughts on the news. Would Rupert journey with them?

'I knew it,' exclaimed Rupert, carefully taking the cauldron off the fireplace with a cotton cloth.

'You knew it was "Arkus Day"?' asked Ralph, astounded. 'And you didn't think to say anything?'

'No, not that,' said Rupert, tilting the amber water into the brewpot before sliding into the chair beside his cousin. 'I knew an adventure was coming. You see, I always crave domesticity before a big journey. This has been the most domestic I've felt in a long while, so I had a feeling a big expedition was on the horizon.'

'So, you'll come with us?' Naldy asked hopefully.

'I wouldn't miss it for anything,' replied Rupert, smiling to reveal his pearly white teeth. 'I already have my boat waiting with the Boat Builder on the east coast. I always knew one day I'd return and finally set sail to Arkus Day.'

'Let's eat up then,' said Betty, placing a board laden with cut fruits and buttered bread on the table. 'We mustn't delay any longer. I'd like to set out once we finish eating.'

'Today?' said Ralph, displeased. 'I thought we'd at

least take a few days to rest.'

'We cannot waste time,' said Betty. 'We will need to gather some advice.'

'Advice?' asked Rupert. 'From whom?'

'From someone who's been to Arkus Day, of course.'

Rupert leant forward curiously.

'I have an old friend,' said Betty, her grey eyes twinkling, 'he lives on the border of the woods. He'll never agree to travel with you, but he might be able to provide us with some useful information. He is a well-known witch, and you may have heard of him —Mortous Flint.'

Naldy recognised the name but couldn't think why. Ralph nodded. Rupert's mouth dropped open with excitement.

'*The* Mortous Flint?' said Rupert, shaking his head, unsure he'd heard correctly.

'The one and only,' said Betty, somewhat surprised by Rupert's enthusiasm. 'It has been some time since I've seen dear Mortous.'

'Who is this Mortous Flint?' asked Naldy.

'He was the first person to travel through the Mortous Woods,' said Ralph, picking up a slice of buttered bread.

'Of course,' said Naldy, realising why the name was familiar.

'He's one of the most respected witches of our time,' added Rupert, his face lit up with excitement. 'He is also one of the founding members of the Seagull Society.'

'Let's hope he can help us,' said Betty. 'Although I fear he may try and talk us out of going.'

After finishing lunch, Rupert lent Ralph some clothes, and Betty gave Naldy some of her old cloaks to take on their journey. Ralph and Naldy didn't have much, as most of their belongings had perished in the Witch House fire. To their surprise, Rupert had already packed most of his things.

'Like I told you,' said Rupert, lifting his rucksack onto his back, 'I had a feeling I'd be off on an adventure.'

They carried their rucksacks into the back garden.

'You'll have to stay here,' said Naldy, picking Smookers up from the grass and squeezing him. 'We've left a window open for you, and you'll have to hunt your own food until Betty returns in a day or two.'

Smookers meowed at Naldy, his furry face squinting in disapproval.

'Don't worry, Smookers. We will come back, too. It will just take us a little longer.'

Smookers wriggled free from Naldy's embrace as if protesting their departure.

It was already late afternoon, but the sun was still high in the sky. Betty fetched the two broomsticks while Rupert busied himself with watering some plants at the last minute.

Naldy felt sad to be leaving the comfort of Betty's home in Heatherton so soon. As she lifted her leather rucksack onto her back, she thought about their last perilous journey through Edengar. She was not looking forward to being on danger's doorstep again.

'Are we ready?' asked Betty, lifting an old leg over her broomstick, hovering mid-air.

'You'll look after the garden upon your return, won't you?' asked Rupert, climbing onto the broomstick behind Betty, taking in the colourful blooms one last time.

'I'm not sure I have your green thumb,' replied Betty. 'I will try, but the sooner you return from Arkus Day, Rupert, the better the garden will be for it.'

Naldy climbed onto her broomstick and felt Ralph clamber on behind her.

'You know,' said Naldy, 'we really need to teach you how to fly, Ralph.'

'I can fly just fine,' he replied, placing his hands on Naldy's waist. 'Just not on broomsticks.'

She kicked off the ground, following Betty and Rupert, and Naldy felt Ralph's grip tighten the higher they climbed. The sky was clear, and the air was fresh on their faces. Naldy could hardly believe a white mist had covered the ground earlier that day.

Few words were exchanged during the flight, and Naldy sensed a shared anxiety amongst them as they glided over the tall pine trees.

A few hours later, the setting sun had broken the sky into a brilliant orange and mauve. Below, a clear stretch of healthy green grass separated the last pine trees of Kirkwood Forest from the dark, thick trees of the Mortous Woods. No houses were built on the lush, grassy plain.

Betty steered her broomstick towards the ground, and Naldy did the same. They landed a little way from the perimeter of the woods.

'We'll need to go on foot from here,' said Betty, dismounting. 'It is dangerous to fly in these parts. We'd best hurry—darkness will be all around us soon.'

This was the farthest east Naldy had ever journeyed. They took quick steps across the soft, springy grass, which seemed nearly untouched, and stopped when they reached the edge of the Mortous Woods. The trees hung low, their branches broad, twisted, and knotted.

'Here we go,' said Ralph, staring at the winding dirt road leading into the woods. 'I already long to see the other side.'

'Let's not linger out here,' said Betty, making her way into the shadows of the woods. 'Day has almost left us, and Mortous's house is still some way. Quickly now.'

The road soon led them to a small castle, wedged amongst the woods. It was made of hefty grey stone, with branches curling along its walls, as though the castle stood long before the trees had ever grown.

'Mortous lives here?' asked Ralph, staring ominously at the ancient castle.

The stone windows had no glass in their frames, and the few with their wooden shutters left open revealed darkened rooms. If Naldy hadn't known better, she would have thought the building was abandoned.

When they reached the castle's wooden front door, Betty fixed her grey eyes on Rupert.

'Do not mention Arkus Day,' said Betty seriously. 'I think he may help us, but we should wait for the right moment before broaching the subject.'

Betty's knock reverberated inside the castle, and they waited patiently. When a short, portly man opened the door, he was unlike what Naldy had imagined the grand Mortous Flint to be.

Mortous was middle-aged, at least forty years younger than Betty, and his wispy brown hair was thin and partially balding. It was combed over in what appeared to be a rushed attempt to flatten it. Underneath his deep green robe, he wore a floral-printed nightshirt with matching silk trousers—the man had likely been preparing for bed before their unannounced arrival. The shape of his waist told Naldy that he didn't leave the confines of his castle much these days.

His face broke into a smile when he saw Betty.

'I would have sent word,' said Betty, returning Mortous's smile, 'but I know you're terrible at correspondence, and we'd be waiting months for an answer.'

'My dear Betty,' said Mortous in a gruff voice, 'I'm very pleased to see you. Glad, indeed, and I see you have brought good company.'

Mortous stepped aside, holding the door open for them.

'Do come in,' he said warmly. 'Darkness is at your heels.'

They shuffled inside, finding themselves in a large stone passage. No candles were burning, and the corridor was cast in dark shadows.

'This way,' said Mortous, closing the front door and tottering past them. They climbed a steep stone staircase, with Mortous breathing heavily as he led the way. When they reached the top, they found themselves in another long passageway where the cobwebbed chandelier was unlit. Mortous ushered them into a nearby chamber.

The only light in this room came from a large fireplace built into the stone wall. Mortous invited them to sit on the sofa before the crackling fire, and they cheerfully made their way across the rough stone floor covered in red and green antique rugs. A few scattered ottomans were against the walls, draped with white fur throw blankets from an animal Naldy didn't recognise. The room had a lot of open space.

Mortous threw open the wooden shutters of the nearest window. Naldy could see the tops of the woods' trees stretching out to the horizon, and she thought they looked much older than those of the Kirkwood Forest. The light had not yet faded, but stars were already appearing in the sky.

'I'll get us something to nibble and sip,' said Mortous, beaming at them before shuffling from the room.

They sat in silence, and Naldy watched as the

sky darkened. Mortous returned carrying an elegant wooden box on a silver tray. He placed it on the stone floor in front of the fireplace.

'I have a special something to welcome my new guests,' said Mortous, the skin around his mouth wrinkling as he grinned.

Mortous bent and carefully lifted the wooden box. He opened it to reveal five small glass phials, each filled with a red, blood-like liquid. Approaching Betty first, he offered the box to her.

'No, thank you,' said Betty, raising a hand in objection. 'I'd like to grow old and depart this place one day, Mortous.'

'I'd hate to offend you,' replied Mortous, and Naldy thought she saw him wink at Betty, 'but you have already grown old, my dear.'

Mortous moved along to Rupert, who was seated next to Betty.

'Thank you,' said Rupert, picking up one of the stoppered bottles and inspecting the thick liquid closely. 'My apologies, Mr Flint, but may I ask what it is?'

'This, oh,' said Mortous, his eyes twinkling with excitement. 'This is a marvellous creation, brewed in the windy south.'

'Veserum,' said Naldy from the far end of the sofa. She had recognised the potion from their travels with Odorf.

'Right you are, young lady,' said Mortous, pleased the potion wasn't unfamiliar to everyone. 'It prevents death from old age, Rupert. A rare concoction to get your pretty hands on. With a trove of gold, it is difficult to come by.'

Rupert stared at the phial with great curiosity.

'If old age is some way off,' continued Mortous, tapping Rupert's shoulder, 'as it is in your case, then it will keep you young. You will forever keep your handsome youth if you swallow one of these enchanting phials during each moon cycle.'

'Does it really prevent death, though?' asked Rupert in awe.

'From old age only,' said Betty. Naldy could sense the disapproval in her voice.

Mortous offered the box to Ralph next.

'No, thank you,' said Ralph, wrinkling his nose. 'I don't think I could stomach drinking a whole spoonful of dragon blood.'

'One per phial, yes,' said Mortous. 'The company you've brought with you, Betty, knows their ancient magic. I'm most impressed.'

'You know my thoughts on Veserum, Mortous,' said Betty. 'No good will come of it, and I think such magic will prove damaging.'

'You are probably right,' said Mortous, moving along and offering the Veserum to Naldy. 'In the wrong hands, such magic may be used for harm. But we are all in good company here. Let us drink and celebrate. One phial will not prevent aging forever —it will pause aging for the current moon cycle. To remain perpetually youthful, one must swallow the potion every cycle, as I do. I only wish I'd started younger.'

Naldy curiously picked up one of the delicate glass phials.

'Goody good,' said Mortous, placing the wooden box back on the tray and picking out a Veserum bottle for himself. Straightening his back, he raised the potion above his head. 'Here's to good company and long, joyous lives,' he continued, uncorking the stopper, 'potion or not.' He drained the potion in one gulp.

Naldy and Rupert uncorked their delicate bottles, and a sweet scent caught their nostrils. They both downed the thick red liquid.

The potion had a peppery taste, and when Naldy swallowed, the liquid warmed her throat. The Veserum was far more pleasant than she had expected.

'Addictive stuff,' said Mortous, putting down his empty bottle and dragging the nearest antique ottoman to the fireplace so he could sit facing the four of them.

'I take it this isn't a courtesy call,' continued Mortous, smiling at them. 'I sense another expedition through the woods might be on the horizon?'

Mortous was mostly eyeing Rupert, whose cheeks had turned red.

'I suppose you already know I am on the board of the Seagull Society,' said Mortous, shifting in the regal ottoman to make himself more comfortable.

'Yes, I do know that, sir,' said Rupert, blushing redder. 'It is an honour to have been invited into such an esteemed Society and to be here in your presence.'

'I had to fight hard to convince the members of the Society to accept someone without magical abilities,' said Mortous, flicking a hand towards the door. '*Arcesso.*'

'I am very grateful, truly. Thank you, sir,' said Rupert, bowing his head. 'I wasn't aware you played such a pivotal role in securing a place for me.'

'Oh, come now,' chuckled Mortous, as a tray laden with fresh brew floated into the room, 'you must call me Mortous.'

'Yes, Mr Flint, sir.'

'All of us must work together,' said Mortous, picking up a metal goblet filled with brew. The tray did the rounds, floating across to each of them before gliding from the chamber again. 'Magic has never teetered on the edge so precariously. We risk losing it entirely—yes, working together is imperative. Your many travels, Rupert, deserve much praise. I'm glad you have pledged your allegiance.'

'We need more than pledges, Mortous,' said Betty in a brittle voice. 'Your Society, although well-intentioned, does little more than hoard Veserum. Action is needed. Now, more than ever.'

'Betty has always disagreed with our practices,' said Mortous, pulling his green robe over his knee. 'Those with age chasing after them tend to have little patience. But we have been around a long time —the Society dates back to The Great Witch Hunt.'

'You talk of protecting magic,' Betty replied calmly. 'But the Devante are on the verge of extinction.'

'Always the pessimist,' said Mortous, chuckling once more. He smiled warmly at Betty before continuing. 'We've tried to welcome Betty into the Society many times, but she always turns us down. It is a pity.'

'There are some members I do not trust. As you are aware, Mortous.'

'Rupert, my dear boy,' said Mortous, pausing to sip from his goblet. 'As our newest member, you will soon be granted the privilege of hearing about our plans and preparations to guard magic.'

'How thrilling,' said Rupert, awestruck.

'It is, yes. Certain other members, although they've officially accepted you into the Society, are wary about divulging our secrets to you just yet. They do not like that you do not have magical abilities. But in time, you will be told all.'

'I am happy to wait,' replied Rupert, bowing his strawberry-blonde head. His hand reached proudly to touch the silver seagull pin on his cloak.

'They have agreed your shipments will arrive in the next delivery, which is undoubtedly pleasing news to you.'

'Shipments?' asked Rupert.

'The Veserum,' said Mortous, raising his wiry eyebrows excitedly. 'Every member receives their supply with the new moon cycle. All of the Society's members are much older than you, and I believe jealousy has played a role in some wanting to delay your shipments.'

'The same members I do not trust, presumably,' said Betty, frowning.

'I think,' said Mortous, 'they had hoped to delay Rupert's shipments until he reached their ripe age, but they cannot deprive him of all membership privileges. They signed off on you receiving Veserum a few nights ago.'

Rupert's mouth was agape, exposing his white teeth.

'You mean, I'm going to'—Rupert gulped—'live forever?'

'You'll live the rest of your life as the strapping young man you are,' said Mortous, pleased by Rupert's elation. 'But I cannot promise you will live forever. No magic can prevent death, and you will not be invincible. However, old age will not come for you.'

'Thank you, sir, truly, thank you.'

'Your previous travels should be rewarded,' said Mortous fondly. 'I am a traveller, as you know. You are the first non-magical person to venture through these woods and return alive, and that is something. And back for more adventures, I see. Taking these lovely witches and wizards with you, huh? But Betty —bless, I don't doubt your talents—but these woods are hardly fit for a witch of your maturity.'

Betty's lips pursed, and she flicked at her grey hair.

'We are not here for sightseeing,' said Betty dryly.

'We have come to you because we need your advice on travelling to Arkus Day.'

Mortous, who had been smirking cheekily, suddenly frowned.

'You must all be hungry after your journey here,' said Mortous irritably. He stood, wrapping his green robe tightly around himself. 'Let us go down and have some supper.'

Chapter Ten

ANSWERS IN ASHES

The dining chamber was a sumptuous affair. A long redwood table was laid with stoneware crockery, dainty silver cutlery encrusted with garnets, and matching metal goblets. A large chandelier hung low over the table, adorned with thick pillar candles that cast a mellow glow over the room. They sat together at the far end of the table. Mortous occupied the table's head, with Betty to his right and Rupert to his left. Naldy sat beside Betty, and Ralph was perched next to his cousin.

Small bowls of creamy pumpkin soup, served as a starter, floated into the room and landed in front of them, each garnished with a green forest leaf Naldy didn't recognise. The soup was delicious, and Naldy finished hers within minutes.

'Oh, dear! How could I have forgotten the wine,' exclaimed Mortous, turning in his chair to scowl at the doors as if they were to blame.

Their empty ceramic soup bowls lifted and drifted past their right shoulders in synchronised movement, floating out of the room.

Moments later, two large carafes of bright red wine glided through the doors. They were followed by several large rectangular trays piled high with fresh green vegetables, potatoes, a selection of roasted meats, buttered bread, and cooked grains.

'Do help yourself,' Mortous insisted, picking up the nearby silver tongs engraved with long-tailed feathered birds.

'You're an Effangale witch?' asked Naldy, surprised to have crossed paths with another. The ability to cast spells without speaking them aloud was thought to be rare amongst witches and wizards.

'Your friend Betty also,' said Mortous through a mouthful of potato. 'I sense it in the boy, Ralph, too. What good company, yes.'

'An outstanding feast,' said Betty, lifting her goblet to her lips. 'As it always is, Mortous. You've always been a fine host.'

'I do like to be prepared for guests,' said Mortous, dabbing his mouth with a white napkin embroidered with the outline of a seagull. 'There was once a time when all witches and wizards were Effangales, did you know? Before The Great Witch Hunt. However, the ability seems to have diminished since that dreadful time.'

'I don't wish to spoil your marvellous supper,' said Betty, watching Mortous to gauge his reaction. 'I know you do not like talking about it, Mortous, but we require your help.'

'The best time to discuss difficult things,' said

Mortous, piling his plate higher, 'is with a plate full of seasoned potatoes.'

'Betty tells us you've been to Arkus Day,' said Rupert eagerly.

'I have,' said Mortous, loading his plate higher. 'There's nothing there but mountains of sand. The lands are empty, and you won't find anything of value.'

'We believe,' said Betty, placing her fork down on her plate, 'the Corium might have been taken to Arkus Day.'

'You are quite right, Betty. We know it has,' said Mortous, beginning to cut his meat into bite-sized pieces. 'But you will not find it. I should not be disclosing such knowledge, and I won't dare ask how you came to know that bit of information. But I suppose it is one less Society secret Rupert will have to wait to learn.'

'You know the Corium is in Arkus Day?' pressed Naldy, her heart racing.

'The Society knows the whereabouts of all the Devante,' said Mortous, a bit of red wine dribbling down his chin. 'We know it resides somewhere in those lands. But there's no point in looking for it. You'll die of thirst before you ever come across it. The heat is unbearable, the sand beneath your feet burns, and the air is so hot it feels impossible to breathe—then, at night, it turns ice cold.'

'There is a wizard,' said Betty calmly, 'in possession of the Aurum, and we believe he is making his way to Arkus Day to seek out the Corium.

We need your help, Mortous.'

'Maverick Gadswell,' said Mortous, his lip curling as he spoke the wizard's name. 'The Seagull Society knows of him.'

'He has succeeded,' said Betty stiffly, 'in destroying six Devante and is currently in possession of the Aurum. He is going after the Corium, and we must stop him.'

'He won't find it,' replied Mortous, a little forcefully. 'Trust me, I tried myself once upon a time.'

'You travelled to Arkus Day to look for the Corium?' asked Naldy.

'It is the only reason anyone risks crossing the sea,' said Mortous, his eyes dropping to his plate. 'But the few who manage to return do so empty-handed. There is nothing but sand as far as the eye can see.'

'But there must be other ways you can help us,' said Ralph, his voice full of optimism. 'I understand you cannot help us locate the book—it could be buried anywhere—but you could at least give us some advice.'

'Book?' remarked Mortous, leaning across the table, fixing his gaze on Ralph. 'The Corium is not a book.'

They all stopped eating, and Rupert nearly choked on his potato. The candles from the chandelier cast a flickering light over Mortous as his thin lips widened into a half-smile.

'Yes, most of the Devante are indeed books,' he continued, sipping his goblet and spilling a little more wine onto his chin. 'However, the top four Devante are not.'

'Not books,' repeated Naldy, confused by what Mortous had said. 'But we've seen the Aurum, and it is a book.'

'And Metallum, too,' added Ralph.

'The Aurum and Metallum are presently in the shape of books,' said Mortous, 'you are right about that. But the books' pages do not hold the magic, and they are unlike the other Devante.'

'But if the spellbook doesn't hold the magic,' asked Ralph, 'then what does?'

'The gold and the metal.'

Naldy recalled the dazzling golden cover of the Aurum. It was one of the most beautiful things she had ever seen. She also recalled the brilliant cover of Metallum—melting into a pool of silver liquid under Maverick's wicked spell.

'The covers,' continued Mortous, his eyes twinkling, 'can be made into any shape—a piece of jewellery, for example—and its magic would still work. They haven't always been books; the Aurum was once fashioned into a golden crown, but that was many years ago.'

'If you know so much about the Devante,' said Naldy, twiddling her silver spoon irritably, 'and you've known their locations, why haven't you stopped Maverick from acquiring them? You claim to want to protect magic!'

Naldy felt Betty place a warning hand on her knee.

'We underestimated the wizard,' said Mortous, giving Naldy a prickly glance. 'Maverick is more skilled than we had thought. But you needn't worry about the Corium falling into his hands. It is lost amongst the sandy mountains of Arkus Day, and even a wizard with his ability will not find it. And that is that. Let us enjoy the rest of this fine meal.'

'And what about the other two?' asked Ralph, topping up his metal goblet. 'What is the Corium if it isn't a spellbook?'

Mortous placed his goblet on the table and leant back into his chair. His green silk robe fell open, revealing his floral pyjamas.

'The Corium, my friends, is a beast. A leagon, to be precise.'

'A leagon!' exclaimed Ralph, his brow scrunched in disbelief.

'Yes, dear boy, a leagon,' repeated Mortous earnestly, wrapping the robe tightly around himself. 'Arkus Day is no small desert, and wild leagons are constantly on the move, so let me assure you, there is little chance you'll find it when you arrive at Arkus Day, and nor will Maverick. It will be forever lost, as it should be.'

'That explains the burning leagons,' said Naldy quietly, more to herself than to anyone at the table. The horrifying image of the leagon on fire, squealing and bolting down the streets of The Great City, entered her mind.

'Maverick,' said Mortous, smothering his potatoes in more gravy, 'was under the impression that the leagon was somewhere in these lands. He has caused quite a mess—swaggering about, setting the poor beasts on fire. But you needn't worry; he won't find it amongst the endless sand dunes of Arkus Day.'

'Of course,' said Betty, shaking her head. 'It was foolish of me to restrict my thinking. Corium translates to "leather"—though some editions list it as "hide" or "skin" in Olde Witchery. We've spent all this time fixated on finding leather books.'

'Maverick abandoned caution,' said Mortous as the carafe lifted itself and topped up their goblets, 'and set alight any poor leagon he came across.'

'And the third book,' said Betty, 'Lignum—it translates to mean—'

'Wood,' said Naldy, her heart pounding in her chest.

'Sadly,' said Mortous, looking directly at Naldy, whose eyes had begun to well with tears, 'we couldn't save the oak tree.'

'Oak was a Devante,' muttered Naldy. She felt numb. 'All this time.'

Her mind struggled to accept the reality of what she had just vocalised. Oak had protected her family's spellbook and had been a Devante himself. She felt Betty place her hand on her knee again. This time, it was gentle and consoling.

'But he can't have been,' said Naldy, noticing the same bewilderment etched across Ralph's face. 'If Oak could do magic without the aid of the spellbook, he would have saved himself from the fire. He would have saved himself from Maverick.'

'We believe he tried,' said Mortous softly. 'It's why it took Maverick so many months to kill him. The wizard used a powerful fire spell created from the Devante.'

Naldy recalled the time she had once returned to warn Oak about Diamone's prediction. The tree had tried desperately to cast a spell to save himself, but the flames burned so fiercely they prevented him from speaking. On that occasion, Naldy had been the one to save him.

'But how can a leagon and a tree be a Devante?' asked Ralph, who seemed unable to believe what Mortous had revealed.

'Hannah Hale was a witch with extraordinary talent,' said Mortous, straightening his back. 'Her efforts to protect the craft are why the Devante hold such power.'

'But how do you use a tree,' said Ralph, letting out a laugh, 'or a leagon, for that matter, to produce magic?'

'It is far easier than you might imagine,' replied Mortous. 'Unfortunately, my boy, you're unlikely to ever possess a Devante to give it a try.'

'Are you feeling alright, Naldy?' asked Rupert gently, meeting her hazel eyes with his brilliant blue ones.

'It's a lot to process,' said Naldy, feeling light-headed. 'One moment we're searching for books, and the next we're running after a leagon.'

'Not just any leagon,' said Mortous, lifting his

gem-encrusted fork. 'The most prized leagon ever to have lived.'

'But how old is this leagon?' asked Ralph. 'Does it drink Veserum to stay alive?'

'The beasts can live hundreds and hundreds of years,' said Betty, the candlelight gleaming in her grey eyes. 'The oldest leagon is thought to be over seven hundred years old. The animals rarely give birth to offspring, and they...' Betty trailed off, having caught sight of Naldy's tear-streaked face. 'Oh, my darling girl.'

'I failed to warn Oak about Diamone's prediction,' mumbled Naldy as Mortous picked up a napkin embroidered with a seagull. 'I could have saved him.'

'You did all you could,' said Mortous, leaning over Betty to dab the napkin delicately on Naldy's cheek.

Naldy took a deep breath, wondering why Oak had never confided in her. Had the tree not trusted her? And why had her parents never said anything? Had they known Oak and the family spellbook were two of the most coveted magical things in existence?

'I've saved the best for last,' said Mortous heartily, clicking his fingers. 'This should cheer us all up a bit.'

At that moment, the old wooden doors at the far end of the room swung open. A crystal bowl of jellied pudding and a plate stacked high with profiteroles glazed in creamy chocolate sauce drifted in to meet them, while their dirty plates lifted from the table and glided out of the room.

'No more talk of sandy deserts,' said Mortous as the food settled in front of them. 'All this dreary talk.

Time for something sweet.'

'You always impress,' said Betty politely, eagerly picking up her polished silver spoon.

'Oh, yes,' said Mortous, gesturing with his hands for them to begin. 'I do like my pudding. I'll say one more thing on the subject. If you refuse to listen to me about the pointlessness of travelling to Arkus Day, you must listen to me about the fastest route through these woods. They are named after me.'

'Any guidance would be much welcomed, sir,' said Rupert, his face glowing with eagerness.

The sweets did little to lift Naldy's spirits, but she placed a profiterole on her dessert plate, wanting to show respect to their host.

'I take it you are journeying to the Boat Builder,' said Mortous, his tone reflecting his fondness for the man. 'It is peaceful out along the east coast. It has been some time since I have been out that way myself.'

'Mortous, my old friend,' said Betty, spooning a generous helping of jellied pudding onto her plate. 'While we appreciate your expertise regarding these woods, what these young ones really need before they set off is advice on crossing the sea.'

Mortous's delight dissipated. He put his profiterole onto his plate and placed his hands on the table's edge.

'These young ones, Betty,' repeated Mortous. 'Do you mean to say you won't accompany them?'

'As you said earlier, Mortous, I am too old for such expeditions. You were some years younger when you made the crossing yourself, Mortous.'

'There's nothing out there,' said Mortous tetchily, his hands gripping the table. 'You're sending the young ones to their death.'

'We know the danger,' said Naldy, sitting upright. 'We are well aware our quest is likely to fail. But we must try, and try we will. With or without your help, Mr Flint.'

Mortous released his grip on the table and smiled gently. He picked up his silver cutlery and ate a large spoonful of jellied pudding.

'Very well,' he said, swallowing. 'You walk to your bitter ends.'

'Maverick is on his way to Arkus Day,' said Ralph firmly. 'He will not stop, and so neither can we.'

'I cannot help you,' said Mortous casually. 'I cannot help you because my journey to Arkus Day wasn't completed with skill. There is no secret to crossing the sea. It was luck. I am lucky to be alive —days and days at the mercy of the ocean, kneeling at Mother Nature's guillotine—begging to be spared. There is nothing I can teach you or tell you that will assist.'

'There must be some guidance you can give,' Betty implored. 'Even something small.'

'May you have good weather,' mumbled Mortous snappily. 'And may your food not rot before the return journey—if you're lucky enough to have one. May luck befriend you all. Now, I don't want to hear another mention of Arkus Day. I'd like to savour this chocolate sauce.'

Silence descended, and only the clinking of Mortous's spoon on his plate could be heard. The candlelight danced over their disheartened faces. Everyone had abandoned their dessert except Mortous.

'Well, it is past bedtime,' said their host, rising from his regal dining chair. 'You'll excuse me. I have some business to attend to before I retire. Betty will show you to your rooms. She's familiar with the guest quarters.'

Before they could bid the man goodnight, he had hurried from the dining room, the doors opening and closing on their own.

'Now what?' asked Ralph, picking out the most chocolate-covered profiterole from the remaining stack.

'We'll try him again in the morning,' said Betty flatly. 'There's bound to be some advice in that old head of his. Perhaps he doesn't want our quest to succeed—envy, maybe. We'll attempt again tomorrow. Hopefully, we'll find him in a better mood.'

Betty led them up the stairs to the guest quarters and bid them goodnight. Naldy was given a room at the far end of the passageway. It was a spacious chamber with a cedarwood four-poster bed draped in red muslin. An open fireplace crackled softly, and the room's wooden shutters were wide open, revealing a view of the starry sky and a quarter moon shining down onto the shadowy trees.

It would not be long before they were sleeping

underneath the tangled trees of the Mortous Woods without any home comforts.

Naldy removed her shoes and clothes, then pulled on the black pyjamas laid out on the bed. She gathered the many decorative plump pillows from the bed, each hand-stitched with delicate embroidery, stacking them neatly on the floor. She sat on the clean linen, realising just how awake she felt. A surge of adrenaline coursed through her body as she thought about the Corium being a leagon and Oak having also been a Devante.

Dinner had ended abruptly, and Naldy felt she hadn't had time to properly reflect on the evening's discussions. She made her way to the door, pulled the ornate metal handle and stepped out into the corridor. Long shadows stretched across the hallway. The stone floor felt cold beneath her bare feet, and when she reached Ralph's guest room, the door was ajar, and she could see him sitting beside the fireplace. He seemed not to have noticed her arrival, focused on levitating an opulent vase, making it rotate slowly in mid-air as he admired its elegant blue hand-painted pattern.

Naldy knocked on the door. Ralph turned in alarm—the vase reunited with gravity, plummeting to the stone tiles and shattering.

'*Restituo!*' said Naldy, flicking her wrists. The vase mended itself until it lay, whole again, neatly on the floor.

'I didn't hear you coming,' said Ralph, picking up the repaired vase.

From the doorway, Naldy could see the cracks in the porcelain where the vase had mended. Ralph seemed unimpressed by her repair job.

'I thought Mortous would be more helpful,' said Ralph. 'He's a well-known witch, and many scholarly articles have been written about him. It's disappointing.'

Ralph deliberately dropped the vase on the stone tiles—the sound made Naldy flinch as it shattered again. Then, the vase repaired itself a second time, and Ralph picked it up from the floor.

'That's better,' he said as Naldy stepped closer to the fire. He was right—only a slight crack could be seen, and the vase was almost as good as new.

'You're getting good at that,' said Naldy, sitting in one of the brocade armchairs. 'A little too good.'

Ralph returned a proud smile.

'Can't sleep either?' asked Naldy.

'It's not our looming trip through the Mortous Woods that worries me,' replied Ralph as the vase glided from his hands and landed atop the fireplace mantle, joining its twin resting on the opposite ledge. 'It's what Mortous said about us needing luck.'

'We're well overdue for some luck,' said Naldy.

'I'm glad we have Cousin Rupert to guide us through these woods,' remarked Ralph. 'Though I've never been on a boat before, and I'm not looking forward to it.'

'It'll be a first for the both of us. For your cousin, Rupert, too, it seems.'

'I don't know if I want any more adventures,' said

Ralph, warming his hands by the fire. 'A part of me wants to walk away from it all.'

'You can,' replied Naldy, watching Ralph lift another log onto the flames.

'I'm in this until the end, Naldy,' said Ralph, the fire casting a glimmering light over his face. 'Bitter or sweet, and whenever it may be.'

'I can't help but think...' Naldy began, but she trailed off into silence.

'What is it?' asked Ralph gently.

'My family's spellbook, Rubrum,' she said, 'and Oak, too—they were both Devante. I can't help but wonder if my parents' disappearance had something to do with this magic.'

Naldy couldn't quell the nagging thought that her parents must have known something.

'Maybe they left to protect you,' suggested Ralph softly.

'They just disappeared,' said Naldy painfully, 'without even leaving a note.'

'Do you think someone abducted them?' asked Ralph.

'I don't know what happened to them,' said Naldy, shifting uncomfortably in her seat. 'But I can't shake the feeling the Devante had something to do with it, and I'm starting to think I might never know the truth.'

'Do you think Maverick played a part?'

Naldy glanced up at Ralph, who was still gazing into the fire. The same thought had crossed her mind.

'We should get some sleep,' she mumbled, rising from her chair. 'We'll have to leave shortly after breakfast tomorrow.'

'I wish we could stay and enjoy the comfort of this place,' said Ralph, stretching tiredly.

'Perhaps we can stay a while when we return,' she said, smiling faintly.

When Naldy made her way back to her room and slumped into the comfortable chair in front of her own fireplace, Mortous's words echoed in her mind: *And may your food not rot before the return journey—if you're lucky enough to have one.*

The mesmerising fire danced in the hearth as sleepiness gradually set in. Her eyes fell shut, and the crackling of a burning oak tree soon seeped into her dreams.

Thick smoke obscured the blue sky as Maverick stood by a clearing, leaning on his black cane, a triumphant smirk spreading across his face. A seagull perched itself high in the branches of a nearby pine tree, its beady yellow eyes watching intently.

Chapter Eleven

BREAKFAST BY THE GARDEN

When Naldy woke, the hearth held nothing more than warm ashes and dying embers. She had inadvertently slept in the chair beside the fireplace. The glittering sun roused her, and through the open window, she glimpsed the knotted treetops, intertwining to create a deep green and brown canopy.

After bathing in the guest bathroom's large cast-iron clawfoot tub, where she had admired the high ceiling decorated with drooping ferns in wicker baskets, Naldy made her way to the dining chamber, where they'd had supper the evening before.

At first, Naldy thought she was the first to wake, as the castle was quiet and the dining room was empty. But Rupert's strawberry-blonde head soon appeared through the doorway, informing her that everyone was patiently waiting outside.

'Breakfast is out on the terrace,' announced Rupert cheerfully. 'It's quite the spread. Wait until you see it!'

Rupert led the way to the spacious covered terrace at the far end of the castle, where Naldy was met with two spectacular views. The first was through a floor-to-ceiling opening in the stone walls that stretched the length of the terrace. She gazed upon a small, well-tended garden boasting ornate fountains, several regal marble statues, and a cobbled path winding between many curious plants. On all sides, the imposing trees of the Mortous Woods flanked the garden.

The second view that impressed Naldy was the lavish banquet spread across the long table. There was enough food to feed a small town: crumpets, eggs, slices of bread, sausages, cheeses, breakfast cakes, fruits, pastries, various delicious-smelling brews, and even a flagon of leagon milk. The air was filled with the mouth-watering aromas of sweet jams and smoked meats.

'Come,' said Mortous, dressed in a frilly lilac shirt. 'Take a seat next to Betty here. We wouldn't dare commence eating without you.'

The tall-backed, elegant chairs were arranged along one side of the table, positioned perfectly to enjoy the view of the sun-drenched garden.

'Do help yourself now,' said Mortous as Naldy crossed the terrace and took the empty seat next to Betty.

The central chair, occupied by Mortous, was grander than the others. Rupert and Ralph sat to his left, while Betty and Naldy were seated to his right.

'I hope you all slept well,' Mortous remarked as they loaded their plates with food, eager to try everything.

'This looks delightful,' said Ralph, balancing some cherries on top of the stack of food already piled high on his plate.

'We can't send you out into the woods on empty stomachs,' said Mortous. 'You'll want to set out as soon as breakfast is done, to get as much walking in while the sun is still high.'

Ralph's shoulders sagged, and Naldy felt equally low-spirited about their forthcoming journey. The memories of Edengar were still fresh in their minds. Mortous seemed to pick up on their lack of enthusiasm, patting Rupert on the back as he declared, 'You have one of the best guides travelling with you.'

'It has been a while,' said Rupert, blushing. 'Many months since I last travelled through these woods.'

'Nonsense,' said Mortous, filling his goblet with orange juice. 'You are a seasoned traveller and one of the few to have made it all the way to the Boat Builder.'

'I suppose,' replied Rupert, sitting up proudly.

'You are rather quiet this morning, Betty,' said Mortous, turning in his throne-like chair to meet the old woman's grey eyes. 'You know, it's not too late to abandon your journey. You'd all be welcome to stay here for a few weeks, and you'd be well looked after. There's no need for gloomy faces. You can trust that neither you nor Maverick will ever find the Corium, for it is lost—and will remain that way forever.'

'I had hoped, Mortous,' said Betty calmly, 'you had better advice to offer.'

'Luck,' said Mortous, biting into a raspberry pastry. 'Is all the advice I can give. But do not waste another brilliant meal dwelling on it. I have a surprise for all of you.'

'A surprise?' Rupert repeated excitedly.

'Maverick,' explained Mortous, 'was sighted before dawn, heading into the woods.'

'Then we are already behind,' said Betty, standing. 'We must not waste another moment. Their journey through the woods must begin right away.'

'An unpleasant surprise,' said Ralph flatly.

'Do sit down,' said Mortous, chuckling at Betty's urgency. 'That is not the surprise. If you insist on setting out, then you must eat first. There is no point in starting anything on an empty stomach.'

'We can't allow Maverick to reach Arkus Day before us,' Naldy insisted impatiently.

'It's unlikely any of you will reach Arkus Day at all,' said Mortous, a smirk playing on his lips. He leant back in his chair, and the top button on his lilac-coloured shirt popped open, revealing tufts of brown hair on his chest. 'Regardless, he won't reach the Boat Builder before you because, well, as I said, I have a surprise for you. A secret, I should say.'

'A secret?' asked Ralph, smiling nervously.

'Yes, boy,' he said haughtily. 'The Mortous Woods holds many secrets, most of which are still unknown, even to me. But I have a secret that will cut your travel time by three-quarters, and it will see you reach the Boat Builder long before Maverick and the fat man he's travelling with.'

'Getergrin,' said Naldy, knowing whom Mortous was referring to.

'What secret is this?' asked Rupert curiously. Everyone had stopped eating, eagerly waiting to hear it.

'The secret of the Versalius Lake,' said Mortous, his eyes widening dramatically. The witch picked up a nearby slice of apple, chewing it as he smiled to himself, as though what he'd just disclosed was something to marvel at.

'But we can't journey across the lake,' said Rupert, also helping himself to a slice of apple. 'They say an evil swims beneath those waters. Nobody has ever crossed the lake and survived.'

'Yes, that is what they say,' said Mortous, chortling. 'But it is not true. I have a boat moored beside the lake, which I once used frequently for quick journeys to the seaside. The lake's water is calm, and it takes just a few days to sail across. You'll be at least a week ahead of Maverick.'

'But surely we cannot cross the lake,' remarked Rupert, his brow furrowed with concern. 'It is well known to be the most dangerous part of the woods, and even getting close to the lake is said to be foolish.'

'You mustn't worry,' said Mortous, as a small ramekin of jam floated towards him. 'Fear is a powerful force that has kept the lake's secret hidden for many years. But it seems the right time to pass the secret on has arrived. If I can't deter you, I shall help you as best I can.'

'I do thank you, Mortous,' said Betty, returning to her morning brew. 'I knew you would be able to offer some guidance. We appreciate your hospitality and your help. And your brew is the finest there is—it is a pleasure to enjoy it with you again.'

'You mean to say it's not dangerous?' asked Rupert, still flummoxed by the news.

'Quite the opposite,' replied Mortous. 'It is the safest place one could be in these woods. Safer than the castle we are currently in.'

'How do you know Maverick entered the woods?' asked Naldy. As she mentioned the wizard's name an anger prickled within her.

'We have our eyes on him,' said Mortous, placing a hand on his stomach to emphasise his satisfaction with the feast he'd prepared. 'It is a matter of time before the secrets of the Seagull Society are passed on to Rupert here. The other members might be bitter that I've divulged this information prematurely, but you are due to find these things out in good time.'

'What an honour, sir,' said Rupert, his cheeks flushed.

'Yes, well, the lake will likely see you arrive at the east coast at least a week before Maverick and his sidekick,' said Mortous cheerily. 'However, there is the issue of a boat. The Boat Builder is strict and won't let you sail away on any vessel—you must build one with him. It could take months.'

'Not to worry,' said Rupert, brushing at his

strawberry-blonde fringe. 'I already have a boat waiting.'

'Of course you do,' replied Mortous, plucking a grape from a nearby bowl. 'How could it have slipped my mind? You spent some time there, didn't you? I must ask—what stopped you from setting sail to Arkus Day last time you were on the east coast?'

'I've always craved adventure,' said Rupert, fingering the silver seagull brooch. 'I wanted to see the world. I want to see as much of it as I can. But the time it took to construct the boat made me reconsider the risks.'

'Yes, many risks,' said Mortous.

'It is getting late,' said Betty, wiping her mouth with a napkin. 'I'm sorry to rush, Mortous, but even with your shortcut, we should prepare them to depart.'

'Not before I've shown Rupert my garden,' said Mortous, standing and picking up his goblet of orange juice. 'I saw Rupert eyeing my Thistle Greniers. Come, let me show you while the others finish their meal.'

Rupert gaily accompanied Mortous into the garden, leaving the others at the breakfast table. They ate in silence for a moment, watching as Mortous, from the far end of the garden, pointed out various plants. Rupert appeared thrilled to be receiving a private tour.

'I don't trust him,' said Betty, narrowing her eyes.

'I thought you said he was a friend,' said Ralph, buttering his third crumpet.

'Old friends, yes,' said Betty, looking down at the table. 'We've known each other a long time, but I fear our friendship isn't a priority for him. His loyalty lies in protecting the Devante.'

'But that's what we're doing,' said Naldy, watching Rupert sniff a flower Mortous held up to his nose. 'We're trying to protect the Devante too.'

'He doesn't trust us,' said Betty. 'I can tell. There is something he is not telling us.'

'Maybe Mortous is right,' said Ralph through a mouthful of crumpet. 'Maybe we are simply wasting our time trying to cross the sea. He knows more about the Devante than we do. We had no idea the Corium was a leagon.'

'Mortous is certainly wise on some matters,' confessed Betty, addressing Ralph solemnly, 'but I fear he underestimates Maverick.'

Naldy saw Mortous slip an envelope into Rupert's hands. The witch leant in and whispered something. Rupert nodded, stuffing the envelope into his cloak pocket. Neither Betty nor Ralph seemed to have noticed the peculiar exchange, and Naldy assumed it was likely related to official Society business.

'I wish you were coming with us, Betty,' said Ralph, biting into a juicy slice of cantaloupe.

'I am an old woman, Ralph,' said Betty gently. 'If I come with you, the odds of succeeding diminish further. I will only slow the party.'

Ralph abandoned his cantaloupe and reached for a pastry, as if trying to get in one last bite of everything.

'You have had little chance to consider what lies ahead,' Betty continued, her tone serious. 'Do not make the decision to go lightly. Neither of you is responsible for saving the Corium, and you needn't go further if you do not wish to.'

Naldy considered Betty's words but couldn't shake the weight of responsibility from her mind. If it was not their burden, then whose?

'I might go and get ready,' said Naldy softly, lifting herself from the chair.

Less than an hour later, they stood on the dirt road outside the castle, the sun reflecting off the building's old stone bricks. Rupert rested his hands on his hips, an eagerness spreading across his face.

'You're too happy for my liking,' remarked Ralph, fidgeting with the leather straps on his rucksack. 'We're about to journey through one of the most dangerous woods.'

'We're off on an adventure,' declared Rupert, lifting his face to the sun's warmth.

Betty and Mortous stood near the castle's front door, deep in a tense conversation. Naldy strained her ears, trying to overhear what they were fervently discussing.

'It's not often I wish we could make the journey on broomsticks,' said Ralph, kicking a small stone.

'The trees grow too close together,' replied Rupert, soaking up the sunlight. 'The flight would be too far, and it would be foolish to risk landing in the treetops.'

Mortous caught sight of Naldy staring and

quickly broke away, strolling over to join them.

'Be on the lookout for a seagull, Rupert,' said Mortous, bouncing on the balls of his feet. 'It will be delivering your first shipment of Veserum. The new moon is but a few nights away.'

'We'll stop by on our way back,' said Rupert with a smile. 'I'd love to spend more time in your garden.'

'Oh, yes,' said Mortous, sounding oddly hesitant. Naldy got the distinct impression that Mortous didn't believe they would be returning.

'I want to see the Night Fennings in bloom,' said Rupert cheerfully.

'It was my pleasure to host you all,' said Mortous. 'I wish you a safe and pleasant journey through these woods.'

Betty wiped her cheeks, tears trickling down them, and Rupert embraced her affectionately.

'Don't worry about us,' said Rupert confidently. 'We'll be back soon enough.'

Betty gently pulled away, then turned and threw her arms around Naldy.

'I don't trust this shortcut,' Betty whispered in her ear. 'Be mindful as you move through these woods.'

Ralph stared ominously at the thick, unwelcoming trees that surrounded them, and Betty pulled him into a comforting hug. Although the sun touched their faces as they stood on the road beside the castle, it couldn't penetrate the unruly canopy of the woods, which lay in darkness.

'It's important you all know,' said Betty, releasing

Ralph from her embrace, 'that you can always stay.'

'I'm going,' said Ralph, touching the emerald jewel dangling from his silver earring. 'Perhaps I'll get a chance to put my skills to the test along the way.'

'I've no doubt you will,' replied Betty.

'I almost forgot,' said Mortous, retrieving a rolled parchment from his cloak, 'you'll be needing this.'

He passed the yellowed parchment to Naldy, and she unrolled it to reveal a familiar list:

H,
Corium
Aurum

'How did you get this?' asked Ralph, glancing over Naldy's shoulder at the parchment.

'Betty told me the list of Devante you carried perished in a fire,' said Mortous. 'Eight of these enchanted lists once existed, created as a companion for each Devante. Of course, they have not been kept together all these years, and some have not survived.'

'My sister's lack of Devante lore led her to give Maverick two lists,' said Betty as a light breeze stirred her wiry grey hair. 'One belonging to Rosea and the other to Metallum.'

'And one of those,' added Mortous, 'Betty tells me Maverick foolishly gave to you, Ralph.'

'You must not be ignorant,' continued Betty. 'Go, knowing full well the danger you are all walking into.'

'Wise words, Betty,' said Mortous, a smile still on his face. 'Do not worry if you lose this list, for the Society has two more in our possession. We do not know the whereabouts of the others, but Betty insists that you should take one with you. You'll need to know if Maverick has beaten you to the Corium.'

'Take care of Smookers when you return to Heatherton,' said Naldy softly. She smiled at Betty, who returned a sad half-smile. Naldy couldn't help but wonder if this would be their final goodbye.

'Be sure to water the Pezileons every fifth day,' said Rupert to Betty, before marching into the shadows of the woods. Ralph hurried after his cousin, not wanting to be left behind.

Naldy took a deep breath, then turned and stepped off the dirt road.

Crossing into the shadows of the woods, Naldy felt a chill on her skin, as if the temperature had dropped several degrees. It took a moment for her eyes to adjust to the darkness as she hurried to catch up to the silhouettes of Rupert and Ralph.

'I can't believe you get pleasure from this,' said Ralph to his cousin, as they navigated the many fallen branches, dead leaves, and overgrown moss. There was no path to follow.

'Don't you find it exciting?' asked Rupert, who seemed to be navigating the uneven ground effortlessly. 'There's no knowing what awaits us. Thrilling, isn't it!'

Naldy tried to catch one last glimpse of Mortous's castle, but it was already obscured by dark tree trunks, and only slivers of light could be seen.

'Oh yes,' remarked Ralph sarcastically. 'Thrilling!'

Chapter Twelve

THE WITCH'S WAY

The further they ventured into the Mortous Woods, the darker it became. The tangled treetops obscured the entire sky.

'We best set up camp here,' said Rupert, stopping between two thick trees that must have been extraordinarily old.

'I thought we'd never stop,' said Ralph, slumping onto a nearby log.

'Cousin, if you fetch some firewood,' said Rupert, inspecting the moss-strewn forest floor before throwing down his rucksack, 'Naldy and I will go find us some food.'

'But we've got food,' said Ralph, reaching into his own rucksack. 'Mortous packed us the loveliest pickled meats.'

'We'll have to save that for later,' said Rupert. 'The further we venture into these woods, the less wild fare there is to be found.'

Ralph groaned, slouching his shoulders.

'Not those ones,' called Rupert sternly, as Naldy bent to pluck a juicy mushroom from beneath a nearby tree. 'Those are poisonous.'

'It seems almost every shrub and growth in this forest is poisonous. How do you know what is and isn't going to kill you?'

'Understanding which vegetation will harm you and which won't,' said Rupert, pointing to a few smaller mushrooms nearby, 'is key to surviving these woods.'

'Gardening,' remarked Naldy, watching Rupert delicately pluck the soft-stemmed mushrooms. 'And how do you know the night is approaching? It always seems dark in here.'

'Can't you sense it?'

'Sense it? It feels like an endless twilight beneath these trees.'

'It'll get darker before long,' said Rupert, reaching into his rucksack to retrieve a small cauldron Mortous had packed for them. 'Travelling at night in these woods would be foolish. We'd best hurry and find more food.'

Naldy and Rupert set off to search for more edible vegetation, leaving Ralph behind to light the fire.

When they returned with a cauldron full of mushrooms and chickweed, they found Ralph had lit an impressive blaze. Naldy, thankful for the warmth, cosied up to the crackling fire as Rupert prepared dinner.

Soon, Rupert was serving them generous helpings of chickweed salad with the fire-roasted mushrooms, dressed in a delicious vinegar wine that Mortous had packed for them. A biting chill set in.

With the darkness came a cacophony of noise: insects calling to one another, night birds humming, and frogs croaking. But the most unsettling sound was the occasional distant screech.

'It's a night-cretingale,' informed Rupert. 'It won't bother us as long as we keep the fire going.'

'How are we supposed to sleep?' asked Ralph, warily eyeing the shadows as if some beast might cross through the curtain of black at any moment.

'You needn't worry,' said Rupert, unperturbed by the forest's liveliness. 'The fire will protect us... at least from most things.'

'Most things?' gulped Ralph.

'Well,' said Rupert, as Ralph slapped his own neck to squash an opportunistic mosquito, 'the insects will have their way, but I have an ointment that will ease any itching.'

'Will it take us long to reach the east coast?' asked Naldy.

'Depends,' Rupert replied, the dancing fire reflecting in his blue eyes. There was a hesitation before he continued. 'I've never taken the route Mortous suggested.'

'What was the letter he gave you?' asked Naldy curiously, recalling the odd exchange between Rupert and Mortous in the garden.

'That,' said Rupert, opening his palms to the fire. 'Just some Society business. It's something for the Boat Builder. He's a member of the Seagull Society too, did you know?'

'I don't understand why Betty dislikes the Society

so passionately,' said Naldy. 'She has the same objective as them—wanting to protect magic—and I don't see why she doesn't join.'

'I don't mean to offend you, Cousin,' said Ralph, swatting at a persistent bug trying to get at his ears, 'but the idea of drinking Veserum and living forever sounds terrifying. It's obvious why she didn't join.'

'I had many conversations with Betty about it,' said Rupert. 'She told me they have a reputation for being ruthless. I tried to press her for more, but she refused to go into detail.'

'I think I agree with Betty,' said Ralph, squashing another mosquito with a loud thwack. 'Did you have to express interest in joining the Society?'

'Oh no, you have to be invited,' said Rupert proudly, as the fire's curling smoke drifted towards him. 'My travels are well known in certain circles.'

'We should set up the tent soon,' said Ralph, stretching his stiff limbs. 'I'll sleep well tonight.'

After only one day of walking, Naldy's muscles ached, too. Their journey through Edengar had been months ago, and their bodies had grown accustomed to the comforts of home life.

'There's no tent,' remarked Rupert, rolling his travelling cloak into a makeshift pillow.

'No tent?' echoed Ralph.

'It's much safer to sleep out in the open,' replied Rupert, lying on the leaf-strewn ground and staring up at the interwoven branches. 'We'll need to keep the fire going throughout the night.'

'You mean we didn't bring a tent?' asked Ralph,

staring disapprovingly at Rupert's modest sleeping arrangement.

'There's no point wasting space in our rucksacks,' said Rupert. 'And who would want a tent when we have such a beautiful ceiling above us?'

Naldy followed suit, folding her cloak into an impromptu pillow. Rupert was right—the forest's canopy was captivating, with the flickering firelight dancing off the red, yellow, and brown leaves above. Each tree's thick wooden limbs twisted and interwove with the next. The night sky was hidden by the exquisite ceiling formed of branches and leaves.

'It's alright for you,' said Ralph, shedding his travelling cloak and bitterly rolling it into a ball, 'the mosquitoes don't seem to like your blood as much as they like mine.'

The sounds of the forest and the crackling fire soon distracted Naldy from her body's aches and pains. Nearby, Rupert and Ralph began snoring softly.

She slept peacefully through the night, and it wasn't until early in the morning that she felt a light nudge on her arm. She rolled over, not wanting to be disturbed.

'It's time to go,' said Rupert, lightly tapping her shoulder.

Naldy sat up, rubbing her weary eyes. Despite the sunlight trying to penetrate the thick curtain of leaves above, it was still dark.

A red apple thumped against her head, bouncing

and rolling to a stop.

'Sorry,' said Ralph guiltily. 'Breakfast.'

'Why'd you go and do that?' snapped Naldy crossly, massaging her head.

'I thought you'd catch it,' said Ralph, shaking out his travelling cloak.

Naldy picked up the bruised apple and polished it on her cloak before biting into it. Its sweet juice trickled down her hand.

'Off we go,' said Rupert, a little too cheerfully for Naldy's liking. 'We've already overslept, and we'll have to eat while walking.'

'Is there any brew?' asked Naldy, pulling on her travelling cloak and hoisting her rucksack onto her back.

'Come on,' called Rupert, ignoring Naldy's question and already setting out. 'We have a wizard to race.'

'My legs feel like their bones have melted away,' groaned Ralph, nearly tripping over one of the tree's exposed chunky roots. 'I'll be glad when we get to this lake.'

Rupert was far ahead of them the entire day, often disappearing behind the thick trees. Naldy was relieved when they stopped again for the night.

'We'll need to pick up the pace tomorrow,' said Rupert, unwrapping some cured meat from butcher paper. 'At this speed, we'll never catch up to Maverick.'

'I'm not sure I can go any faster,' said Ralph honestly. 'I thought you said we needed to save the meat for later.'

'You both look like you need cheering up,' said Rupert, reaching into his bag and pulling out a small loaf of ale bread. He broke the dark-coloured loaf into three pieces.

They ate in silence, lacking both the energy and morale for conversation. Naldy knew Rupert was right—even with the shortcut, they'd have to pick up the pace if they planned to reach Arkus Day before Maverick. After dinner, Naldy fell asleep as soon as her head hit the makeshift pillow.

The following day, Naldy awoke to the orange flicker of a burning fire and the spiced scent of freshly boiled brew. She was grateful Ralph didn't wallop her with another apple but instead held one out, a sleepy smirk on his face.

'Hold it for me, would you?' asked Naldy. 'I need the washroom before we go.'

'The ensuite is that way,' Rupert replied, his voice croaky with sleepiness.

She ventured deeper into the woods and came upon a gigantic tree. Before she could lift her cloak, she felt the soft, cold touch of something on her neck. Naldy gingerly turned her head to find a purple, tentacle-like vine slithering along her left cheek. She froze.

'Rupert?' she called, hoping her voice wouldn't startle the strange plant.

The tree's trunk looked similar to the others but was much wider. As Naldy glanced up, she noticed about fifty purple vines extending from its main trunk instead of branches. Each thick vine gently swayed, as if moved by a light breeze—though there was none. One of the vines had come down to meet her.

Rupert appeared, and when he saw Naldy, his eyes widened in horror.

'Don't move,' instructed Rupert, reaching into his cloak and pulling out a small pocket knife. 'I don't want to panic you, but if it stings you, it can be deadly. If you move too quickly, it may take hold.'

The tentacle was now inching over Naldy's black hair, and she couldn't help but admire the alluring purple flowers growing on the vine's tendrils.

'You'll have to slice the tentacle,' said Rupert, sliding the knife across the ground. 'Make sure you do it in one quick motion.'

Naldy gingerly reached for the pocket knife and flicked the blade open. Without hesitation, she slashed it across the plant. Purple slime oozed from the vine, and the severed tentacle retreated up the tree to join the many other flowery creepers stretching out above. Naldy moved out of the tree's reach.

'How do you feel?' asked Rupert, panicked. 'Do you feel light-headed?'

'I feel angry,' said Naldy, briskly brushing the folds of her black cloak with her palms. 'You told me the ensuite was this way.'

'So, you don't feel nauseous?'

'I told you,' Naldy repeated, 'I feel furious with you. Trying to get me killed!'

'We need to return to Mortous's castle,' insisted Rupert.

'Go back?' said Naldy, shocked. 'We're not going back.'

'You made contact with the Kineleek tree,' said Rupert seriously. 'It's a matter of time before you'll become very sick, and you'll need rest and proper care to recover. Are you sure you don't feel dizzy?'

'We don't need to go back,' said Naldy calmly. 'Both Ralph and I are immune.'

'Immune?' repeated Rupert, raising an eyebrow. 'Not many people have built immunity to the Kineleek tree. They're native to these woods, and there's only one way to build your immunity.'

'By drinking the tree's stewed bark,' said Naldy.

'How do you know that?'

'Barbra served us Kineleek brew when we first met her. The same sitting where she served us poisoned scones.'

Rupert laughed in relief, embracing Naldy tightly.

'You are so lucky,' said Rupert happily, hugging her tighter. 'I can't believe you've both had Kineleek brew. It's rare to come by. Barbra has saved your life. She'd be furious with herself if she knew it.'

'Can you point me towards a tree that isn't trying to poison me?' asked Naldy. 'I still need to use the loo.'

'Sorry, yes,' said Rupert, releasing her from his hug.

After Naldy returned from a tree that wasn't

trying to harm her, they enjoyed some brew by the fire before strapping the heavy rucksacks onto their sore backs and setting out through the trees.

'He tells us to stay close,' said Ralph to Naldy, swatting away a fly, 'but he's the one walking ahead of us.'

'Maybe he is checking if it's safe,' said Naldy, though she didn't admit she also felt uneasy that they were always lagging behind.

The deeper they ventured into the woods, the gnarlier the trees became. On the rare occasions when the sun had an unobstructed path to the forest floor, they would all rush towards its glow, squeezing together in the small pools of light, happily soaking up the sun's soothing warmth.

Naldy thought it was odd that the woods had such a terrible reputation amongst Kirkwood Forest folk, as they hadn't encountered any other dangerous plants or threats since the Kineleek tree incident.

Rupert continually impressed them with his extensive knowledge of the wood's native flora. He knew the names of every type of tree, which barks could be stewed to make comforting brews, and which mushrooms were edible or poisonous. He could name every kind of wild grass and even the sprawling moss they passed.

'I can smell smoke,' said Ralph to Naldy one dewy morning. Rupert was some way ahead of them, as he usually was.

Naldy took a deep breath of the moist morning

air, detecting a dry smokiness. Rupert turned and marched briskly towards them, his body tense.

'What's wrong?' asked Ralph, his face wrinkled with worry. 'Is it smoke from Maverick's campfire?'

'It's from a chimney,' said Rupert, leading them back the way they had come.

'A chimney?' asked Naldy, puzzled.

'Yes,' replied Rupert, irritated. 'We'll have to go around. We shouldn't risk getting too close to the house.'

'House?' pressed Ralph, a quiver in his voice. 'Whose house?'

'Mortous isn't the only witch living in these woods,' said Rupert sourly. 'We can't risk introducing ourselves. The people who live out here in these remote parts of the woods tend not to welcome company.'

Naldy peered between the gaps in the twisted trees. In the distance, she thought she could make out the grey stone bricks of a house wedged between the wood's thicket.

'This way,' said Rupert, veering left. He was already well ahead of Ralph and Naldy. 'Come, we mustn't linger.'

'How does he know which way to go?' asked Ralph, stepping over exposed tree roots. 'This wood all looks the same to me—dark and ominous.'

They hurried to catch up with Rupert, not wanting to be left behind.

'Once we find the Corium,' said Ralph, sounding somewhat sceptical, 'what are we going to do with it?'

'Do?' said Naldy, her legs aching. 'We're going to protect it.'

'A magical leagon is much larger and might be easier for us to find than a book,' said Ralph, trying not to slip on the mossy ground, 'but a leagon is going to be much harder for us to keep hidden from Maverick.'

'Books aren't on the move,' replied Naldy, doubting the leagon would be easier to find. 'I don't know, the Boat Builder might have some ideas.'

'How do you use the magic of a leagon anyway?' wondered Ralph, raising one of his strawberry-blonde eyebrows.

'Perhaps,' said Naldy, smiling as she considered the possibilities, 'you just ask it to do what you want.'

Ralph broke into a smile and giggled. His chuckle was contagious, and Naldy found herself laughing too.

'Pumpkin-and-potato pie, please, leagon,' quipped Ralph.

'I would like you to rebuild the Witch House,' giggled Naldy. 'Without the clutter. Build it for me, please, magical leagon.'

Their laughter was short-lived—a few metres ahead, Rupert was hoisted upside down by a rope attached to his ankle.

'Cousin!' cried Ralph, about to run to Rupert's aid, but Naldy grabbed his shoulder.

'There could be another trap,' she said, but he

broke away, racing to his cousin.

Naldy followed cautiously, peering left and right at the shadows between the surrounding trees.

'Rupert?' called Ralph, staring up at his unconscious cousin. 'Naldy, he's not moving.'

Rupert's hands flopped limply over his head, gravity pulling at his travelling cloak. His strawberry-blonde hair dangled.

'I don't like this, Ralph,' said Naldy, her hazel eyes scanning the nearby trees again. 'I feel like someone's watching us.'

'*Secare,*' said Ralph, and the rope snapped, sending Rupert tumbling to the mossy ground. Ralph leant over his cousin.

'Careful with him,' said Naldy. 'You could have at least softened his fall.'

'He's still got a pulse, and he is still breathing,' said Ralph.

He moved to loosen the rope wrapped around Rupert's ankle.

'Don't touch it,' exclaimed Naldy, placing a hand on Ralph's shoulder to stop him.

'What is it?'

'Look,' she said, pointing to the peculiar way the rope was fastened to Rupert's leg. It wasn't secured with a knot—instead, it was snaked around his ankle, almost as if it were holding on.

'The rope seems easy enough to undo,' said Ralph.

'It's not a rope,' replied Naldy, encouraging Ralph to look closer.

'Oh, it's a plant,' said Ralph, backing cautiously away from his unconscious cousin.

'I have Rupert's pocket knife,' said Naldy, reaching inside her travelling cloak.

Ralph scrutinised the treetops for other vicious plants.

Naldy cut the vine, carefully keeping the sharp blade away from Rupert's leg. The vine shrivelled as it released its grip.

'Is it a Kineleek tree?' asked Ralph.

'I don't think so,' said Naldy, noticing for the first time that Rupert's knife had colourful flowers etched onto its blade. She wondered if it had been specially designed to cut wild plants.

'He's still unconscious,' said Ralph, gently tapping Rupert's cheek. 'But at least he's breathing.'

'We'll have to carry him,' said Naldy, brushing Rupert's hair down with her hand. It seemed as if he were peacefully sleeping. 'I don't think there's anything we can do. Maybe the Boat Builder will be able to help revive him.'

'If we ever make it to the coast,' said Ralph sadly. 'We don't know where to go without Rupert guiding us.'

'I'll check his rucksack,' said Naldy, rolling Rupert gently onto his side so she could reach his bag. There were plenty of supplies for their journey, including food, rope, and warm clothes, but there was no sign of a map or even a compass.

'Maybe he'll wake up soon,' said Naldy, though she sounded unconvinced. 'We have to give it time.'

'We're lost,' said Ralph, lifting his hands and burying his face. 'This is hopeless. We're lost in these woods. We can't sit around waiting for him to wake up. We have no idea which direction we're meant to go.'

Naldy could see Ralph's tears escaping through the gaps in his fingers.

'Oh, Ralph,' said Naldy, throwing a comforting arm around his shoulder. 'It's okay. We will find our way. Rupert will be okay, I promise.'

'You can't promise that,' snapped Ralph, his voice gritty with emotion. 'We're lost in the middle of the Mortous Woods with no idea which trees might kill us and which won't.'

'We managed to make our way through Edengar,' said Naldy gently, trying to dab Ralph's cheeks with her sleeve. 'We did that together, remember. We'll manage.'

'I'm not sure our luck extends this far,' said Ralph, brushing away Naldy's hand. He stood and walked away but only managed a few steps before stopping.

'What is it?' asked Naldy, alarmed.

'Look,' said Ralph, bending to the ground to pick something up.

'It's the letter for the Boat Builder,' said Naldy, recognising the envelope Mortous had handed him in the garden. 'It must have fallen from Rupert's pocket.'

'But look closer,' he said, holding up the envelope. 'It's not addressed to the Boat Builder.'

'It's addressed to Rupert,' said Naldy curiously,

noticing the sprawling black ink. 'But why did Rupert tell us the letter from Mortous was for the Boat Builder if it was for him?'

'Secret Society business,' suggested Ralph, passing the envelope to Naldy.

'I'm opening it,' she replied, upturning the flap on the small envelope.

She removed the delicate sheet of folded parchment enclosed. As Naldy unfurled the paper, her hand instinctively sprang to her mouth, and she gasped at what she saw.

Chapter Thirteen

A BOAT INTO DARKNESS

R alph squealed with delight. The thin paper held a beautiful hand-drawn map of the woods. No paths were drawn, as none existed throughout the inner woods, but certain trees were sketched in impressive detail.

'We're saved,' said Ralph, jumping joyfully. 'We still have some work to do figuring out exactly where we are in the woods, but you needn't be so miserable, Naldy! We have a map.'

'Yes, but look *there*,' said Naldy, her heart thumping in her chest. Her patience was thinning.

'Look at what?'

Naldy placed her finger on the sketch of a small compass with the words '*you*' written underneath it.

'Even better,' said Ralph cheerily. 'An enchanted map that tells us exactly where we are. I can't believe Rupert's been hiding this from us.'

'Yes,' said Naldy, irritated, 'but it's not the only thing he's been hiding.'

Ralph's forehead wrinkled as he took a moment to inspect the map.

'Oh,' muttered Ralph, his smile vanishing as he realised why Naldy wasn't celebrating.

'We are nowhere near the lake,' said Naldy, glancing sourly at Rupert, still lying unconscious. 'Your cousin has been taking us in the opposite direction.'

'But I don't understand'—Ralph took the map from Naldy—'why would Rupert take us the wrong way?'

'I don't know,' said Naldy, recalling Rupert and Mortous's private exchange in the garden. Had Rupert decided to betray them? Was the Seagull Society trying to hinder their quest?

'I'm sure it's just a mistake,' said Ralph, staring at the map as he tried to find an explanation for why they were so far from their desired destination. 'Perhaps it's because we took a detour around that house in the woods.'

'We don't have time to sit and ponder why,' said Naldy, snatching the map from Ralph's hands. Even with the detour, it was clear they were nowhere near where they needed to be. 'We must get moving. We've got a lot of catching up to do.'

'But surely he didn't intentionally lead us astray.'

'We should leave Rupert here, and he can find his own way home when he wakes up.'

'*Arcesso,*' muttered Ralph, somewhat bitterly. Rupert's body lifted a few inches off the ground. With outstretched palms, Ralph guided his cousin, whose travelling cloak dragged along the ground as he floated.

'You're getting quite good at that,' said Naldy, surprised Ralph could produce magic strong enough to carry Rupert with little effort.

'I practice every moment I can get,' said Ralph, walking proudly alongside Naldy.

They were silent for some time, with Rupert drifting ahead of them. Each step felt heavy. Naldy could tell Ralph was deep in his own thoughts—perhaps pondering why Rupert had led them away from the Versalius Lake. A few hours passed before either spoke.

'It couldn't have been by accident,' said Naldy softly. 'Rupert had a map disclosing exactly where we were. He was deliberately ignoring Mortous's shortcut.'

'Maybe he was protecting us?' suggested Ralph, stepping carefully over the uneven ground.

'Protecting us from what?' asked Naldy, unconvinced Rupert's intentions were for their benefit. 'And, if he was, surely he should have told us?'

'When he wakes, we can ask him, but until then, I'd like to get on the lake and away from all these trees.'

They continued on for some time. It wasn't until Naldy smelt smoke again that she stopped.

'Can you smell that?' asked Ralph, glancing at the map in Naldy's hands. 'Is there a house on the map?'

'That's not smoke from a chimney,' said Naldy, pointing at the gap between a few large, knotted trees. 'It's coming from there.'

Something blackened and burnt lay on the ground between the trees. Soft grey wisps of smoke curled into the air, but there was no flame. The fire had gone out some time ago and been left to smoulder.

Ralph kept his unconscious cousin close as they drew nearer.

'Maverick's been here already,' said Ralph, staring at the charred bones of the leagon's ribs.

'He's not taking any chances,' said Naldy, feeling sorry for the poor animal.

'We have to reach Versalius Lake, Naldy,' replied Ralph, placing his cousin gently on the ground. 'It's our one chance of beating Maverick to the east coast. Let me take a look at the map.'

Naldy passed the map to Ralph, whose face scrunched as he inspected it. She couldn't peel her eyes away from the circle of black ash, where grey bones jutted out. The fire must have been started some time ago, and Maverick was likely a whole day ahead of them.

'If we go this way,' Ralph said, almost to himself, 'we could reach the lake by sunset in three, maybe four days.'

'Do you think Maverick is also heading towards Versalius Lake?'

'No, I don't think so,' said Ralph. 'We've been veering north because of the thicket, but if we push through this section of trees, we should be able to get back on course.'

'Let's keep moving then,' said Naldy. 'I can't stand

the sight.'

'Or the smell,' added Ralph, folding up the map.

Naldy was glad no other plants tried to attack them as they trudged under the dark shadows of the trees. Her legs were tender from all the walking, and each evening she nursed painful blisters on the heels of her feet.

They didn't dare pick wild mushrooms or berries for supper, fearing they'd accidentally choose something poisonous, and instead rationed the dry crackers they'd fished from Rupert's rucksack.

'What will you do?' asked Naldy one evening as they sat beside the crackling fire, the darkness hugging their campsite.

'Do when?' asked Ralph.

'What will you do if we manage to find the Corium? I know we've joked about it, but is there anything you *actually* want?'

'We're finding it to protect it,' said Ralph. 'That's what I plan to do.'

'Yes,' said Naldy, in a light tone, 'but we can protect the leagon *and* invent a few new spells. You are a wizard, after all.'

'We should focus on finding the leagon first.'

'What do you think, Rupert?' asked Naldy, turning to face Ralph's unconscious cousin. They had propped Rupert up against a large, knotted tree. Rupert obviously couldn't respond, but Naldy nodded and said, 'Yes, I think you are right, Rupert. Discussing which spells we will invent is imperative to our quest.'

'I'd like another flying carpet,' Ralph said, smiling. 'I do miss mine. What spells will you invent, if we ever find this leagon?'

'What I'd really like,' said Naldy, warming her hands by the fire, 'is to find my parents... or at least find out what happened to them.'

'But Naldy—'

'I know, Ralph,' interrupted Naldy, staring into the dancing flames. '*Knowledge* is a *Banned Spell*— we can't use the Corium to find someone's location. But I might be able to invent something to help find them. Or I could...'

'You could what?' he asked, his voice rigid with concern. 'What were you going to say, Naldy?'

'Don't worry about it. We should both get some sleep.'

'Were you going to suggest breaking the *Banned Spells?*' pressed Ralph, shaking his head. 'It would be too risky. If someone has another Devante, they could use it for bad.'

'You know there is only one other Devante,' said Naldy, fidgeting with the frayed ends of her travelling cloak. 'We've let all the others be destroyed.'

'I suppose you could try,' said Ralph, avoiding eye contact with her.

Naldy could tell from Ralph's tone he thought it unlikely they'd be able to work out how to break Hannah Hale's *Banned Spells.*

'We should set off as early as we can tomorrow,' said Ralph sleepily.

He bundled his travelling cloak into a makeshift pillow. Naldy, not yet ready for sleep, remained sitting by the fire.

'If we get our hands on this leagon,' Ralph continued, staring up at the contorted branches, 'I'll invent a spell to turn cloaks into comfortable pillows. That's something we can do without breaking any *Banned Spells*.'

Naldy laughed softly. She sat by the fire for some time, staring at the glowing red logs as they were consumed by flames, thinking about her parents. It had been over six years since she had last seen them. Had they changed as much as she had? Would she recognise them if she saw them? Naldy was certain the Corium could help her find them, and a surge of determination welled up inside her.

Ralph began snoring heavily. Naldy added more wood to the fire, which crackled in the heat of the flames. She glanced at Rupert, who looked as though he were peacefully sleeping, and wondered if the vine's effects would wear off on their own or if he would remain unconscious until they found a spell or potion to revive him. They had even tried *Sanitatem Restituere*, the healing spell created with the Devante, only to discover it couldn't wake someone from unconsciousness.

Naldy rolled her cloak into a pillow. She lay her head down for a moment, then lifted it again and unfurled her travelling cloak. Reaching into its pocket, she retrieved the list Mortous had given them. Both the Aurum and the Corium were still safely on the list. There was still hope, even if it were slim.

The next day, Naldy was relieved Ralph refused to give up the duty of levitating Rupert. Her brain felt too foggy from sleep deprivation to safely guide him around the trees.

'I don't know where you find the energy,' said Naldy, carefully avoiding the slippery toadstools growing in abundance in this part of the woods.

'I told you, I practise every chance I can get,' said Ralph, stretching out his palm proudly, causing Rupert to drift along a little faster.

'When have you had the time to practise?' Naldy asked, adjusting the straps on her rucksack.

'I'm always up hours before you,' said Ralph. 'And I know you think Olde Witchery is pointless, but I've found translating it has greatly improved the potency of my spells. I am a scholar—I have a pretty good memory.'

'This is why townsfolk are more afraid of wizards than witches,' said Naldy, accidentally stepping on a red toadstool and nearly losing her balance. 'All you wizards are obsessed with magic.'

'I'm not obsessed. I'm simply studious.'

Naldy pursed her lips, hitching up her travelling cloak to better dodge the fungi.

The truth was, she felt a pang of jealousy. It had taken her an entire childhood to master the art of casting spells, and Ralph seemed to have surpassed her with only a few months of practice.

As the faint light began to fade in the ever-dark

woods, Ralph let Rupert drop to the ground.

'It's not quite dark,' said Naldy. 'We can get at least another half-hour of walking in.'

'There!' Ralph shouted excitedly, pointing ahead. 'Through the trees, Naldy—there!'

They could see the dark blue water peeking through the tangled trunks.

As they made their way to the edge of the lake, both gasped at how vast it was. The water was eerily still, without a ripple disturbing its surface, and the shore was lined with river stones. Old, gnarled trees ran along both sides of the bank.

'It doesn't look this big on the map,' said Ralph, gently laying his cousin on the shore. 'I can't even see the other side.'

'It'll be dark before long,' said Naldy, glancing up at the sky, now tinted a deep shade of blue.

'The water's unusually still,' remarked Ralph. 'It almost seems like glass.'

'Surely that's not the boat,' said Naldy, catching sight of an old wooden rowboat resting on the river stones a few metres to their left. They had been so mesmerised by the lake's size that neither had noticed the pitiful vessel.

'I can't see any others,' said Ralph unhappily, staring at the grey lichen growing up the rowboat's sides. 'Should we set up camp here for the night?'

'The sky is clear of clouds,' said Naldy, approaching the rickety boat. 'We should set out. We don't have time to waste. Maverick's already ahead of us, and it looks like there'll be a full moon, so we'll have plenty of light.'

Ralph groaned, and Naldy knew he didn't like the idea of setting sail with night approaching.

'I think we will be safer on the water,' said Naldy. 'I don't want to spend another night beneath those trees.'

The rowboat had been poorly cared for, its aged wood faded to a dull grey. Naldy wondered if it would float.

Inside the little boat, they found three planks serving as precarious seats, and only one oar with tiny cracks in its wooden blade.

'This can't be the boat,' whined Ralph from behind Naldy. 'It must have washed up here by accident.'

'Do you see any others?' asked Naldy, moving to the other side to inspect it further.

'But we'll drown in that! Maybe if we walk along the bank, we'll find another one. Something less ancient.'

'I'm certain this is it. There's no tide—look at it! It's the stillest water I've ever seen. Anyway, I think it'll float just fine.'

'*Restituo*,' said Ralph, palms outstretched.

The weaker sections of the boat thickened, while the cracks in the oar's blade smoothed over. The vessel changed from its sombre grey to a gleaming, polished brown.

'Show off,' remarked Naldy.

'Let's not take any chances.'

Naldy shook her head, trying to mask her envy

—Ralph appeared to have endless energy, even after carrying his cousin all day.

She tugged on the rowboat, struggling to pull it towards the glass-like water.

'Let me help,' said Ralph, and without him raising a palm, the boat slid into the lake.

'I don't need your help,' snapped Naldy.

'I'm sorry, I didn't mean to—'

But Ralph stopped. The boat's polished nut-brown wood was transforming back to its original dull grey, and the sections he had reinforced with magic were returning to their weakened state.

'The lake must be enchanted to prevent magic,' said Ralph, shocked.

'At least we know it floats,' said Naldy, staring at the little rowboat, which had barely made a ripple upon entering the water.

'Let's see if it floats with us inside,' said Ralph, raising his palms. Rupert lifted off the river stones and was gently guided into the rowboat.

'I'll row first,' said Naldy, stepping carefully into the boat as she made her way to the middle plank.

Ralph climbed in behind her and settled onto the back seat.

'Are we ready?' asked Naldy, picking up the fragile oar.

'I don't think I'll ever be ready for this,' said Ralph, gazing at the vast stretch of motionless water ahead.

Naldy dipped the oar into the lake, and the boat glided away from the bank. With each stroke, the oar moved smoothly through the water, producing a few tiny silvery ripples on the surface, which vanished less than a metre from the rowboat.

'If you want to get some rest, Ralph, I can wake you when I get tired,' suggested Naldy from her seat.

The light was fading, and the knotted trees lining the bank had become grey silhouettes.

'I don't think I'll be able to sleep,' replied Ralph uneasily. 'This is my first time on the water.'

It was Naldy's first time travelling by boat too, but she felt instantly at peace on the lake. The expanse of still water stretched into the twilight, its surface mirroring the full moon rising in the darkening sky.

Rowing the boat was far easier than Naldy had anticipated, and she knew this must be due to some magical property the lake seemed to possess. Her oar moved effortlessly through the water, and the rowboat glided steadily along. Soon, Ralph snored peacefully, and Naldy had no doubt that the gliding motion had lulled him to sleep.

Before long, she could no longer see the trees, which had become distant, murky black shadows as the lake gradually widened. Many twinkling stars came out to greet her, the water sparkling with the night sky's reflection. Naldy rowed for hours, enjoying the tranquillity.

She knew morning was approaching when she heard stirring from the bow.

'You can keep resting,' said Naldy, glancing out at the water. 'I don't think I'll be able to sleep until the sun rises, and it won't be far off.'

'Where are we?' asked a faint, croaky voice—but it wasn't Ralph's.

Naldy had forgotten that Rupert was the one lying on the front plank. He had woken, lifting his head drowsily.

'You're alive!' Naldy shouted excitedly, nearly dropping their oar into the water.

Ralph woke at Naldy's outburst.

'What's happened?' he asked, looking around in fear before spotting Rupert, who was wiping his sleepy eyes. 'Cousin! You're alive! I'm so glad to see you're alright!'

But as Rupert slowly lifted himself from the floor of the old wooden rowboat, Naldy saw dread spreading across his face.

'What is it?' asked Naldy.

'Cousin? Is everything okay?' muttered Ralph, reaching past Naldy to place a hand on Rupert's shoulder.

'We have to get off the lake.'

—*Chapter Fourteen*—

THE SECRET OF VERSALIUS LAKE

R upert rested his hands on the edge of the rowboat, peering out into the darkness as he tried to gauge the distance to the bank.

'Naldy, grab the oar—quick,' he urged. 'Make for the shore.'

'We're miles away from the shore,' replied Naldy, puzzled by Rupert's eagerness to get off the lake. Had his extended period of unconsciousness caused him to lose his mind?

'Mortous said to cross the lake,' Naldy said nervously.

'Mortous didn't tell you everything,' replied Rupert, meeting her gaze with a weighted look.

'What do you mean he didn't tell us everything?' she asked, recalling how Mortous had whispered something to Rupert as the two of them strolled alone through his garden.

'We are not safe on the lake,' said Rupert, slumping onto the floor of the wooden rowboat.

'Not safe... how?' asked Ralph, worry spreading across his face. 'What do you mean, Cousin?'

'The Society never wanted us to actually take this

route,' said Rupert, his voice heavy with exhaustion. He shook his head, searching for the right words. 'They believe the Corium is best left in Arkus Day. They don't think we, or Maverick, will find it there.'

'Mortous said this was the quickest way,' said Naldy. 'He told us to come this way.'

'It is the quickest route to the east coast,' replied Rupert. 'But Mortous only wanted you to believe we were coming this way. He wanted me to actually take you the safer way.'

'The *slower* way!' exclaimed Naldy. 'You took us in the wrong direction. We found your map.'

'Yes, because the lake holds a secret,' continued Rupert. 'A secret Mortous didn't disclose to you.'

'What secret?' asked Ralph, exchanging a tense look with his cousin.

'The secret,' said Rupert, his blue eyes widening, 'is that the lake is home to the Great Fairy Queen.'

'You mean water fairies live on this lake?' Ralph groaned.

'Not any old water fairy, but the Great Fairy Queen herself.'

'Fairy Queen?' asked Ralph, edging towards the centre of the wooden plank, as though fearing water fairies might suddenly leap from the lake. 'Why didn't you tell us all this before you fell unconscious?'

'Why did Mortous not tell us?' demanded Naldy irritably. 'What do you mean he wanted you to take us along the slower route?'

'He knew he could not stop your journey,'

explained Rupert. 'Mortous told you about the lake's shortcut to earn your trust. The shortcut is not a lie. He wanted me to make you believe we were going this way. But, don't you see, the Society believes the Corium cannot be found in Arkus Day. They have tried to seek it there before and have failed. There is no point in rushing to Arkus Day and facing unnecessary danger when we will not find the Devante. To keep us safe, Mortous told me that I must take you the safe way.'

'If this is the quickest route,' snapped Naldy, rolling her eyes, 'then we should have always come this way—Fairy Queen or not.'

'I thought you would say that,' said Rupert.

'What is that supposed to mean?' growled Naldy.

'You are willing to risk too much,' he replied.

'I'd like to be on solid ground again,' said Ralph, staring ominously into the water. 'If this fairy is more dangerous than the woods, maybe we ought to turn back and go the way Rupert and The Society wants us to go.'

'We must go the fastest way,' said Naldy bitterly.

'It was for our protection,' said Rupert. 'I know the dangers lurking in those woods. But I do not know the dangers of this lake.'

'You should have let us make up our own minds,' said Naldy, raising her voice, 'instead of pretending to take us the quickest way while actually leading us along the slowest path through the woods.'

'I was leading us along the safest path,' he shot back.

'You can row, Rupert,' said Naldy, accidentally swaying the boat as she climbed over Rupert, passing him the oar. 'We're not turning around. If you want to go back, you can jump out and swim. Ralph and I spent the last few days carrying you, so if you're staying, it's time you pull your weight.'

'I'm sorry,' said Rupert, squeezing past Naldy to reach the middle seat.

'I'll row,' said Ralph, carefully standing. 'Switch places with me, Cousin. You probably need rest.'

'It's okay,' replied Rupert. 'I've slept long enough. It was a ganark vine that got me. It can knock you unconscious for a few days, but there won't be any lasting effect. A night-cretingale might have had me for dinner if you'd left me there, but I'm fine to do the rowing. If you both want to go this way, we'll continue—just don't say you weren't warned.'

Naldy curled up on the floor, resting her head against the front plank, though she was too angry to sleep. How could Rupert have misled them? A Fairy Queen wasn't going to scare them off. Did Mortous not believe they were up to the task of handling a shortcut? They had faced far worse trekking through the Edengar mountains—they'd confronted fire-breathing dragons!

Her heart ached as Odorf's wrinkled face came to mind. They had paid a high price during that journey, and for a moment, Naldy wondered if Rupert was right. Was she willing to risk too much to save the Devante?

She knew they'd fall too many days behind

Maverick if they turned back now. Besides, she found some comfort in knowing that Mortous had considered this route the quickest—even if the old witch doubted their courage and had chosen to keep the lake's secret from them.

Naldy pushed the pestering questions from her mind and let the gentle movement of the boat lull her into a deep sleep.

She didn't wake until the midday light cast a bright glare over the lake. As she lifted her head, brushing her long black hair from her eyes, she saw Rupert still rowing while Ralph sat slumped on the back seat, humming a slow tune to himself.

'You'd better not have turned us around while we slept,' said Naldy, stretching her arms.

'Morning,' said Rupert, smiling at her while his broad shoulders worked the oar. 'There are dry biscuits for breakfast.'

Naldy wanted to open up to Rupert—to tell him she was glad he'd woken—but she was still too upset with him and ate her dry biscuit in silence.

Hours drifted by without anyone exchanging words. Naldy watched the powdery clouds drift across the lake's reflection as she breathed in the cool air.

When it was Ralph's turn to row, he seemed to thoroughly enjoy it, showing no sign of wanting to relinquish the duty anytime soon.

As the late afternoon approached, the sky gradually turned a golden haze. Naldy was fixated on the reflections in the water when a bird caught her attention. She realised it was the first bird she'd seen flying over the lake.

She squinted, trying to determine what type of bird it was, then quickly realised it was a seagull.

'Look there,' said Naldy as it began descending.

'What's it doing out here?' asked Ralph.

The seagull's wings were outstretched as it headed towards the rowboat. They moved back to give it space. The gull landed on the edge of the boat, tucking its wings behind its back and meeting Rupert with its beady yellow eyes.

'There's something around its neck,' Ralph observed.

'I think it's for you, Rupert,' said Naldy.

Rupert slowly moved his hand towards the bird, and the seagull lifted its orange beak, revealing a leather satchel draped around its feathery neck. Rupert gently unbuckled the satchel's fastening and removed a familiar, small glass phial filled with a red, blood-like liquid.

'Veserum,' said Naldy. 'The Society has already forgiven you for failing to lead us in the direction they wanted.'

The bird elegantly turned and leapt from the side of the rowboat, spreading its grey wings and flying off into the distance.

'It must be the new moon cycle already,' said Rupert, holding the delicate phial up to the fading light to admire its deep colour.

He uncorked the bottle and swallowed the thick red liquid in one gulp. Ralph shuddered squeamishly as he watched Rupert down the potion.

'I can take over the rowing,' said Naldy from the bow, standing to stretch her cramped legs.

'No, I'm not done yet,' insisted Ralph.

All three settled into a comfortable silence, soaking up the sun's last warming rays. Things remained calm and quiet for a long time—until Ralph shouted in distress.

'What is it?' asked Naldy, who had been watching the orange sky above.

'The oar,' said Ralph in disbelief. 'It's gone.'

'What do you mean, gone?'

'Something took it,' Ralph replied, leaning over the boat and studying the water.

'What do you mean *something* took it?' asked Naldy, hoping this was some cruel joke and that Ralph had merely hidden the oar from sight.

'I don't see anything,' said Rupert, cautiously peering into the murky blue water.

'Something yanked it from my hand,' said Ralph, his blue eyes tense with fear. '*Arcesso.*'

No oar came floating up from the depths below.

'You don't think it was the Fairy Queen, do you?' asked Naldy.

'I hope it isn't,' said Rupert, frowning.

'What are we going to do without an oar?' asked Ralph, moving away from the sides of the rowboat.

'I'll go in,' said Naldy bravely. 'Surely, it is just sitting at the bottom.'

'The lake is too deep,' replied Rupert. 'But I fear Ralph is right—I believe something took it. Let us hope it wasn't the Queen herself.'

'We'll die out here,' said Ralph, his face pinched with worry.

'We'll simply have to use our hands, Cousin.'

'I'm not dipping my hands in there,' said Ralph, scrunching his face in objection. 'I'm not putting any of my limbs into that water if there's something down there.'

'We should wait,' suggested Naldy. 'In case whatever took the oar is still below us.'

A few moments passed as they stared at the glass-like water. A light breeze brushed their concerned faces. Naldy noticed the wind didn't stir up the slightest ripple on the lake.

'Whatever took our oar is long gone,' said Rupert, gripping the boat's edge to steady himself. He leant over, ready to plunge his free hand into the water. 'Well, we can't float around here forever. Here goes.'

Rupert cupped his hand and dragged it through the water, but the lake barely quivered. To their amazement, the rowboat didn't move at all. Droplets dripped from Rupert's wet hand as he lifted it out of the water.

'Let's try it on both sides,' said Rupert, readying his hand again. 'Naldy, you take the other side. On my count.'

Naldy dangled her hand over the edge, waiting for Rupert's signal. Ralph watched, his strawberry-blonde eyebrows raised.

'Now,' said Rupert.

Naldy broke the water's surface with her cupped

hand—it was ice cold as she ran it through the water.

'We didn't move at all,' said Ralph tensely. 'The lake is cursed. Rupert was right—we should have stayed in the woods.'

'What do we do now?' asked Naldy, turning to face Rupert.

'I don't know,' said Rupert, his face plagued with worry. 'I don't know if there's anything we can do.'

'There must be something,' said Naldy.

'I need to think,' said Rupert, sitting on the plank and putting his head in his hands.

As night approached, the sky bloomed into a deep purple. They exhausted themselves trying to think of any possible solution. Naldy's thoughts kept returning to an image of three lifeless skeletons lying at the bottom of a lake—where they'd stay for eternity.

'I'm going to try swimming,' said Rupert, unfastening his travelling cloak.

'You can't get into the water,' said Ralph firmly. 'There's something down there.'

'It'll be too deep for me to reach the bottom,' said Rupert, pulling off his green jumper. 'We won't be able to retrieve the oar, but I'll try to push the boat.'

'Maybe we can wait for the next seagull,' suggested Ralph, his brow creased with anxiety.

'We'll be long dead before the next moon cycle,' said Rupert, unbuttoning his white shirt. The skin on his lean but muscled torso was paler than the skin on his face.

'There must be some other way,' said Naldy.

Rupert dropped his grey trousers onto the growing pile of clothes.

'I don't want to go into that water any more than you do,' said Rupert. 'But if we stay here, we'll all die.'

Rupert tossed aside his underpants before diving headfirst into the water. He disappeared beneath the surface with barely a splash, and for an unnerving moment, Ralph and Naldy couldn't see him. They stared at the reflection of the purple sky.

'Where is he?' asked Ralph, his hands firmly gripping the boat's edge.

When Rupert's face emerged from the water —gasping for air—it was paler than before he'd jumped in. Naldy thought his lips had a blue tinge.

'It's s-s-so c-cold,' said Rupert in a quivering voice, his teeth chattering.

'You should have gone in slowly,' said Ralph in a reprimanding tone, 'instead of diving in like that.'

Rupert did a few breaststrokes with his head above water until he reached the rear of the rowboat. He tried to push it while still in the water—but the boat wouldn't budge.

'It's too c-cold,' said Rupert, breathing a mist. 'I n-need to g-g-get out.'

They helped lift Rupert back into the boat. Ralph wrapped his travelling cloak around his cousin's glistening body, and the colour in Rupert's face gradually returned to normal.

'The water is colder than ice,' said Rupert, shivering.

'I told you it was a silly idea,' said Ralph, dropping

defeatedly onto the middle plank of the boat.

'I don't know what we are going to do,' said Rupert, sounding exhausted.

He began dressing, his posture hunched, almost crestfallen, as droplets slid from his strawberry-blonde hair. His torso shuddered. Naldy reached into her bag to fetch dry biscuits for their supper.

The sky shifted from bruised purple to midnight blue as stars began to populate above. They watched the orb-like moon making its journey across the darkness.

'We should ration the food carefully,' said Rupert.

'It won't last long,' said Naldy, finishing her biscuit and gathering the fallen crumbs from her cloak. Just as she was about to eat them, the boat trembled—intense ripples appearing on the lake's surface.

'What's happening?' shouted Ralph, gripping the edges of the boat.

The small vessel shook—slowly at first, then so violently that Naldy feared it might splinter apart. The water sloshed around them, sending the rowboat jolting left and right. Waves sprayed over them as they clung on as tightly as they could.

Then, the lake ceased its harsh attack, and the water gradually returned to a standstill.

'What was that?' asked Ralph, his voice cracking.

'I don't know,' whispered Rupert.

'That was the lake,' said a figure, rising up from the still water. 'She is not happy with you.'

The woman was slightly taller than Naldy. She

wore no clothes, but her wet blue hair was long enough to wrap around her like a garment. Her skin seemed to glow, as though soft lights were shining beneath it. She rose until only her feet remained submerged—it was as if the lake itself was lifting her up.

'And why have you come to the lake?' asked the woman in a husky voice. 'Few live to tell of such bold decisions.'

'You're the Great Fairy Queen,' said Ralph in a small, shaking voice.

The woman had an alluring face with striking green eyes—Naldy couldn't look away from them.

'We need your help,' said Rupert, standing in the cramped rowboat. 'If you would be so kind as to give it.'

Tucked behind her back, the woman had large wings resembling fragile glass, though she did not require them as she glided across the water's surface, moving closer to them.

'You have stolen from the lake, and she is most displeased with you.'

—Chapter Fifteen—

THE PRICE OF PASSAGE

The Fairy Queen smiled tenderly down at them, and they stared in awe at her beauty.

'You have upset the water,' said the Fairy Queen, reaching into the lake and lifting out the old wooden oar. 'You do not belong here.'

'We are sorry,' said Rupert, holding his hand out to take the oar. 'We will make our way to the nearest shoreline. We do not mean to disturb you or the lake.'

'And how do you propose you'll make your way to the shore?' asked the Fairy Queen, still clutching the oar, her pink lips smiling affectionately. 'The lake has claimed your paddle, and she does not want to return it.'

The woman's translucent wings unfurled, stretching out high above her head, each the size of her body. She let the oar fall back into the water with barely a splash.

'You should not take from the lake,' said the woman, her deep green eyes fixed on them.

'But that's not fair,' protested Ralph. 'The lake took it from us first.'

'You'll find,' replied the woman gently, folding her wings again, 'you were the ones who took it from her shoreline.'

'We didn't steal it,' said Ralph defensively. 'We only borrowed it, and we didn't know it belonged to the lake.'

'But you knew it did not belong to you,' said the Fairy Queen.

'Please,' said Naldy, calmly placing a hand on Ralph's shoulder as she addressed the woman. 'We do not mean to intrude. We are just trying to make our way to the other side. We don't want any trouble.'

'Do not let me stop you,' she said, turning and gliding gracefully along the water's surface.

'Wait,' called Naldy, and the Fairy Queen halted. 'Please, we need your help.'

The Fairy Queen pivoted, smiled tenderly, and floated towards them.

'Do tell me,' the woman said, sinking until the waterline was at her hips and her eyes were level with Naldy's. 'Why should I offer my help to you, Naldy?'

'How do you know my name?' she asked in awe.

'The lake shares many things with me.'

'We are trying to protect magic,' said Naldy.

'Your kind is foolish,' said the Fairy Queen, her voice tinged with sourness. 'Your kind has allowed so many spells to fade into forgotten places. Much magic has been lost.'

'There is a wizard who is looking for—'

'The Corium, yes,' interrupted the Fairy Queen. 'Many pass who pursue this treasure, but they will never find what they seek. The lake's waters flow to the sea, her arms stretch far, and she knows much.'

'He carries a Devante with him,' said Ralph, his tone heavy. 'Aurum.'

The water on the lake trembled.

'She is angry with you,' said the Fairy Queen as the ripples settled. She rose until only her toes were submerged in water. 'Your kind has created an evil that could ruin all things beautiful. How dare you pass here, expecting the lake to help you find what could destroy her.'

'Please,' begged Naldy.

'The lake does not trust you. She has made up her mind—you will not leave freely.'

'But we are trying to protect the Corium,' said Ralph desperately. 'We want to stop it from falling into Maverick's hands. He is the one that wants to destroy all magic.'

The water surged, violently lifting the boat before dropping it with a mighty splash, hurling them onto the floor of the rowboat. Naldy's shoulder slammed painfully into the wooden seat. The water became still again.

'We don't mean to cause any offence,' said Rupert, standing again. 'We have no way of surviving out here on our own, please, we mean no harm.'

'Surely there's something we can offer in return for your help,' said Naldy.

'You have nothing left but'—the Fairy Queen

paused, a sly smile curling at the corners of her lips —'yes, alright. I will persuade the lake to let the rowboat cross safely. But I want something from you in return.'

'Anything,' pleaded Naldy. 'You can have everything we have.'

'I do not want everything,' said the Fairy Queen. 'I want one thing. Promise me the most valuable thing in that rowboat, and you will be granted safe passage to the other side.'

Ralph's hand moved to his emerald earring, while Rupert and Naldy exchanged looks of pity.

'There must be something else,' Rupert implored. 'What if we brought you something on our return journey?'

Ralph shook his head, his expression filled with dread. The Fairy Queen's gaze lingered on him, a strange fondness glimmering in her eyes.

'Without it, I cannot produce magic,' said Ralph meekly. 'A wizard can't replace his Imporiom.'

'There has to be another way,' said Rupert, taking a small step forward. 'We could bring you back gold, silver—anything you want.'

'I have told you what I want,' said the Fairy Queen in a husky voice.

'Please,' whispered Ralph, 'I can't part with it.'

The Fairy Queen glanced at the stars before slowly sinking into the lake until the water touched her knees.

'Wait,' called Naldy, stopping the Fairy Queen. 'Please, don't go. Give us a moment to consider your offer.'

The glowing Fairy Queen nodded.

'We have no other way of beating Maverick,' said Naldy, offering Ralph a look of tender understanding. 'This may be our only chance.'

'I fear she is right,' said Rupert, 'we'll die out here without the Fairy Queen's help.'

Tears streaked slowly down Ralph's pale cheeks, and his expression softened, as if conceding there was no other way.

Ralph reached up to his right ear and detached the small silver chain. In the dim light, the emerald stone appeared almost black—until he held the earring over the water, where it flashed a dazzling green, reflecting the Fairy Queen's glow.

'Your Imporiom is not the most valuable thing you possess,' remarked the Fairy Queen, turning her cheek. Ralph was relieved.

'Then what is?' asked Rupert, glancing around the rowboat, astonished he had overlooked what the Fairy Queen truly desired.

'The most valuable thing is not Ralph's Imporiom,' said the Fairy Queen, lowering herself into the water until it reached her hips. 'It is not something material.'

'What else could it be?' asked Ralph curiously.

'The most valuable thing you have is your life.'

Naldy's stomach churned. Tension spread across Ralph's face, while Rupert chuckled nervously but quickly stopped, realising the Fairy Queen's seriousness.

'You're asking too much of us,' said Rupert, unable to mask his frustration.

She sank until the water rested above her navel. Her long, mesmerising blue hair floated out on the water's surface in strands.

'You're asking one of us to give up our life?' asked Rupert, his voice cracking with disbelief.

'Every life holds great value,' said the Fairy Queen, sinking further until the water reached her chest. 'If you want me to help you safely reach the other side of the lake, then one of you must be willing to make the sacrifice.'

They watched as she descended further until her entire body, except for her neck and head, was underneath the lake's surface.

'A sacrifice too great, it seems,' said the Fairy Queen bluntly. 'What a pity, for I see no other way for you to reach the shore.'

The Fairy Queen sank until her head disappeared, and her long blue hair was pulled towards the place she'd been moments before, slipping beneath the water. As the last strand vanished, the faint glow she had emitted faded, leaving only the soft light of the moon.

'We'll find another way,' Naldy said quietly, settling onto the front seat.

'There isn't any other way,' said Rupert, taking in the vast stretch of dark water.

'We will work something else out,' replied Naldy softly. 'Something will come along. We always find a way.'

'I don't think the Society believes you'll succeed,' said Rupert, his voice sounding firm and weighted. 'It's their job to protect magic and, as a member, my job too. I think you might be our last real chance.'

'I don't care what the Society thinks,' said Naldy, her gaze fixed on the still water.

'You're our best shot,' said Rupert, his eyes gleaming with a strange intensity. 'Even if Mortous doesn't believe in you, I do. You mustn't fail, and I must do everything I can to help you succeed.'

Rupert stepped onto the wooden plank and, with one swift motion, dove headfirst into the icy water, fully clothed.

'No,' cried Naldy, clutching the side of the old wooden rowboat. She stared into the black water, its surface already still and unrippled. There was no sign of him.

'I'm going in,' said Ralph, shrugging off his travelling cloak.

Warm tears slipped down Naldy's cheeks and into the lake.

Before Ralph could dive, the boat lurched forward, as if pulled by an invisible rope. Ralph stumbled backwards.

'I won't leave him out there,' he cried, scrambling to his feet.

Naldy lunged to grab hold of him, terrified he would also jump into the water.

'You can't, Ralph,' pleaded Naldy urgently. 'Please, it's too late.'

'I won't leave him,' shouted Ralph, trying to push

Naldy away.

'If you jump into that water,' said Naldy, her heart pounding, 'you'll never make it back to the boat.'

'I don't care,' Ralph shouted, wrenching free of Naldy's hold. 'I have to try.'

'The boat's moving faster than you can swim, Ralph!'

'I'm not going to leave him out here to drown.'

'It's too late,' cried Naldy, panic rising in her voice. 'The boat's moving—it's too late, Ralph. Please.'

Ralph moved to get up, ignoring Naldy, but she gripped his leg as tightly as she could.

'Get off me!'

'I can't do this alone,' said Naldy, sobbing. 'Please, Ralph, I need your help.'

Ralph kicked her off with his free foot and tried to get up again, but Naldy was quicker, lunging forward again and pinning him down.

He stopped struggling, his whole body convulsing as he wept. His flushed, tear-streaked face was etched with anguish as his bloodshot eyes met Naldy's with a distraught look.

'I'm so sorry,' whispered Naldy, her voice hollow and drained. 'I'm so sorry, Ralph.'

He buried his face in his hands, and Naldy wrapped an arm around him. Together, they sat silently on the floor of the rowboat, the cool night air flowing over them as it glided across the still lake.

They stayed like this for what felt like hours, until their emotions were raw from all the weeping and their breathing had slowed.

Naldy's eyes stung with tiredness, but she knew she wouldn't be able to sleep even if she tried. She stared at the wooden bow of the rowboat, its outline becoming a shadowy silhouette as thick clouds obscured the moonlight and the night became darker.

The rickety boat propelled them forward, not slowing its pace.

'He'll find a way,' Ralph murmured softly as the first light of morning flashed on the horizon.

'Maybe,' Naldy replied, though she knew they were hoping for too much.

The boat skimmed across the water as the golden haze of light spread across the sky. Naldy retrieved two dry biscuits from Rupert's rucksack and handed one to Ralph. He took it but didn't eat.

They didn't speak all day. Naldy knew no words could ease the pain, and she feared she would become a blubbering mess if she tried to talk.

Ralph still clutched his uneaten biscuit at the end of the day, when the sun vanished and night surrounded them.

Naldy curled up between the front seat and the central plank, trying to sleep. She dipped in and out of consciousness. When she woke—for what must have been the twentieth time—Naldy saw the navy tinge of the sky and knew it was almost morning again.

Ralph was seated on the back seat, staring blankly at the endless expanse of water ahead. He still clutched the same dry biscuit Naldy had given him the day before, and she noticed his eyes had a grey lustre, framed by puffy lids.

She helped herself to another biscuit from Rupert's rucksack and tried to eat, but the sight of his things caused a heavy sadness to wash over her, making her throat feel sore and dry.

They didn't speak for another whole day, but the silence wasn't uncomfortable. Naldy could tell Ralph wanted to be alone with his thoughts.

When the sun set, Ralph placed his uneaten biscuit on the plank and lay down on the wooden floor, pulling his travelling cloak over himself. Soon, he was snoring softly. Naldy lay beside him, tucking herself beneath her own cloak.

When Naldy woke, she was pleased to see Ralph had eaten half his biscuit. He sat perched on the back seat, staring out at the glistening lake, a light breeze tousling his strawberry-blonde hair.

The morning was chilly, and the sky was a soft baby blue spotted with fluffy clouds. Naldy looked at him warmly, and Ralph returned the tiniest hint of a smile.

'Maybe he'll live at the bottom of the lake with the Fairy Queen,' said Ralph, his voice hoarse from not having used it for a few days.

'Maybe,' Naldy replied, a sob catching in her throat as she spoke.

'I can't allow myself to believe that he is actually gone.'

'He is with the lake now,' said Naldy. 'It's a

beautiful place to rest.'

They fell silent once more, not speaking until the late afternoon, when the air had grown warmer.

'Naldy?'

'Yes,' she replied, turning to see Ralph holding the other half of his biscuit.

'We're here,' said Ralph, nodding towards the horizon.

Naldy had been too preoccupied with her thoughts to notice the thick, knotted trees appearing in the distance. Their rowboat sailed towards the shoreline. The dark umber trees of the wood stretched along, looking almost like a tall, sinister fence. When the boat reached the bank, it slid up along the small river stones and came to a halt.

After gathering their belongings and climbing wearily out of the little boat, Naldy scanned the water, hoping to get one last glimpse of the mysterious Fairy Queen, but there was no sign of her. Upon turning back, she caught sight of Ralph staring at Rupert's lone rucksack.

'I can carry his things,' said Naldy, gently squeezing Ralph's shoulder.

'I think we should leave his personal things,' he said softly, lifting Rupert's bag from the boat. 'In case he needs them.'

'Alright,' she replied quietly.

Together, they sorted through Rupert's items, making two piles: one for what they would take and another for what they would leave behind.

Naldy had plenty of extra room inside her bag now that most of the food had been eaten, but Ralph insisted on splitting the load evenly. Naldy tried to sneak more into her rucksack, wanting to ease Ralph's burden, but he caught her and wouldn't allow it.

After they re-packed their bags, Ralph carefully folded Rupert's clothes into a neat pile. He placed Rupert's metal bowl, spoon and empty Veserum bottle on top. Naldy stood by, watching as Ralph carried the neat pile to the water's edge and gently laid Rupert's things on the river stones, just inches from the still water.

'I'll miss you, Cousin,' Ralph whispered, his voice strained. 'We won't fail you. I promise you that.'

Naldy's chest tightened as grief swelled within her. She picked up Rupert's empty rucksack and carried it to the water's edge, resting it beside the pile of his belongings.

'It doesn't feel real,' muttered Ralph, taking Naldy's hand. 'I don't believe he's... how can he really be gone?'

'We can stay here the night if you like,' she said delicately. 'We can stay here as long as you need.'

'No,' replied Ralph, releasing her hand. 'I won't let his life be sacrificed for nothing. We can rest once we've beaten Maverick to the Corium.'

Ralph picked up his own rucksack, swung it onto his shoulders, and stepped beneath the shadows of the knotted trees. Naldy followed close behind.

The cover of the trees felt strangely comforting.

It was just as dark and eerie on this side of the lake as it had been on the other, but Naldy welcomed the change from the bright, open water.

They trudged through the woods, their legs stiff after days cramped in the small rowboat. Ralph held Rupert's map as he navigated the way.

Some days, Naldy convinced herself Rupert was perhaps trailing behind them. But at dusk, as they stopped to light a fire, the truth that Rupert was no longer with them set in—and her heart ached.

They had little food left, but neither seemed to care. Their hunger felt insignificant next to their grief.

Ralph set a brisk pace, eager not to let any time go to waste, and they rose at the first sign of light. Naldy struggled to keep up, occasionally losing sight of him as he vanished behind thick trees.

'You're pushing yourself too much,' said Naldy one evening as she finally caught up to Ralph, who had come to a halt.

Out of breath from walking, Naldy dropped her bag in relief. The dull light was fading, and she bent to pick up a nearby branch to start a fire.

'You won't need that,' said Ralph, watching as she collected fallen branches.

'Ralph, I know you want to reach the coast as quickly as possible, but we can't walk through the night. It's too dangerous, and we need to light a fire before it gets dark.'

She kept scanning the ground for sticks and twigs for kindling.

Ralph motioned with his hand for her to approach him.

'Look at the ground there,' he said, with a brightness in his eyes which Naldy hadn't seen for many days.

She gasped. Beneath their feet, the grey soil blended into yellow sand.

'The beach,' she said, smiling.

'We're here,' Ralph said. 'I've never seen the sea. Want to race?'

Without waiting for Naldy's reply, Ralph darted away, weaving between the sturdy trees. Naldy went after him, leaping over chunky, exposed tree roots protruding from the sand. They ran, adrenaline fuelling their pace. Minutes later, they reached the edge of the Mortous Woods.

They found themselves standing atop a tall sand dune. The view was disarming—the undulating blue sea stretched endlessly to the horizon, where the last sliver of daylight slowly faded. The sky was a deep purply-blue, flecked with brilliant orange and pink, dotted with the first stars of the night. Below, gentle waves lapped at the golden sand.

The shoreline was scattered with beached boats —at least a hundred of them—varying in size and age, but all made of the same dark wood. Many appeared unfinished, some decaying after years of exposure to the unkind weather, while others seemed recently completed. A few older boats were sunken into the sand, their weathered wood splintered and broken in places. Some ships had tattered masts, while others bore freshly stitched, bleach-white canvas that fluttered boldly in the salty breeze.

Nestled amongst the boats was a small white cottage. A plume of grey smoke billowed from its chimney, and warm lights twinkled invitingly in its windows.

'I've never seen the sea,' said Ralph, his blue eyes glistening as he gazed at the water. 'I can see why Rupert spoke so fondly of this place. It's relaxing just to look at.'

Together, they slowly descended the slanting sand dune, their feet sinking into the dry, slippery sand, while the sound of the soothing waves lapped rhythmically at the shore.

Naldy glanced back, but from this far down the slope, the trees of the Mortous Woods were no longer visible.

Orange bricks had been embedded into the beach, forming a sunken path half-buried in sand, leading to the back door of the white cottage.

Naldy took a deep breath before knocking on the door.

They heard shuffling inside the house, and soon, footsteps approached to greet them.

Chapter Sixteen

MASON

T he man in his mid-thirties didn't look surprised to see them when he opened the door, as though he were accustomed to strangers arriving unexpectedly. His long, dark dreadlocks were the same colour as his rugged, scruffy beard. Dark brown eyes sparkled beneath his wiry brows, and his chocolate-brown skin flaked like the cracked paint on the house's exterior—dry from prolonged exposure to the salty sea air.

'So, then,' said the man, a smirk half-hidden behind his wiry beard, 'you want to cross the Easterly Sea and have yourself a little adventure?'

'We need to travel to Arkus Day,' said Naldy. 'We need to leave as soon as possible.'

The man stepped aside, gesturing with an outstretched hand to invite them in. They entered a candlelit hallway, its dark, polished wooden walls reflecting the warm, flickering light.

'The second door on the right,' said the man.

The kitchen matched the hallway, lined with the same umber wood panelling. Beneath a window overlooking the boats resting on the sand, a large stove held a pot bubbling away. The sweet aroma of fish stew filled the air. At the centre of the room stood a round table.

'Take a seat and make yourselves comfortable,' said the man, making his way over to the pot and stirring it with a large wooden spoon. 'There's water on the table.'

Naldy picked up the ceramic jug and poured a glass of fresh water for herself and Ralph. They drank thirstily. Ralph leant back comfortably in his green-cushioned dining chair.

'Thank you,' said Naldy kindly.

'You've come just in time for dinner,' said Mason, turning towards a nearby cupboard to collect three ceramic bowls, each painted with a different blue ship. 'We require introductions. I was named Mason, but many call me the Boat Builder.'

'I am Naldy, and this is Ralph. We appreciate your hospitality, Mason.'

Their host retrieved three silver spoons from a nearby drawer before serving generous helpings of the pungent fish stew.

'No need for manners,' said the man, placing the bowls of stew in front of them before taking his seat. 'You must be hungry after your journey. The woods can be a wicked place.'

The stew was the first hot meal they'd enjoyed in a long time. The fish was tender, steeped in a rich tomato broth, with aromatic spices that perfumed the air and comforted them.

'So, you're hoping to find the Corium?' asked the

Boat Builder.

Naldy and Ralph both lifted their faces, startled by his question.

'Did Mortous contact you?' Ralph asked.

'No,' Mason replied, taking a sip of the broth. 'The only reason anybody comes by here is to set sail to Arkus Day. And everyone who wants to sail to Arkus Day is after the same thing.'

'The Corium,' said Ralph.

'Many desire it, but the few who return do so with nothing more than sand in their shoes.'

'We appreciate your hospitality,' said Ralph with a faint smile, 'and yes, you are right. We, too, are seeking the Corium.'

'I know I am right,' said the Boat Builder, scratching his black beard. 'Only one person has ever come by here who wasn't dreaming of finding the Queen of the Devante.'

'Rupert,' Ralph said knowingly, his smile fading.

'You know of him?' asked the Boat Builder, his brown eyes curiously meeting Ralph's blue ones.

'He is my cousin,' explained Ralph, his voice cracking as he spoke.

'Yes, I can see that now. You look much like him.'

'We lost him,' said Ralph, almost choking on his words. 'On the Versalius Lake.'

The Boat Builder placed his spoon on the table and bowed his head respectfully before speaking.

'I am sad to hear this terrible news. I would have liked to have welcomed him back.'

'He may find a way home yet,' Ralph said meekly.

From the Boat Builder's doleful expression, Naldy could tell he didn't believe Rupert was alive—and that Ralph was clinging to false hope. They ate in silence for some time.

'We've come because we need to use my cousin's boat to cross the sea,' said Ralph seriously.

Mason shifted uncomfortably in his seat but said nothing.

'It's no good,' said Naldy, turning to face Ralph. 'He's part of the Seagull Society—just like Mortous. He probably believes the Corium is safer left where it is, in Arkus Day. Am I wrong?'

The Boat Builder lowered his chin, studying her curiously.

'Well,' said Naldy, her voice quiet but firm.

'You are not wrong,' Mason replied. 'I am part of the Seagull Society.'

'Do you actually help people cross the sea?' asked Naldy, bitterness blooming in her voice. 'Or is it your job to pretend to help while making sure the boats never reach Arkus Day.'

'The sea between us and Arkus Day needs no help hindering those who wish to cross.'

Without another word, the Boat Builder left his seat and exited the room, leaving Naldy and Ralph alone at the wooden dining table.

'We shouldn't irritate him,' said Ralph. 'We need his help.'

'He won't help us,' said Naldy, flatly. 'All the members of this Seagull Society think they know better.'

'He didn't say he wouldn't help us,' whispered Ralph, finishing the last of his stew. 'Just try not to upset him. We can't do this without him.'

'I don't like this,' she murmured, half to herself.

Ralph eyed the pot—clearly pondering whether there was enough time to help himself to seconds before the Boat Builder returned. But as he made to stand, Mason re-entered the room carrying a lantern with a thick wax candle burning inside.

'Once you've finished your dinner,' said the Boat Builder, 'I want to show you something. You'll need your travelling cloaks.'

Naldy stood without hesitation, while Ralph reluctantly followed, casting a forlorn glance at Naldy's abandoned bowl of fish stew.

The Boat Builder led them back along the wood-panelled hallway and out the front door. They stepped into a night that had turned dark and unwelcoming. A cold, roaring wind blew in from the sea, cutting through their clothing and chilling their bones.

'Where are we going?' asked Ralph, tightly wrapping his travelling cloak around himself to shield against the harsh weather.

The Boat Builder led them a few metres along the sand before stopping. He held up the flickering lantern, its light casting eerie shadows on the towering hull of a tall ship looming over them. Naldy hazarded a guess it would take at least twelve people to sail the ship.

Mason passed the lantern to Naldy, its flame

flickering violently in the wind, precariously close to being extinguished.

'You're welcome to take any ship you like,' he said, a smile peeking through his wiry beard. With those parting words, the Boat Builder turned on his heel and walked back towards the comforting glow of his cottage.

Holding the lantern high, Naldy circled the towering ship Mason had shown them.

'You're not serious,' called Ralph over the howling gale. 'Let's go back, Naldy. We can't set out in this weather, and we certainly can't operate a boat this size.'

'There are boats along this stretch that aren't so large, Ralph,' said Naldy, the tails of her black cloak thrashing in the wind. 'We can find a smaller boat.'

'It's too windy to set sail,' cried Ralph, hurrying after her along the beach.

'We're a week ahead of Maverick at best, Ralph,' she said, spinning to face him. The quivering flame cast a sombre light upon his troubled face. 'I'm not going to sit around in the Boat Builder's cottage waiting for him to help us. We don't have time.'

Ralph swallowed hard, his face paling under the lantern's light. Naldy continued up the stretch of sand, and Ralph ran to keep up.

'We need the Boat Builder's help,' he said meekly. 'We can't do this without him.'

Naldy felt tears dampen her cheeks. She knew Ralph was right—commandeering a ship in the windswept night wouldn't improve their situation or help their quest.

'Okay,' said Naldy, stopping, her voice so quiet she doubted Ralph had heard her.

She turned, making her way back towards the cottage. When Ralph caught up to her, he tenderly gave her arm a comforting squeeze.

They re-entered the cottage together, closing the door behind them and leaving the howling wind outside. They heard the Boat Builder's guttural humming drifting from a room at the far end of the central passage. As soon as he saw them enter, Mason stopped humming.

They found themselves in a sitting room furnished with two small lapis-blue sofas. The walls were adorned with nautical artefacts: a sea captain's brass spyglass, a polished wooden ship's helm, and an assortment of ship lanterns in various sizes. Warmth radiated from a small black tin inglenook fireplace, where the Boat Builder stood with his back to the fire.

'If you require my help,' said the Boat Builder in a composed manner, 'I am happy to offer it.'

'We need your help,' replied Ralph politely, 'and we are grateful for it.'

'You'd have had no luck tonight anyway,' said Mason, gesturing for them to sit. 'The wind, for starters, would have worked against you.'

As Naldy lowered herself onto the sofa, she noticed three cups and a pot of brew already waiting on the small side table.

'Of course, then,' the Boat Builder continued,

'there's the enchantment.'

'The enchantment?' asked Ralph as the brew poured itself into delicate blue cups.

'Yes,' replied Mason. 'The boats are enchanted to set sail only if those aboard have had input in the construction of the vessel.'

Naldy's stomach twisted.

'You mean they won't float unless—'

'They won't move,' said the Boat Builder, taking hold of his blue saucer, which had floated up to meet him. 'Everyone who comes by here must build their own boat before taking it to sea. This should be no surprise—it is no secret.'

'Build our own boat?' repeated Ralph, his forehead wrinkling with anxiety. 'But my cousin has already done the building. We were hoping to set sail in his boat. We just need your help learning how to captain it.'

'Building in groups is, of course, fine,' said Mason, taking a small sip from his cup. There was an elegance to the way he drank his brew. 'I've had many visitors before who intended to journey as a team. You aren't required to build a boat each, but the boat you construct must have had input from everyone. It will take approximately six months—'

'Six months,' Naldy exclaimed, nearly spilling her brew.

'Even if the boat is for one,' said the Boat Builder calmly, 'it must be large enough to withstand the ire of the sea.'

'But we don't have six months,' Naldy said

desperately, springing to her feet. 'You don't understand. There is a wizard who is going to be here in a week, possibly sooner!'

'He too will be required to construct his own ship.'

'He has a Devante,' said Naldy, her voice rising. 'There will be no stopping him. He plans on destroying the Corium.'

'There are no shortcuts to Arkus Day,' said Mason sternly, taking another delicate sip of his brew. 'Everybody must—'

'We are trying to save magic,' Ralph interrupted, standing. 'We don't mean to disrespect you, but we do not have six months.'

'I know who Maverick is,' said the Boat Builder, making his way to the nearest sofa and taking a seat. He calmly crossed his legs. 'The Seagull Society has been watching the wizard for some time. But you needn't worry yourselves. He is not the first of his kind to venture this way.'

'Okay,' said Naldy dryly. 'We will do it your way.'

'Naldy,' said Ralph, outraged, 'we can't sit around assembling wood for months!'

'We do it the way it's always been done,' said Naldy, flashing her hazel eyes at him. 'Can we start tomorrow?'

'Tomorrow?' repeated Ralph piercingly. 'Naldy, we don't have time to waste!'

Inside, Naldy was just as incensed at the Boat Builder's reluctance to speed up the process, but she knew that arguing would only escalate the tension.

'All you Seagull people,' said Ralph, glaring at the Boat Builder, 'you think you're helping. But we'll all lose magic if we don't act with urgency.'

The Boat Builder took another sip of his brew. Naldy couldn't discern his expression, concealed by his bushy facial hair.

'There's a reason,' began Mason in a soothing voice, 'why most boats along the shoreline are unfinished and abandoned. Few have made it to Arkus Day and returned. Life-and-death decisions, my friend, are best ruminated on. The wisest of those who come by here decide not to make the crossing.'

'We don't have the luxury of rumination,' replied Ralph, clearly displeased with the Boat Builder's words.

'If you've both finished your brew, I'll show you to your sleeping quarters.'

Naldy felt relieved that the Boat Builder showed no inclination to turn them out of his house, even after their argument. She supposed Mason was accustomed to such outbursts from visitors eager to depart.

The Boat Builder led them to a cosy room at the end of the passage, its windows overlooking the open sea. Two twin beds, dressed in sea-green linen, stood ready for them.

'Breakfast will be at seven,' said Mason kindly. 'The bathroom is across the hall if you want to wash.'

He left, closing the door behind him. Ralph

opened his mouth to speak, but Naldy held up a finger, silencing him. They listened as their host's footsteps retreated and finally faded altogether.

'Naldy, why would you agree to his conditions? We don't have time.'

'Because you were right,' said Naldy. 'We need his help, Ralph, and bickering isn't going to do us any good. You're the one that said it's best not to irritate him—and then you went on and on.'

'But six months, Naldy. We can't give up now. Every minute matters.'

'We're not giving up,' she replied, hanging her travelling cloak on the peg on the back of the door. 'We just need to find a way to earn the Boat Builder's trust. Then we can convince him to let us sail sooner. Besides, we both need a good night's rest. I'm going to freshen up before bed.'

Naldy left Ralph in the bedroom, his face sour and glum. She made her way across the hall to the bathroom.

—*Chapter Seventeen*—

REFLECTIONS IN HOT WATER

T wo rust-gold wall candelabras illuminated the large bathtub. Naldy removed her shoes and stepped barefoot across the blue-marbled tiles flecked with gold. She turned on the hot water and, while the tub filled, approached the square sink, where an old round mirror reflected her weary face.

She was startled by how tired she looked. The skin beneath her eyes was tinged grey, and her long black hair had become a greasy, matted nest. She splashed her face at the sink, half expecting the grey circles to wash away. But as the water dripped down her cheeks, she conceded that only a long sleep would banish them.

Naldy found several small waxed candles embellished with seashells inside the bathroom's cabinetry. She also discovered a foaming solution and lime-green bath crystals, which she sprinkled liberally into the bath's hot water. After lighting the candles, she removed her travelling clothes and climbed into the soothing water.

Her mind kept drifting to the faces they had lost

along their journey: Odorf's wrinkled smile, Oak's moss-green eyes, and Rupert's white-toothed grin. Then there was the Witch House, burnt to cinders, and the many Devante—all but two—destroyed.

She gently played with the surface of the soapy water, wishing she could go back in time—longing for the chance never to have set out on the quest to begin with. To distract herself from the painful thoughts, she studied the sizeable old map fastened to the wall at the foot of the tub, enclosed in an industrial metal frame.

Random numbers were scribbled in untidy black ink across the time-worn parchment, seemingly in no particular order. Faintly drawn grid lines marked the coordinates. She wasn't sure what place the map represented, but she guessed it might be Arkus Day. A wave of doubt washed over her as she wondered if they would ever reach it. Naldy sank lower into the tub, but even the warmth of the water couldn't ease her worries.

Nearly an hour later, when Naldy returned to the bedroom, she found Ralph tucked into one of the twin beds, snoring steadily. His muddy travelling clothes lay discarded in a messy bundle on the floor.

She climbed into bed, but despite her exhaustion, she knew sleep would elude her. She couldn't shake the feeling that more failure was to come.

The next morning, after a hot breakfast of fried mackerel on toast, Ralph and Naldy followed Mason along the shoreline, their feet leaving streaks in the dry sand. The wind had passed and the hot sun reflected off the cracked wood of the tall ships.

'It will take us years to build one of these,' Ralph muttered, eyeing the nearest cutter boat, its white canvas sails stretching several metres into the air.

'We won't quite be building one that large,' the Boat Builder called from slightly ahead. 'A boat for two will be half that size, with one less sail.'

'Only half the size,' echoed Ralph, horrified, before leaning in to whisper to Naldy. 'If you don't convince him by lunch to let us sail without having to construct one of these monstrosities, I'll resort to magic.'

'He's a witch, Ralph,' said Naldy, turning her angular face towards him. 'And if he's part of the Seagull Society, he's probably quite a good one.'

'Here we are,' said the Boat Builder, stopping in front of a vessel that stretched several metres long and stood at least eight metres tall, including its masts. The two sails had been lowered and tied securely to the booms for protection.

'Will we be building one like this?' asked Naldy, looking up at the large boat. 'Whose was this?'

'Rupert's,' said Ralph instinctively, reaching out to touch the oiled wood.

'I thought you might like to see it,' the Boat Builder said kindly. 'He was a fine craftsman, as you can see.'

Ralph's eyes sparkled as he gazed up at his cousin's boat.

They couldn't help but be impressed by the skilled artistry that had gone into the vessel's construction. Rupert had evidently paid meticulous attention to every detail—from the intricacy of the hemp rigging system to the railing's refined finish.

'Can we go up?' asked Ralph eagerly, a hand resting on the rope ladder which still hung from the side of the ship.

The Boat Builder smiled, and Ralph climbed the ladder, Naldy close behind. Mason remained on the beach. Once they were standing on the deck, they were struck by how spacious everything felt.

'Rupert was going to sail this alone?' asked Naldy, watching as Ralph stepped into the ship's open wooden wheelhouse.

'I can picture him here,' he said, gripping the cylindrical wooden spokes of the ship's wheel and gazing at the choppy waves rolling in from the sea.

Naldy entered the wheelhouse and picked up a hammer resting on the wooden bench beneath the helm's window. A few silver nails lay abandoned beside it, as though Rupert had gone on a lunch break and never returned to finish securing the bench.

'I could spend six months here. Longer,' said Ralph softly, a heaviness in his voice. 'If only we had the time. Do we have a plan, Naldy?'

'I'm working on it,' she replied, her tone tinged with unease. 'I need some time to think of a way to convince him.'

'Well, I suppose we ought to start on our own little boat—or big boat, I should say—at least until we figure out how to convince Mason. I wish we could stay here and build something this beautiful, like Rupert did.'

Leaving Ralph by the wheel, Naldy climbed down the rope ladder, and stepped back onto the beach, her shoes pressing into the dry sand.

'I thought I'd give him a moment alone,' said Naldy to the Boat Builder.

'That's kind of you,' replied Mason, the hot sun giving his brown skin a satiny lustre. 'You needn't worry, Naldy.'

'Worry?'

'About Maverick,' said the Boat Builder, meeting her eyes. 'Many a powerful witch and wizard has come by before, and many have expected special treatment. But all have had to yield to tradition. Six months, at a minimum.'

'Have you ever had a witch or wizard stop by with a Devante in their pocket?' asked Naldy boldly.

The Boat Builder winced, just barely, but then he smiled warmly at her.

'When he's done,' said Mason, nodding towards the tall sand dunes, 'meet me up by the edge of the woods.'

Once Mason had climbed the nearest sand dune and disappeared from view, Naldy turned her gaze to the shimmering sea. The rolling waves broke confidently against the beach. She wondered if Ralph had been right—would forcing Mason with magic be the only way to convince him to let them sail without needing to construct their own boat?

Nearly twenty minutes later, Ralph descended

the ladder, his eyes puffy and red, a wet streak glistening on his cheek. Without a word, they climbed the slanted sand dune together, their foreheads beaded with sweat by the time they reached the top.

The Boat Builder was perched comfortably on a tree stump, his bearded face tilted back to soak in the sun's warmth. As Naldy glanced around, she was startled to see thousands of bare stumps stretching parallel to the edge of the woods.

The evening prior, when they had first emerged from the woods, they had been too awestruck by the sight of the ocean to notice the many chopped trees.

'Take one each,' instructed the Boat Builder, gesturing towards a selection of axes and silver sharp-toothed saws laid out on the sand near his feet.

'There's got to be a spell for felling trees,' said Ralph, eyeing the metallic tools with disdain.

'There's not,' replied Naldy, bending to examine the saws. 'The spell to cut down trees didn't survive The Great Witch Hunt.'

'We need to get our hands on a Devante,' said Ralph, picking up a long axe with a dark walnut handle.

Naldy settled on a lean crosscut saw with pine wood handles attached at each end.

'Ralph will be executing the front cut, then,' said the Boat Builder, rising to his feet and walking over to Naldy. 'And you and I will take care of the back cut.'

Mason led them into the gloominess of the woods, instructing them to be on the lookout for tall, slender trees.

'They all seem chunky to me,' remarked Ralph.

'We want to begin with the leanest ones,' explained Mason, 'until you build up your strength.'

As lunchtime approached, they had yet to fell a single tree. Ralph repeatedly lodged his axe firmly in the trunk, needing Mason's help each time to free it. When it came to Naldy and Mason's turn to finish severing the remaining attachment, Naldy strained her back muscles multiple times working the saw, requiring Ralph to use *Sanitatem Restituere* to heal her.

Despite their efforts, the tall, dark tree still stood when they paused for lunch. Ralph and Naldy's clothes were soaked with sweat.

'You both look like you've gone for a dip in the sea,' remarked the Boat Builder cheekily as they returned to the cabin for food.

When they came back an hour later to finish the job, they discovered the tree had fallen on its own.

'One down,' said the Boat Builder, running his hands over the tree's cracked branches. 'How's your back, Naldy?'

'Ralph's spell seems to have done the job of easing the pain.'

'Good to hear.'

'How many trees?' asked Ralph flatly. 'How many do we need to build our boat?'

'I think about fifty should do the job. More, if

they're all this slender.'

'Fifty!' Ralph exclaimed, his mouth agape.

By sunset, they had successfully felled another four trees. As they walked back to the house, the Boat Builder tried to lift their depleted spirits, assuring them it would become easier with practice.

'I don't think I can do weeks of this,' said Ralph wearily, 'let alone months.'

While Mason cooked a coconut crab curry in the kitchen, the mouthwatering aroma wafting through the cottage, Naldy and Ralph rested their aching limbs in the sitting room by the fireside.

'We've wasted a whole day,' whispered Ralph, seated on the floor with his arms dangling limply at his sides. 'An entire day—good gracious!'

'I don't have any ideas, Ralph,' Naldy admitted reluctantly. 'I hate to say it, but I think you might be right. We may have to force the Boat Builder to help us. I can't see any other way.'

'Maverick will arrive any day now, and we won't even have the bones of a boat,' said Ralph, the firelight flickering across his pale skin.

The Boat Builder's voice floated along the hall from the kitchen. 'Dinner is ready.'

'Let's give it another day of thought,' said Naldy, as she lifted herself and made her way to the door. 'I'm too exhausted to duel Mason tonight.'

They ate mostly in silence, too drained for conversation. The food was spicy and comforting, its warmth spreading through their tired bodies.

'The first day is always the hardest,' said the Boat

Builder gently. 'We'll go straight to bed after dinner. You both need a good rest after the day's work.'

But Naldy didn't go straight to bed after dinner. Instead, she ran another hot bath for herself.

For hours, she stared at the large map fixed to the wall, her thoughts drifting to Maverick and how he had once conjured a ball of smoke, convinced she knew the location of the Corium—before she had even learnt it was hidden in Arkus Day. Naldy wondered if a solution to their problems lay dormant within her. Was there more information about the Corium hidden in the depths of her mind somewhere? A forgotten memory, perhaps?

'Arkus Day,' she murmured, eyes fixed on the framed grided parchment. Naldy sat upright in the bath. 'It's not a map of Arkus Day. It's a map of the sea between here and there.'

Looking more closely, Naldy realised that the edges of the two jagged lines at the diagonal corners of the parchment represented the inverse of what she had initially thought. The land was on the outside, while the sea made up the bulk of the map.

She was still unsure how to interpret the many dotted numbers scattered across the parchment. They seemed chaotically distributed, without any discernible logic; the number 6 was scrawled just centimetres away from one as high as 124.

'I need to stop fretting about *what* we'll be travelling in,' said Naldy to herself. 'I need to start focusing on *how* we'll reach Arkus Day safely. We need to learn how to read sea charts.'

The sun was punishing the following day. Ralph stood in the shadow of the broadest tree, trying to escape the stifling, unmoving air. He wiped sweat from his brow while Naldy worked the two-person saw with the Boat Builder.

'Do you need more than a compass, then?' asked Naldy breathlessly, her hands gripping the wooden handles of the sharp-toothed saw as she pushed and pulled.

'You need luck,' the Boat Builder replied, seemingly unbothered by the heat.

Naldy wanted to press him for more details— surely it took more than good fortune to navigate the sea—but she was too out of breath to speak further.

The wood let out a sharp cracking sound, prompting them to step back, retreating to the safety of the tree where Ralph was sheltering. The cracking grew louder, intensifying until the tree splintered and collapsed with an ear-splitting crunch.

'That's number nine,' said the Boat Builder cheerfully. 'We're ahead of schedule.'

'More than luck,' said Naldy, catching her breath. 'There's a map in the bathroom riddled with numbers—they must mean something. It can't just be luck.'

'They do mean something,' replied the Boat Builder, turning to face her with a curious expression. 'But let's take it one step at a time, shall we? We need a vessel first, then I'll teach you how to sail. Time for lunch.'

The scorching sun reflected off the blonde sand as they made their way back to the house. Naldy wished she had been more tactful when questioning the Boat Builder, but the relentless heat was making her irritable. She resolved to try again over lunch.

'How many times have you been to Arkus Day, then?' asked Naldy once they were seated around the table. She took a bite of her slow-cooked octopus.

'I've never been,' replied Mason, looking up calmly.

'You've never been?' repeated Ralph, aghast. 'But if you've never been, how are you supposed to teach us how to get there?'

'I know enough about the sea,' said the Boat Builder placidly. 'Enough to know the journey isn't worth the risk. I'm not foolish enough.'

'Not worth the risk,' said Ralph, wiping sweat off his nose. The residual heat from the oven kept the house stuffy, even with the windows thrown open. 'But you can't teach us if you've never been yourself.'

'Oh, I know plenty about sailing, and I know everything you need to know about boats,' said Mason, topping up their water glasses and lowering his voice. 'But only fools take the gamble of crossing the ocean to Arkus Day. You must decide if you're a fool. If you are, may luck be kind to you.'

Ralph chewed his octopus slowly, as though it had suddenly lost its flavour.

Four days passed, and with each one, the weather grew hotter, refusing to cool even at night. They returned to the house each evening with sore, stiff limbs. The Boat Builder opened all the cottage's windows in a futile attempt to stir the sweltering air.

After a cold dinner of seaweed salad served in large clamshells, they retired to their bedrooms. Naldy waited until Ralph was sound asleep before retreating to the bathroom and climbing into the large tub. The cool water soothed her inflamed muscles. These nightly baths had become her way of gathering her thoughts.

They had cut down nineteen trees in total, but the stifling heat had slowed their progress, leaving them far short of the required fifty.

Maverick could arrive at any moment, and the boughs hadn't even been stripped of their bark.

Naldy reclined in the bath's tepid water, her gaze fixed on the framed map of the journey they had pledged to undertake—a quest that felt increasingly hopeless with each passing day.

'Are we meant to confront Maverick on this hot, sandy shore?' Naldy wondered aloud. But then the inner voice of reason interjected—*if it comes to that, you'll surely meet the same fate as Rupert. It will all have been for nothing.*

In an attempt to clear her thoughts, she sank beneath the bathwater. The room's slanted corrugated iron ceiling blurred and shimmered above the rippling surface as she let her head slip deeper into the cool water.

'Depth,' her mind sparked. She lifted her head

from the water, inhaled deeply, and rubbed her eyes. Her gaze fixed on the numbers scribbled across the map on the wall. 'The numbers indicate the water's depth—of course—it's so obvious now I see it.'

Naldy climbed out of the tub and dried herself with a towel before slipping into her lightweight cotton dressing gown. She reached for the metal frame on the wall, awkwardly lifting it from its hooks. Placing the large frame onto the tiles, she unfastened the latches and carefully removed the glass casing. Without pausing to think, she rolled the parchment, replaced the glass in the frame, and hung it back on the wall, now bare of its map.

She carried the metre-long rolled-up map back to the bedroom, where Ralph was already asleep. His snoring breaths were barely audible over the gentle sound of waves breaking on the nearby shore.

Naldy perched on the end of her bed, resting the rolled map against her leg. Moonlight filtered through the open window, casting a muted glow across the room.

The urge to wake Ralph, pack their bags, take the map, and push one of the smaller boats into the water grew stronger with each passing moment. But then she remembered the enchantment—the boats wouldn't move. She couldn't bear another day of chopping trees, and the need to act was rising inside her.

Hours slipped by as Naldy sat motionless at the foot of the bed, the untouched sheets tucked rigidly beneath the mattress. She remained deep in thought—the past uncoiling in her mind as she contemplated everything that they had been through. Everything that had led them to this remote sandy shore. Surely something had been overlooked. Surely a solution was waiting to be uncovered if only she gave it enough attention.

The moonlight gave way to a navy hue, signalling the approach of dawn.

'You're up early,' Ralph said sluggishly, his hair sticking up at awkward angles.

Naldy hesitated—afraid her words might dissolve into tears if she tried to speak. There had been so many tears in recent weeks, and she didn't want to give in to them again.

'What's that thing?' asked Ralph, nodding at the rolled-up map. Before waiting for an answer, he pulled the covers over his head.

'It's a map of the sea.'

For a moment, Naldy thought Ralph had fallen back asleep, but his drowsy voice soon drifted out from beneath the covers. 'Did you sleep at all?'

'I've failed us, Ralph. I've brought us on a quest that's doomed, but I've been too stubborn to admit it.'

'It's still so early,' said Ralph softly. 'Go back to sleep. We'll figure out a way to convince Mason when we wake up.'

'There is no way,' said Naldy. The muffled sounds of the Boat Builder pottering around in the kitchen reached her ears. 'We can't stay here and definitely shouldn't be here when Maverick arrives, which could be any day now. I think... we should go back.'

'Go back?' repeated Ralph, sitting upright again, shaking his head firmly. 'We can't have come all this way just to give up now.'

'Perhaps the Society is right,' said Naldy sadly. 'Perhaps the Corium is best left in Arkus Day.'

'You need some rest,' Ralph said with a yawn. 'Today, while we work on our boat, we will try to convince the Boat Builder. We can't give up.'

Naldy's thoughts weighed too heavily for her to sleep, but Ralph laid his head down and was soon snoring softly again. She decided to take a walk along the beach while the sun rose. Picking up the map, she slipped out the back entrance so the Boat Builder wouldn't see her leave the cottage. Walking across the dry sand barefoot, Naldy felt glad to be alone.

To her surprise, a cold breeze swept in from the ocean, signalling that the weather was finally cooling. The sky bloomed a brilliant yellow as she walked along the wet sand, the waves lapping at her feet as they broke. Naldy stopped when she reached Rupert's ship and decided to climb the ladder. She made her way to the helm, the spot where Ralph had stood just days earlier. Naldy unfurled the map across the wooden wheel and stared out at the vast expanse of rolling blue.

Was the sea to Arkus Day the path they were meant to take? Was there any path left that could lead them to save magic? Were they destined for failure?

'We can't do this without you, Rupert,' said Naldy, her eyes fixed on the horizon where the deep blue ripples met the golden sky. 'I guess our only option is to go back. I'm sorry we failed you.'

She turned to leave, but a flash of silver caught her attention—glinting in the early morning sun lay Rupert's abandoned hammer and nails. Naldy's heart fluttered.

'It couldn't be that easy, surely,' she murmured.

Slipping one of the small nails into her pocket, she returned to the cottage.

—Chapter Eighteen—

FOOL'S CROSSING

R alph was already seated at the kitchen table, fully dressed and sipping his brew.

'How was your walk?' asked Mason, busy at the frypan.

'The ocean is beautiful in these early hours,' replied Naldy, pouring herself a cup of the toasty-smelling brew.

'I see you've decided to borrow my wall décor,' said the Boat Builder, nodding towards the rolled-up map still in Naldy's hands. 'We've got a few months of work ahead before you'll be ready for maps.'

Naldy reached into her pocket, retrieved the small nail she'd taken from Rupert's ship, and placed it on the table. The Boat Builder glanced at it, then turned back to add more mackerel to his sizzling frypan.

'We're not ready for nails either,' said Ralph, his strawberry-blonde eyebrows raised. 'We've still got thirty-one trees to fell, not to mention stripping, cutting, and sanding them.'

'He never finished his boat,' Naldy said, keeping her focus on the back of the Boat Builder's head.

'You knew that, didn't you? Rupert hadn't finished it when he decided to give it up and return to Kirkwood Forest.'

'Yes, but Rupert's not here to finish it,' replied Ralph heavily.

'But we are here,' said Naldy. 'We all travelled together. You and I can pick up where Rupert left off. The Boat Builder conveniently left that bit out.'

Mason turned around, the frypan in one hand, his face becoming cold and stern.

'It is better you take the time to build your own boat.'

'I remember you saying,' began Naldy, not breaking eye contact with him, 'groups of people could work on a single boat, and, well—'

'We are a part of Rupert's group, yes,' Ralph finished for her.

'You don't understand how important it is,' said Mason in a slow, serious tone, 'to take your time. The six months are crucial—not just for building the boat, but for considering your choices. This isn't a decision you want to rush.'

'We don't have the luxury of time,' said Naldy bluntly, realising the Boat Builder's response was an admission that a few nails were enough to consider them worthy of sailing Rupert's ship.

Mason served the mackerel onto their plates, then took a seat. Naldy sensed he was deliberately taking his time, carefully weighing the situation.

'Okay,' Mason said at last. 'I'll help you. But you must spend six weeks with me, learning the ropes.'

'Six weeks!' exclaimed Naldy, her fork clutched tightly. 'We're leaving after breakfast, and we won't be stopped by you or anyone else.'

'You are right,' said Mason, his voice steady. 'I've known for a while that a few nails were all it would take to get Rupert's boat to sail. But if you want the best chance of survival, then—'

'Don't you see?' she interrupted impatiently, 'Maverick is no ordinary wizard. The Devante might have been safe, lost in the sands of Arkus Day for all this time, but the Corium can no longer stay there. I don't care if the Seagull Society believes the leagon is best left where it is—I just know it's not.'

The Boat Builder nodded, but Naldy caught the disappointment clouding his eyes.

They finished the rest of their breakfast in silence, accompanied only by the sound of waves and Ralph's slow chewing of mackerel. When the plates were cleared, Naldy and Ralph headed to their room to pack.

'We're really doing this, then,' said Ralph, sitting on the edge of his unmade twin bed. He offered her a melancholic smile.

'Maybe it's silly,' said Naldy, tossing her pyjamas into her leather bag.

'No, I don't think it is,' replied Ralph, standing to search for his belongings. His things had been scattered across the room after only a few days. 'It feels like we're wasting time here, Naldy. If Rupert were with us, we'd already be on our way.'

She finished collecting her things and watched as

Ralph hunted for the rest of his.

'I think that's everything,' he said, pulling the leather straps closed.

'If you've forgotten something, we can collect it on our way back.'

When they re-entered the kitchen, they found three large wooden crates beside the door, filled with supplies: food, bedclothes, fishing gear, brew, and plenty of glass bottles of fresh drinking water.

'This is yours,' said Naldy, handing the rolled-up map she'd pinched from the bathroom to the Boat Builder.

'You'll need it more than I will,' Mason replied, directing his palms at one of the crates which lifted off the ground. 'Everybody take a crate with them.'

'You'll help us then?' asked Naldy.

'I'll do what I can, but I must be frank with you— if you really plan on setting sail today—I fear all that I can do won't be enough.'

The mood was tense as they walked across the beach, the crates drifting ahead of them. They passed the tall wooden ships, standing like skeletal monuments gleaming in the sun.

When they arrived at Rupert's vessel, the Boat Builder and Ralph set their crates down on the sand and climbed the ladder to the deck. Naldy used her magic to lift each wooden box, guiding them onto the ship. Ralph took them one by one, stacking them neatly.

The Boat Builder hoisted one of the ship's spectacular white canvas sails, which fluttered in the breeze.

'I hope you're both fast learners,' said the Boat Builder, fastening the rope of one of the sails. 'Because I'm going to try and teach you months of knowledge in one morning, and we've no room for error.'

'I thought you said it was all luck,' said Naldy, grinning cheekily as she climbed the ladder to meet them on the deck.

'Mostly,' the Boat Builder replied, smiling back. 'I hope you understand what you're undertaking.'

'Trust us,' replied Naldy. 'We've had many months to weigh the risks.'

'The weather's finally cooled,' said Ralph, holding his face high in the wind. 'The beginning of our good luck.'

As the sun climbed the sky, they practised tying ropes, hoisting the sails, reading maps, and pretending to steer the ship despite the vessel being on dry land. The hard work took a toll on their bodies, and by late afternoon, they were drenched in sweat.

The Boat Builder made crab sandwiches, and they ate on the ship's deck. Naldy worried she had forgotten most of what she'd been shown.

'Building your own boat would have helped build up your fitness,' said Mason through a mouthful of sandwich. 'The journey across is two or three days —if you don't get lost. Hopefully, the weather stays kind, though she often is not.'

'We should spend another day reviewing

everything,' said Ralph nervously. 'I feel I should have written it all down.'

'Yes,' said Naldy, her cheeks flushed from the day's work. 'It's much more difficult than I'd expected. I'm beginning to see why you wanted us to take more time. It was silly to think we could set out today.'

The Boat Builder stood and disappeared into the open wooden wheelhouse, returning moments later with a hammer. He held the hammer out to them.

'You were right,' said Ralph, staring at the hammer without accepting it. 'We're not ready.'

'What is it, Mason?' pressed Naldy, sensing an unease in the Boat Builder.

'I've had word Maverick will be arriving sometime tomorrow,' he said.

'Tomorrow!' exclaimed Ralph. 'But we'll never keep ahead of him. He has the Aurum!'

'I'll delay him,' said Mason. 'For as long as possible —six months if I can. But you should depart as soon as you can.'

'Why are you helping us now?' asked Naldy, surprised at how quickly the Boat Builder had forsaken the idea of constructing their own vessel.

'You were travelling here with Rupert,' said Mason, holding out the hammer again. 'He was the first to come by without the desire for the Corium. He was a good man, and I can see goodness in your hearts, too. I see there's no stopping you. If you're to set sail, you must go while the weather is forgiving, and before Maverick arrives.'

Naldy didn't take the hammer but instead reached into her pocket and pulled out the silver nail. She held it out to Ralph.

Ralph's eyes sparkled as he accepted Mason's hammer and Naldy's nail. He made his way to the small wooden wheelhouse. Three heavy blows echoed as he drove the nail into place.

'Your turn, Naldy,' Ralph called from the helm.

Naldy joined him, standing beside the wooden wheel. He held the hammer out, and she took it from him, picking up another small nail. With a few heavy blows, she embedded the nail into the wooden bench—securing the final piece of Rupert's ship.

Naldy paused, expecting sparks or some sign the magic had worked—something to signal the ship would set sail at their command. But there was nothing, only the light sea breeze blowing across their faces.

'How do we get it to sail?' she asked, turning to find the Boat Builder no longer sitting on the deck.

'Where's he gone?' asked Ralph.

'Do you think he was fooling us?' said Naldy. 'Making us believe we could set sail, knowing all along we wouldn't be able to get the boat off the sand?'

'Maybe we just need to tell the boat to sail,' said Ralph, gripping the ship's wheel. 'Sail!'

The boat did not move.

'The tide doesn't reach this far up the beach,' said Naldy, moving to the rail to check if the Boat Builder was standing below.

'I'm getting darn good at magic, Naldy, but I'm not nearly good enough to shift this boat with it, and neither are you. Can you see the Boat Builder?'

Before Naldy could answer, the vessel began sliding across the golden sand, and she nearly lost her balance. They were making their way towards the vast bluish-green ocean.

It was nothing like the smooth, tranquil gliding of the tiny rowboat they'd sailed on Versalius Lake. This was turbulent and somewhat frightening.

Ralph gripped the wheel tightly as the vessel splashed into the water. The sails billowed in the breeze, pushing the boat forward and breaking through the sea's rolling waves.

'I think we should turn back,' said Ralph anxiously.

Naldy glanced at the beach and was surprised to see how far from the shoreline they were already. Amongst all the stationary boats lining the sand, there was no sign of the Boat Builder.

'Let me steer for a bit,' said Naldy, stepping into the open wheelhouse and relieving Ralph of the captain's duty.

The sea breeze smelt of fish and salt, and Naldy's long black hair whipped wildly.

'We did it,' said Naldy, joy rushing through her as she gazed ahead.

Ralph retrieved the map from one of the large crates—the one that had hung in the bathroom—and Naldy used heavy seashells to pin it to the bench beside the wheel. She flipped open the silver compass. The boat jostled as it cut through a stretch of choppy water.

'It's quite exhilarating, isn't it?'

'I think I'm going to be sick,' returned Ralph, leaning against the wooden panelling of the wheelhouse.

The ship jerked as it hit another rough swell, and Ralph rushed to the railing.

'Are you feeling okay?' asked Naldy.

Ralph heaved, his head hanging over the side of the boat. Naldy sent him down into the boat's small cabin to rest.

As evening approached, she stood proudly behind the wheel, guiding the ship through the swells of rippling water. The open sea invigorated her, and for the first time in a long while, she felt free of stress or worry.

A bluish moon soon replaced the warm sun, and the sea's rough waters calmed as night fell. Ralph's seasickness quickly improved.

'Have you ever seen a sky that clear?' asked Naldy, lifting her head to the twinkling stars as she breathed in the cool, refreshing air.

'It's so beautiful,' said Ralph. 'I've never seen stars so bright.'

'I've never seen a sky quite like it,' she agreed.

'I don't think I should have looked up,' said Ralph, his hand moving to his stomach.

Naldy glanced at the compass and consulted the map before slightly adjusting the ship's wheel. She didn't need a light to read the map—the glowing beam of the moon was more than enough.

'I can play captain while you nap,' said Ralph. 'You've been sailing all evening.'

'Okay,' said Naldy, passing the compass to him. 'I'll have a short nap while the water is calm, but please wake me if you start to feel sick again.'

Naldy made her way into the boat's cabin. The belly of Rupert's ship had a comfortable double bed. There was also a door leading to a small lavatory.

She happily collapsed onto the soft pillows, pulling the large green knitted quilt over herself. The gentle motion of the sea soon lulled her to sleep.

She hadn't been asleep long when a deafening rumble jolted her awake. Heart pounding, she sat up and listened as the sound faded. Relief washed over her as she felt the ocean's waters were still calm beneath the ship—it must have been part of her dream.

'Naldy,' Ralph's strained voice called from above. 'Naldy!'

She leapt out of bed, hurrying up the narrow stairs to the deck, where Ralph stood behind the wheel staring at ominous grey clouds obscuring the stars in the distance.

'We need to turn around,' said Ralph, his voice trembling.

'Here, let me see,' said Naldy, pulling the map closer. She studied it for a moment before shaking her head. 'There's no point, Ralph. We need to go right through it.'

A powerful crack split the sky, accompanied by a

blinding flash of lightning.

'Naldy, we can't sail through a storm that large. It's too dangerous.'

'Tighten the ropes on the sails, Ralph,' said Naldy, taking the wheel from him and lashing it in place with rope. 'We knew it wouldn't be smooth sailing, and we're not turning back now.'

As they neared the grey clouds, the boat jolted as the sea grew more turbulent. Ralph's face turned pale again.

Strong gusts blew, causing the sails to thrash violently on their poles. The boat jerked upwards as it collided with an enormous swell, then plunged down the wave with a tremendous crash, nearly sending them overboard. Water poured into the boat, drenching them.

A flash lit up the sky nearby as the boat surged upwards again. Thunder rolled overhead, vibrating the vessel while it nosedived down another choppy wave. The wind roared, and the sails looked ready to tear free from their masts at any moment.

The rope on the ship's wheel loosened, and Naldy gripped the wheel tightly, struggling to keep hold of it. Ralph stood near the helm, clinging to the bench and working to stay upright.

The map was so wet its ink was running, and the arrow on the silver compass pivoted wildly as Naldy struggled to keep the boat travelling in one direction. The pull of the sea's unpredictable current was so strong that she failed to keep the wheel steady.

A burst of forked lightning lit up the ashen clouds. Thunder, deep and threatening, filled the sky above.

Another rope must have come undone, as one of their sails had half broken free of its pole, flapping in the harsh weather. The boat twisted until it was parallel to an oncoming seven-metre wave.

'Ralph, take the wheel,' cried Naldy over the roar of the wind and the crashing sea.

He did as he was told, and Naldy rushed to the mast, trying to resecure the loose sail—but the boat jerked. She slipped. Her head collided with the deck.

There was no time to assess the damage. She raised her hands and caught the rope thrashing about in the storm. Pulling it with all her strength, she desperately tried to recall the Boat Builder's lesson in tying knots. The rope burned her hands as it slipped across her skin until she finally managed to weave it around the pole. She secured the knot, but then noticed her clothes were covered in blood. She was already so wet from the seawater that she hadn't realised her head was bleeding.

'Turn the wheel, Ralph,' called Naldy, watching as a wave twice the size of their boat rose up.

It was too late—the boat only managed to spin halfway before the sea came crashing down on them. Naldy reached for the pole, but she lost her balance, and the water carried her to the far end of the deck, slamming her into the wooden railing.

Thunder clapped and lightning flashed as Ralph struggled to grip the wheel.

The last thing Naldy remembered seeing was the map lying wet beside her—drenched in seawater, running ink, and blood.

Chapter Nineteen

HOUSE AWAY FROM HOME

Naldy dreamt she was back inside the Witch House, with its comforting clutter and faint musty smell. She was lying on the well-used sofa in front of the old stone fireplace. It was a warm day, so the fire hadn't been lit, and only cold, charred wood rested in the grate. She knew it was daytime because the sun penetrated the edges of the heavy drapes, which had been pulled closed, leaving the room shadowy, with only a few candles flickering. She sat up and stared at the yellowed spellbooks scattered on the small table before her. The sound of someone flitting about the kitchen could be heard, and the smell of fresh brew soon filled the air.

'Hello *you*,' said Ralph, and Naldy swivelled her head to see him perched in the nearby armchair, his eyelids drooping as if he'd also just woken up from a nap.

The dream felt eerily lifelike.

'How's your head?' asked Ralph in a soft voice.

Naldy tilted her head in confusion. She felt no pain, but a tiredness lingered in her body.

'Let her sleep,' came a familiar voice from the kitchen. She knew that voice but couldn't quite place it. It was soft and silvery, yet strong at the same time. 'Come away, Ralph.'

That's my mother's voice, thought Naldy.

The last time Naldy had heard or seen her mother, she had been twelve years old, and her mother had been thirty-six. Naldy eagerly glanced towards the doorway as her mother stepped into the archway—tall and beautiful, with long black hair— holding a silver tray laden with delicate cups and a brewpot.

This is a good dream, thought Naldy.

Her mother smiled warmly, and Naldy's vision blurred as tears welled in her eyes. Her mother's gaze twinkled with affection.

I want this dream to last forever.

Her mother had aged slightly, with faint wrinkles etched into her kind face. It had been so long since Naldy had last seen her.

'I've missed you,' said her mother softly, rooted in the archway.

'I miss you too,' replied Naldy. She wanted to stand, leap up, and hug her mother, but she was scared she might wake up if she moved, and she didn't want everything to disappear.

Her mother made her way towards the sofa. Naldy blinked, and tears fell, dripping onto her lap.

'I'm so sorry, Naldy,' said her mother, placing the tray on top of the yellowed books scattered across the small table. She sat beside Naldy, reached out her pale arms, and held her daughter tightly in an embrace.

'This doesn't feel like sleeping,' Naldy said aloud, her face resting on her mother's shoulder.

Ralph laughed faintly—or maybe it was a sob.

'Tarren saved us,' said Ralph, coming to sit on Naldy's other side.

When her mother let go, Naldy saw Ralph's face was wet too.

'You're not asleep,' said Ralph, as if answering Naldy's bewildered look. 'It seems luck was on our side after all.'

Naldy stood. She wanted some distance from both Ralph and her mother, so she made her way to the unlit fireplace.

How could this be real?

'During the storm,' said Ralph tenderly, 'you knocked your head quite hard on the boat.'

Naldy's hand sprang up to her forehead. There was no pain, no blood, no open wound—not even a bruise or a scab.

I must be dreaming. Or maybe I'm in some sort of coma.

'I did the best job I could with *Sanitatem Restituere*,' said Ralph. 'I stopped the bleeding, but you were still in a bad state, and I couldn't get you to wake up. It was horrible. Tarren used powerful magic to heal you properly. I've never seen magic like that before.'

'We wanted to be with you when you woke up,' said her mother, standing and making her way to

Naldy. She reached out and rubbed Naldy's shoulders with both hands. 'But now that you're awake, why don't you go upstairs to your room and lie down for a bit? There's some time, I think, and once you've rested properly, we'll explain everything.'

'Rest?' said Naldy, an anger swelling within her. 'I'm not going anywhere, and I can't rest. I want to stay in this dream forever with you.'

'You are not asleep,' Ralph said slowly, looking at his feet.

'Then someone explain everything,' replied Naldy impatiently. 'I couldn't rest now—not until this makes some sense. The Witch House has perished in a fire—how can any of this be real?'

She had wanted to forget there was nowhere for her to return to. But now it seemed the Witch House had survived—or maybe they had travelled back in time somehow?

'We are quite real,' said Tarren calmly. 'I suppose an explanation is long overdue. Come and sit.'

Naldy was breathing heavily. Tarren seated herself calmly in the armchair, and Naldy sank onto the sofa.

'Let us have some brew,' said Tarren softly.

She poured the brew just as Naldy remembered from when she was a little girl: first placing the spoon into the cup, then filling it with hot liquid, adding a dash of cold water, and stirring. Her mother always served the brew at drinking temperature, exactly as Naldy had liked it when she was younger.

Tarren held out a cup and saucer to Naldy. She took it, half expecting her hand to pass through the cup—but it didn't. It felt solid. Real.

'I think,' said Tarren softly, passing Ralph some brew, 'it is best for Ralph to begin. For I would like to know what happened on the ship. He's already told me a little about how you came here, but I would like to hear the rest.'

'But here doesn't exist,' said Naldy, her frustration increasing. 'Our home perished in a fire. How can we be here?'

'All will be told,' said Tarren. 'But you must have patience, Naldy. You will have all the answers you have been looking for, but first, let us listen.'

Naldy sipped the warm brew, leaning back into the comfortable sofa.

Ralph sat forward, perching on the edge of his seat, and for the first time Naldy noticed how dirty and worn his travelling clothes were.

'We entered the storm,' said Ralph, wincing. He halted for a moment. 'Should I go back further?'

'No,' answered Tarren kindly. 'You may begin there. There will be time later to talk about everything that came before.'

'We lost control of the ship,' said Ralph. His cup rattled on his knee. 'I couldn't see anything through the wind and all the water—there was so much water. The boat was being tossed around, and at times, it was almost completely on its side. I was calling out to you, Naldy, but the roar of the waves and the thunder was too deafening. Then, I couldn't see you, and I thought you'd gone overboard.'

Naldy saw a flicker of pain cross Ralph's face. He took the rattling cup and saucer from his knee and placed them on the small table before him. Despite this, his leg kept shaking.

'Drink,' said Tarren kindly. 'It will help ease your troubled mind.'

Both Ralph and Naldy took a sip of their brew.

'It went on and on like that,' continued Ralph, staring at the cold ashes in the hearth. 'For hours, it went on and on, and I thought it would never end. I was so cold and wet and sick. It was miserable, and my hands were torn from gripping the ship's wheel.'

Ralph's hands showed no sign of damage, and Naldy wondered if her mother had used magic to heal them.

'There were times I wanted to throw myself overboard,' said Ralph darkly. 'I didn't think I could go on like that any longer. I thought the sea had already taken you, Naldy. But then, suddenly, the waves ceased, and the sky cleared. I was shocked to see it was daytime—the black clouds had made everything seem like night. I could see the sun high in the sky. The wind stopped, and the air became still. Then I saw you there.'

Ralph paused, and Naldy saw the anguish in his expression. His lips trembled as he continued.

'You were curled up in the corner of the ship, shivering in a pool of blood,' said Ralph quietly. 'There was so much blood. I tried to speak to you, but you wouldn't answer me. I used *Sanitatem Restituere* to stop the bleeding, then carried you into the cabin and laid you on the blankets. You were breathing, but your body was so bruised. You had a fever and were mumbling something, but I couldn't make out the words.'

'I was trying to secure the sail, and...' Naldy trailed off. She couldn't remember anything after that.

'You did manage to,' said Ralph, smiling faintly. 'You saved both our lives. I hate to think what might have happened if the sail had been left loose. After I laid you on the cabin bed, I knew I had to return to the wheel and try to find land. But the map and compass were gone, and all our water and food had been lost overboard, too.

'The sun became so hot, the air dry. There was barely a breeze to catch in the sails, and the boat drifted slowly across the ocean. Afternoon came, and that's when I saw it—golden, under a brilliant sunset... land. The boat drifted closer, and I saw sand dunes the size of mountains stretching across the horizon.

'We finally touched the sand. I was so exhausted, but I knew I had to find us drinking water. You were in and out of sleep, and I knew you wouldn't make it if I didn't find water and food. So, I lowered the anchor, left you there, and went searching, and...'

Ralph choked up. He took a moment to sip his brew. Neither Naldy nor Tarren interrupted, knowing he needed a moment to regain his composure.

'There was nothing,' said Ralph in a hollow voice. 'Just stretches and stretches of endless sand. No river, no lake, not even a tree or any sign of life. It was hopeless. It was so hot, my skin burned and cracked, and the air was so dry I could barely breathe. We were going to die. And then it got worse. I couldn't find my way back to the boat. All I could see were peaks of sand—sand everywhere. I'd left you alone in the ship's cabin, and I thought we would both die. I didn't think I'd ever see you again.'

Ralph could no longer hold back his grief. The floodgates opened, and he wept into his hands.

Naldy wrapped her arms around him, pulling him into a hug and holding him tightly. They sat together, Ralph crying into her shoulder, until his sobs subsided. Naldy didn't let him go. She held him close.

After a few minutes, Ralph lifted his head and gently pulled himself from her embrace.

'I think I can take it from here,' said Tarren tenderly.

Naldy took a few sips of the comforting brew as her mother continued. 'I found him wandering in the desert. Another day in the heat, and he would have been dead. He kept mumbling *I've left her in the boat.* I brought Ralph home, then went back out to find the boat. My heart raced when I saw you. At first, I thought I was hallucinating. I brought you back here.'

'Back here—but where is here?' asked Naldy, suddenly panicked. 'Do you mean we're no longer in

Arkus Day? We need to be in the desert. We need to be in Arkus Day to look for the Corium.'

'Do not worry, Naldy,' said Tarren in her silvery voice. 'We are still in Arkus Day. If you need proof, you can take a peek out the window.'

Naldy stood and made her way to the thick curtains blocking the sunlight. She pulled them back, blinking as the sun's blinding brightness momentarily obscured her vision. When her eyes adjusted, she saw a vast desert of sand stretching endlessly outside the window, with massive dunes sloping up and down.

'I'm either sleeping or I've gone mad,' muttered Naldy to herself. 'This cannot be real.'

'You are neither,' Tarren replied calmly. 'And neither was I when I found you in the boat's cabin. Though I can understand why it might seem like a dream to you. It's been so very long, and I have wanted to reach out and tell you everything. It seems the time for telling can no longer be put off. Come now, Naldy. Sit, and I will tell all.'

'But how can this not be a hallucination?' asked Naldy, her anger bubbling to the surface again. 'Everything here is exactly as it was in the Witch House when it stood at the edge of Kirkwood Forest —the same chairs, the same books, the exact same wallpaper—everything!'

'All of this,' said Tarren calmly, 'looks exactly the same because it was made with powerful magic. It was created, Naldy, with the Corium.'

Ralph's mouth fell open in shock, and Naldy felt

more certain than ever that she must be trapped in some kind of dream.

'You have the Corium?' asked Naldy, raising her eyebrows in disbelief.

'There is much to tell you, my girl,' said Tarren, a slight tremble in her voice. 'I have wanted to tell you for so very long. But it was not safe for me to do so. Let us go into the kitchen, have something to eat, and I'll pour us some wine. It seems the time has finally come.'

Ralph stood eagerly and made his way into the kitchen. He appeared completely at home. Naldy couldn't help but recall the months he had spent with her at the Witch House, searching through trunks for the Corium.

In some ways Ralph had been right—the Corium had been inside the Witch House all along. Just not the house on the edge of Kirkwood Forest.

'Come and take a seat at the dining table,' said Tarren as she made her way under the archway into the kitchen. 'I will try to answer all your questions. I am sure you must have many.'

Naldy's mother was right—her head was reeling with questions, and her heart felt heavy with mixed emotions. She was overjoyed to be reunited with her mother, but she was also disappointed that her parents had disappeared, never once attempting to reach out to her. Could any explanation possibly ease the deep wound they had left behind?

And the Corium—how had her parents come to possess it? Had they had it all along? A sadness washed over her, as she thought of all the lives that had been lost in the search for a leagon her parents had apparently guarded. And where was her father? Was he upstairs somewhere? Or out wandering the desert?

'I will make us your grandmother's butternut pumpkin and potato pie,' said Tarren, as Ralph began setting the table without needing to be asked. 'It was always your favourite. We'd best talk as I prepare the food, though, for I fear we have less time than I originally thought.'

Chapter Twenty

LEATHER AND BLOOD

R alph was told to return the crockery to the cabinet and fetch grandmother's antique silverware from the cupboard in the hall. Naldy had never eaten from these family heirlooms; as a young child, her parents had strictly forbidden the use of her grandmother's silverware.

As Tarren prepared the pie, she asked questions about Ralph and Naldy's quest. This suited Naldy fine, as although she had many questions of her own whirling around in her head, she was too shocked to decide which to ask first.

The familiar smell of sweet roasted pumpkin filled the air, and Naldy felt as though she'd been transported back to childhood.

'Naldy has made this dish for me before,' remarked Ralph, licking his lips with anticipation, 'but it's never smelt this delicious.'

Naldy laughed, and Tarren smiled as she added the filling to the pastry. By the time her mother was serving them generous helpings, Ralph had finished recounting their journey in search of the prized Devante.

Twiddling her grandmother's silver fork, Naldy voiced the question she most feared to ask.

'And is Dad joining us for dinner?' she asked in a small voice, betraying she'd already guessed the answer. Ralph had set out three places at the table, and Naldy's mother hadn't corrected him.

Without the aid of magic, Tarren returned the leftover pie to the warm oven before descending into the cellar. She emerged with a carafe of red wine. After filling their crystal goblets, she took her seat at the round table. Neither Naldy nor Ralph touched their pie.

'He has been buried at the back of the house,' said Tarren softly, her eyes heavy with sadness.

A silence settled over them as Naldy let the news of her father's death take hold. Despite the wonderful meal, she suddenly didn't feel like eating. Ralph stared sadly at his plate.

'I'll take you to see him afterwards,' added Tarren tenderly, reaching for her daughter's hands.

'How did he... you know,' asked Naldy, so quietly it was barely a whisper.

'This place may look deserted,' said Tarren, picking up her fork, 'but it is full of dangers lurking out of sight. Beasts prowl the sand.'

'But you have the Devante,' said Naldy, her voice rising. 'Not just any Devante—you have the Corium.'

'I tried to make this place feel like home,' said Tarren softly. Their food and drink remained untouched. 'But you know your father—he hated being isolated in one place.'

'No,' said Naldy bluntly. 'I didn't know my father. I hardly know *you* either. You left without any explanation or warning. I was only twelve years old.'

'I am sorry, so very sorry, Naldy,' said Tarren, her face pained. 'We owe you an explanation. Do not think we love you any less, for it is precisely why we left—because of love.'

Naldy had spent so long dreaming of the day she would find her parents and be reunited. But now, sitting with her mother, she wasn't sure she wanted it anymore. She felt bitter, angry, and hurt.

'You must both be hungry,' said Tarren, gesturing kindly for them to start eating. 'We'll feel much better with food and wine in our stomachs.'

Ralph began to eat slowly, but Naldy only prodded her slice of pie with her fork.

'I am pleased to hear,' said Tarren, picking up her crystal goblet, 'that you both know much more about the Devante than I expected. You've been on quite the journey—across Edengar to see dragons! I've never gone so far myself.'

'You made it to Arkus Day,' said Ralph in polite disagreement.

'Yes, but I did it with the aid of a Devante,' replied Tarren, smiling warmly at him. 'You have both come this far without one. Of course, it hasn't been without its struggles.'

Ralph bowed his head, and Naldy understood he was thinking about his cousin, Rupert.

'You've both been through a great deal,' said Tarren. 'There is much to tell you, but now I'm unsure where to begin.'

'You could begin with why you left,' Naldy said, though it came out sharper than she intended.

'Yes,' said Tarren. 'I will start there. From Ralph's account of your travels, I see you're both well aware that the Devante are highly sought-after. People will entertain all sorts of evils to get their hands on one. Most seek them for power, but this Maverick fellow has other plans.'

'He's a brute,' said Ralph heatedly. 'Rupert, Oak, Odorf, and the Witch House would all still be here if it weren't for him.'

'Have pity,' said Tarren gently. 'It takes a broken soul to welcome such darkness. I do not know why Maverick desires to end all magic. Perhaps we will never know, but his intention to do so is clear. Come, Naldy, you should eat.'

'I'm not hungry.'

'Please, you must eat something,' said Tarren in a motherly tone. 'You're going to need your strength.'

Naldy took a small nibble of the pie, and tears welled in her eyes. She had forgotten the taste of her mother's cooking, but that single bite opened a floodgate of childhood memories.

'Your father and I had to leave, Naldy, for the same reason you've sailed here to Arkus Day.'

'To find the Corium?' asked Naldy, still not quite understanding. She took another bite of the comforting pie.

'To save magic from being destroyed,' said Tarren, her silvery voice calm but resolute. 'There is one aspect of your Devante knowledge you've both gotten wrong. The Corium is not a leagon. Corium in Olde Witchery does mean leather or skin, but it doesn't refer to the hide of any beast.'

Ralph accidentally knocked over his crystal goblet, and the delicate glass shattered, sending red wine dripping from the round table onto the floor.

'Not to worry,' said Tarren. The sharp edges of the broken crystal floated up and rejoined. The beautiful goblet was restored to its original form. The spilt liquid evaporated, and Ralph's glass was refilled with fresh wine.

'You're an Effangale witch,' noted Naldy, shocked she hadn't already realised her mother could cast spells without uttering words or gesturing with her hands.

'So are you, Naldy,' said Tarren with a soft laugh. 'I thought by now you'd have worked that bit out on your own.'

'I'm not an Effangale witch,' said Naldy firmly. 'I've tried to cast spells without speaking aloud, and it's never worked for me. How can I be an Effangale?'

'You only need to try,' said Tarren warmly.

'Are you saying what I think you're saying?' asked Ralph, picking up his repaired goblet and marvelling at it. There wasn't the slightest sign of a crack. 'The Corium is... it is...'

'It is a person, yes,' said Tarren.

'It's you,' said Naldy, locking eyes with her mother. 'You're the Corium. Aren't you?'

'For now, I am, yes,' admitted Tarren.

'But how can a person contain the magic of the Corium?' probed Ralph, his mouth open in shock.

'And if you are, you should have stayed to protect me,' said Naldy, her hands trembling as her thoughts spiralled with more questions. 'If what you're saying is true, it doesn't explain why you and Dad left—without so much as scribbling a note.'

'Ralph spoke earlier about a woman you both met on your travels—Betty,' said Tarren, pausing to take a sip of wine. 'You mentioned how her family's tradition was to pass the Devante down to the eldest girl. Our family followed the same tradition with our Devante: Rubrum, Lignum, the Aurantiaco and the Corium.'

'I don't understand,' mumbled Naldy, her breathing heavy. 'Oak was Lignum—how could he have been passed down? And the Aurantiaco was at the Bleckdale museum until Maverick stole it and destroyed it. What do you mean *our Devante?*'

'Your great-aunt Geraldine is rumoured to have pinched the Aurantiaco long ago,' said Tarren. 'They say she sold it to the museum for a fraction of what it was truly worth.'

'You mean our family once possessed four of the eight Devante?' asked Naldy, her head spinning. 'And the Corium's magic... it's inside you?'

'Well, Rubrum and Oak have always remained in the forest together,' said Tarren, a twinkle in her eye as she remembered the old tree. 'They have always taken care of themselves. I took you there when you were a child, just as your grandmother took me.

I introduced you to the secret at the heart of the forest, as has been done for generations.'

The hot sun outside must have begun to dip below the sandy mountains, as the light in the room slowly faded.

'Olde Witchery,' said Tarren softly, 'is an ancient language, and many books get the translation wrong. By "leather," they mean "skin." To be more specific, they do not mean the very skin stretched over our bodies, but the bodies themselves—and the blood within them. The Corium, Naldy, is a bloodline.'

'A bloodline?' repeated Naldy, her chest tightening. 'You mean... are you saying what I think you're saying? Is the Corium within me?'

Tarren glanced thoughtfully towards the kitchen window, where the open curtains revealed the sand dunes casting long shadows.

'I was twenty-four,' Tarren continued, 'when my mother first told me about the Devante and their powers. She told me on the day you were born.'

'I never met my grandmother,' said Naldy, her irritation rising. 'You always told me my grandparents were dead.'

'I am sorry we kept so much of the truth from you,' said Tarren with a remorseful stare. 'You see, I also believed they had passed. But I received a lucurn candle the day you arrived into this world— your grandmother told me about the Devante and their power. She said it was the reason she had disappeared when I was younger. She told me not to reply, for fear any further messages would be intercepted.'

'But why did she have to go?' pressed Naldy. 'And why did you and Dad have to go?'

'The Corium, Naldy,' said Tarren slowly, 'it is not within you yet. But one day it will be. The magic of the Corium is inherited by the eldest daughter when her mother dies.'

'Does that mean…' began Naldy, but she couldn't bring herself to finish the sentence.

'Yes,' said Tarren. 'The day I die, the magic of the Corium will be passed on to you. You see, four Devante were entrusted to our family and four to another. But that is a history lesson for another time.'

Naldy felt a lump rise in her throat. It was hard to believe everything her mother had just told her, and more than ever, she felt as though she must be dreaming.

'Years later, your father and I were playing cards,' said Tarren, pensively running her fingers along the edge of the table. 'It was late, and you were asleep in bed. You were only twelve years old. We were sitting right here. Then I felt it. Your grandmother had died, and the magic had come to me. Your father wanted to stay and explain—'

'Then why didn't you?' snapped Naldy. 'Why didn't you tell me?'

'Because you were a child,' said Tarren, her voice steady.

'Oh, you think that was better, do you?' retorted

Naldy. 'To disappear without a trace in the middle of the night? You left me alone.'

'We left you in the care of Oak,' said Tarren. 'He was a Devante, and we knew he could protect you.'

'He couldn't protect himself,' replied Naldy angrily. 'You were a Devante—the most powerful—*you* should have protected me!'

'I became the most hunted person overnight,' said Tarren, sounding wounded. 'With the Corium's power comes a responsibility greater than I can put into words. Staying with you would have put you in danger. Some know about the bloodline, and if they discovered we were family, they would hunt you, too. If the worst were to happen to me, the power would be best protected if you were far away. We couldn't tell you we were alive—you would have come looking for us. For your own protection, Naldy, and for the protection of the Corium, we had to leave you. The Corium was not safe in Kirkwood Forest.'

'Why didn't you take me with you?'

'To Arkus Day,' replied Tarren wistfully. She looked at her daughter with adoration. 'This sandy desert would have been no life for you.'

Naldy took a moment to process everything. Her cheeks felt flushed. She would one day become the Corium—the thought was almost incomprehensible. The candles on the table suddenly sparked, their flames bursting to life. Naldy wasn't sure whether Tarren had lit them or if Ralph had done so, perhaps in the hopes of distracting her from her rising anger. She glanced out the rectangular window above the kitchen sink and saw twilight setting over the sand.

'That explains something that's been bothering me,' remarked Ralph as he set down his fork, having finished his pie. 'It's why Maverick's ball of smoke thought Naldy knew the location of the Corium when we were in Edengar.'

'It is also why Naldy could penetrate the *Banned Spell of Knowledge*,' said Tarren, she met Naldy's gaze. 'When you tried to find the Corium using Barbra's scroll—the page torn from Metallum—you were able to penetrate the *Banned Spell* because the magic of the Corium lies dormant within you, Naldy. It offered you the answer, albeit a little jumbled—*ask Audry.*'

'There's more,' said Naldy, sensing a hesitation in her mother. 'There is something else you are not telling us.'

'For generations, Hannah Hale's magic has been kept safe,' said Tarren, shifting uncomfortably in her chair. 'There have been many moments in history when the books have fallen into the wrong hands. Sadly, some have been used for evil. But apart from The Establishment, long ago, who sought them in the hope of eradicating them, no one since has hunted them with the intention of destroying them completely.'

'Maverick,' said Naldy and Ralph in unison.

'He'll have to deal with us first,' added Ralph boldly. 'We know he's hoping to get his grubby fingers on the Corium's magic, but you needn't worry. He won't get past us.'

'I appreciate your resolve,' said Tarren, smiling affectionately at Ralph. But Naldy sensed unease behind her mother's expression. 'I do not like to burden you further, but I fear you are both right. Maverick's plan is to undo the *Banned Spell of Death* and bring an end to all magic. Permanently. Magic will become extinct, and there will be no way to restore it.'

Tarren stood and carried her plate to the kitchen sink. She gazed out the window where the light was nearly gone.

'Naldy,' said Tarren, still staring at the sand dunes with her back to them, 'you should know our family wasn't chosen to carry this burden by accident. Hannah Hale is your great-great-grandmother.'

Naldy remained silent, letting the revelation —her great-great-grandmother was the legendary Hannah Hale—wash over her. Then, irritation surfaced as she considered the reality: it was her family who'd caused this mess. Naldy fixated on her mother's words: *Magic would become extinct.*

A wave of nausea surged through her as she realised what Maverick would need to do to ensure the permanent removal of magic couldn't be reversed: he would need to destroy the Corium.

'Let us go outside now,' said Tarren, turning to face them again. 'We are running out of time, and I want to take you to see your father before you have to leave.'

'Leave?' repeated Naldy. 'We're not going

anywhere.'

Tarren ignored her and made her way along the hall leading from the kitchen. They followed in silence. At the back door, Tarren picked up a lantern resting beside the overburdened shoe rack. She led them outside into the starry twilight. Naldy was startled by how cold it had turned. With every breath, mist floated up from their mouths.

Tarren stopped a few metres from the house, standing in front of a beautiful tombstone carved from grey rock. She placed her lantern beside it on a patch of young green grass thriving amidst the dry, yellow sand. The inscription, etched in shiny gold cursive lettering, gleamed in its light:

In ever loving memory of
Jacob Elahline
1596–1644

A pang of sadness went through Naldy's heart. Tarren gently took her daughter's hands in her own. Between their hands, from thin air, a bouquet of yellow garden peonies bloomed. Naldy laid the majestic bouquet on her father's grave. She knelt by the tombstone as darkness surrounded them. When she finally rose, Ralph placed a comforting arm around her shoulders.

'Why don't you bring him back?' asked Naldy, turning to face her mother. 'If you have the magic of the Corium, you can bring him back.'

Tarren avoided meeting Naldy's hazel eyes.

'It is something we discussed,' said Tarren

quietly. 'He did not want to return once he passed to the other side.'

'But he didn't know I was coming,' said Naldy. 'If he knew I was here, he might want to come back.'

Tarren fell into a heavy silence, her gaze lingering on Jacob's grave, her brow creased in thought.

'There's something I've been wanting to ask you,' said Ralph, gently removing his arms from Naldy's shoulders. He took a few steps closer to Tarren.

'I know what it is you ask of me, Ralph,' said Tarren, her face strained. 'But I cannot. It is not wise.'

'Wise,' repeated Ralph, his voice rising. 'We've lost so many people on our way here, and you have the power to bring them back. It's not a *Banned Spell*.'

'There are many spells that are not banned,' said Tarren, bending to pick up the lantern from the ground, 'but that does not make them harmless.'

'I admit I didn't know Odorf or Oak well,' said Ralph. 'But Rupert—he's my cousin. I know he would want to return. He would be of great use to us, and I know he would help protect you.'

Tarren winced slightly, as though Ralph's words troubled her.

'You could bring back Oak,' remarked Naldy, trying to decipher her mother's tense expression. 'Ralph is right—bringing someone back from the dead is not a *Banned Spell*.'

'It would not restore the magic of Lignum,' said Tarren, moving towards the back door, her black cloak billowing as she walked. Ralph and Naldy were close behind. 'Once the bearer of the Devante passes, bringing them back does not revive the magic. And I know Oak would not want to return. You must understand—bringing someone back from death upsets the balance of things.'

'What balance?' Ralph snapped. 'It is without Rupert the world has become unbalanced.'

'Come inside,' said Tarren, holding the back door open.

Naldy walked past her mother without a word, stepping into the house, but Ralph remained where he was. He stood firmly on the sand, framed by the jewel-like stars scattered across the sky.

'Ralph,' said Tarren, looking at him tenderly. 'I understand your desire. But you must believe me when I say that awakening the dead is a dangerous act.'

'Please.'

'Your cousin made a deal with the Fairy Queen,' continued Tarren, 'and I would advise you not to betray her. Let your cousin rest—he is at peace now.'

For a moment, Ralph didn't move, his posture stony. But slowly, he softened, his shoulders lowering as he walked past Tarren and into the house.

Naldy could sense that—though Ralph had dropped the subject for now—the idea of bringing Rupert back hadn't entirely left him.

Once they were all gathered inside by the back door, Tarren hung the lantern on the cloak rack.

'Let us go back down the hall,' said Tarren. 'Our

time together is almost up.'

'You keep saying we are running out of time,' said Naldy, 'but we've only just arrived.'

'And you'll have to go soon,' replied Tarren solemnly. 'Maverick has landed on the shores of Arkus Day.'

—Chapter Twenty-One—

BURDEN AT SEA

Naldy was surprised to find two rucksacks, packed full of supplies, already resting beside the front door. Fresh travelling clothes lay neatly folded on the dining table.

'Put them on,' said Tarren, stepping into the kitchen and carefully wrapping two slices of leftover pumpkin pie in white linen napkins.

'How do you know Maverick has landed on the shore?' asked Ralph, pulling off his shabby travelling clothes to change into the fresh set. 'I thought the *Banned Spell of Knowledge* prevented you from knowing someone's location. Unless you've broken it?'

'I've wrapped some pie for you both,' said Tarren calmly, her hands steady as she collected two glasses from the cupboard beside the pantry. 'It should keep your spirits up while you depart.'

'But aren't you coming with us?' asked Naldy, ignoring the clean clothes.

'The reason I know Maverick has landed on the shore,' explained Tarren, filling the two glasses with water from the sink, 'is because a higher-ranking

Devante knows the location of a lower-ranking one. And, as you well know, Maverick is carrying the Aurum.'

'We're not going without you,' said Naldy firmly. 'We're not leaving you here. You must come with us.'

Ralph's fingers fumbled with the buttons of his starched white travelling shirt, which was still half undone.

'You should change, Naldy,' said Tarren, setting the glasses on the kitchen table. 'And finish doing up your buttons, Ralph. You must both go now.'

'Maverick thinks the Corium is a leagon,' said Ralph, abandoning his shirt's buttons as he picked up the two glasses of water. He passed one to Naldy and stood beside her. 'Even if he finds us, he doesn't know you hold the Corium's magic, and he won't stand a chance against all three of us.'

'I fear he would have extracted the truth from the Boat Builder,' said Tarren, seating herself at the kitchen table, her posture upright and tense. 'Finish your water. You will need to go.'

'You mean the Boat Builder knows you are the Corium?' asked Naldy, shocked.

'There are some in the Seagull Society who have always helped protect the Corium,' said Tarren quietly. 'They have dedicated their lives to the task and keep secrets well. But do not trust them all. Many have been corrupted by the desire for power, and the Society is not what it once was.'

'I agree with Ralph,' said Naldy, lifting her angular face. 'We'll be stronger together. We can face

Maverick and be rid of him for good.'

'We're not leaving you here, Tarren,' said Ralph resolutely.

'I know you want to stay,' replied Tarren quietly. 'I wish we had longer, but protecting magic from extinction must be the priority. I fear Maverick is a more skilled wizard than you might believe.'

'We've gone up against him before,' said Ralph.

'He has defeated some of the most powerful people I knew,' said Tarren. 'Odorf was lauded for her magical ability, and killing a dragon takes significant skill.'

'Yes, but he had the power of a Devante to help him,' said Naldy. 'And you have the magic of the Corium—the highest-ranking!'

'Even so,' said Tarren, 'his powers are alarming. He has managed to find and destroy all the other Devante, including Oak—and he knew how to defend himself.'

'It doesn't matter,' said Naldy, placing her untouched glass of water on the kitchen table. 'We're not leaving you here, and we can face Maverick together.'

'It is our duty,' said Tarren in the most severe tone she'd used yet. 'We must not allow Maverick to get his hands on the Corium's power. Our best chance is to separate.'

Tarren stood and turned her back on them.

'I won't lose you again,' said Naldy, choking on her words. 'We won't go without you.'

'My darling,' Tarren replied in a pained voice, her

back still turned. 'I do not want us to be separated. I never wanted us to be separated. But it must be so.'

'You're wrong,' said Naldy, her voice trembling. 'I won't go.'

'We're staying to fight,' said Ralph, his eyes narrowing with determination.

'If you are here,' said Tarren, turning to fix them with a hard glare, 'and something should happen to me, you will have had no practice with the Corium's magic. Don't you see, Naldy? Maverick will win too easily. By leaving, you give the Corium its best chance of survival. If you both go, as you must, I will do everything in my power to fight him off. And if I succeed, I shall come and find you.'

'And if you don't?' asked Naldy, her voice cracking.

'You will both be far away, in the middle of the ocean, safe.'

'And what if he manages to take your magic for himself?' asked Ralph. 'If we all stay together, there's less chance of him getting it.'

'His intention is to end magic,' warned Tarren darkly. 'If he succeeds, all magic will vanish from every corner of the world. The highest-ranking Devante will hold the only power to reverse it.'

'But then what are we to do?' protested Ralph.

'If Maverick casts a spell to destroy all magic,' said Tarren, 'and if my assumptions are correct, he intends to ensure nobody can ever reverse this evil. To do this, he—'

'He will destroy the Corium,' whispered Naldy,

finishing her mother's sentence. She felt the blood drain from her face. 'He intends to kill you so his evil can never be undone.'

'He will destroy the Aurum first,' said Tarren slowly, 'which is good news for us.'

'Good news?' repeated Ralph, his face pale with worry. 'To have another Devante ruined, and then for him to murder you? We won't leave. Not without you. We should all go together if we're to go at all.'

'He will come after us,' said Tarren. 'He will not stop. He will never stop.'

'I don't understand,' said Ralph. 'Why is it good if he destroys the Aurum?'

'Because,' said Naldy, knowing the answer, 'Maverick will be left without the power of a Devante.'

'Exactly,' said Tarren, smiling warmly at her daughter. 'First, he will use my power to see all magic become extinct. Then he will destroy the final two Devante—the Aurum and the Corium. He will assume he has succeeded in eradicating magic permanently, but he will be wrong because—'

'If you die,' said Ralph, lifting his blue eyes to meet Naldy's hazel ones. 'Naldy will become the Corium.'

'Yes, the Corium's magic will transfer to Naldy,' remarked Tarren. 'The firstborn female of the Hale line.'

'I don't want it,' said Naldy, her anger flaring again. 'It is a curse.'

'A burden we must carry,' said Tarren, moving to

the front door to pick up the rucksacks. 'Put these on now.'

'If we stay, then we can fight,' said Naldy as her mother lifted one of the rucksacks onto her back.

'And if we lose all magic?' asked Tarren. 'Not just ours, but all magic everywhere. Our family has been tasked with carrying this responsibility. One day, Naldy, if you choose to have children and bear daughters, the magic will pass to them. Only when the female bloodline ends will our duty to the Devante also end. Until then, we must do everything we can to ensure it is not used for evil—especially not irreversible evil. That is why you must both go.'

Tarren opened the front door and led them out onto the old porch. She pulled Ralph into a warm embrace, kissing his cheek, before turning to Naldy and wrapping her arms tightly around her. Naldy wanted to stay in her mother's warm hug forever. Her long black hair smelt of sandalwood, just as Naldy remembered. There was so much she wanted to say, and so many questions still lingered unasked.

'Ralph, come here and take this,' said Tarren, breaking away from Naldy's hug.

Tarren held out what appeared to be a long wooden peg, and Ralph stared at it, perplexed.

'Take out one of the wheel spokes when you get to the ship,' explained Tarren, speaking quickly. 'Replace it with this. It will handle the steering for you, so you shouldn't run into trouble at sea.'

Tarren made her way to the edge of the porch and bent to touch the sand. A soft blue glow spread through the sand beneath her hand, and a line of vibrant, luminous blue shot forward, trailing off into the distance.

'It will guide you back,' said Tarren. As she rose, a gust of wind caught her cloak, swirling it around her.

To Naldy, her mother looked like a warrior preparing for battle—her face focused and determined.

'Follow the trail,' said Tarren firmly. 'You must set sail at once. Do not wait for me. I will find you if all goes well.'

Ralph took hold of Naldy's hand, and together they stepped off the porch onto the dry sand, running as fast as they could along the glowing blue line. Naldy's heart pounded, each step growing heavier as they left the Witch House behind. She glanced back, longing for one last glimpse of her mother. But it was too late—the wind picked up, and swirling sand veiled the house from view.

She wanted to stop, but Ralph pulled her forward. Soon the sound of the sea reached them, and they ran down a steep dune, slipping at times as they made their way to the shore. The reflection of the stars glimmered in the rolling waves.

They half expected to cross paths with Maverick and Getergrin, but they didn't pass anyone or anything on their way to the sea. Rupert's boat was waiting on the beach, tilted slightly on one side.

Ralph had begun climbing the rope ladder, but Naldy hesitated, staring back at the glowing blue line in the sand they had followed.

'Are you coming?' Ralph called from the boat's deck, watching her intently.

'This isn't right,' Naldy muttered to herself.

She went to retrace her steps, but after a few strides, the blue line faded and vanished. The wind had erased their footprints, and Naldy realised there was no path back to her mother.

'Naldy?' called Ralph.

'But how will we get it into the water?' she asked, climbing the rope ladder. She pulled herself onto the deck. 'We should wait here for my mother. I don't want to leave her behind.'

Ralph stepped into the open wheelhouse. He grabbed one of the ship's wooden spokes and tried to wiggle it free from the wheel.

'Do we have to go?' asked Naldy weakly, though something deep inside her knew they must.

'It's stuck,' said Ralph, bracing his leg against the wheel and tugging harder.

'You're a wizard, remember, Ralph,' said Naldy, chuckling softly.

'I don't know a spell for this.'

'Move aside and let me,' instructed Naldy, pleased there was magic she had learnt that Ralph hadn't yet mastered. She held out her hands. '*Solvere.*'

The spoke cracked, and Naldy pulled it free from the wheel.

'And you, Naldy,' remarked Ralph cheekily, 'are an Effangale witch, remember.'

'Pass it here.'

Ralph handed Naldy the wooden peg. She took a deep breath before slotting it into the wheel. It clicked into place, and the ship moved instantly, sliding across the sand before crashing into the dark, shimmering blue sea. The boat carved through the frothy waves.

The urge to jump overboard swept over Naldy. The thought of leaving without her mother felt unbearable, and she knew there would be no turning back once they were out at sea. She longed to swim back to shore, but it was already too late—the boat had sailed far from the beach.

'I don't see Maverick's ship,' said Ralph, standing with one hand on the wheel as he looked back over his shoulder.

'It must be further up the coast,' replied Naldy, peering at the shadowy mountains. In the dim light, they didn't look like sand. 'You don't need to keep holding the wheel, Ralph. I think it'll steer itself.'

Ralph let go of the wheel and stepped back cautiously. He moved to stand beside Naldy, watching as Arkus Day slowly disappeared into the darkness of the night.

When they could no longer see any sign of land, Ralph settled on the weathered planks beneath the sails and helped himself to another slice of pumpkin pie from the rucksack Tarren had packed for them. Naldy wasn't hungry. Unable to relax, she paced the deck, her thoughts racing. Maybe her mother had been wrong. Perhaps Maverick hadn't reached Arkus Day. After all, they hadn't seen his ship along the shoreline.

'Come and sit,' said Ralph gently. 'Your pacing is making me anxious. Have some food. You barely ate at dinner.'

'I don't want to sit,' said Naldy, agitated. 'I can't stand all this waiting and not knowing.'

Ralph smiled affectionately, but there was a hint of pity in his eyes. Naldy eventually slumped beside him.

'Was any of it real?' she asked softly. 'It all felt like a dream. A wonderful dream. And now the nightmare has taken hold.'

'She will be okay,' said Ralph tenderly, the sea breeze tousling his hair. 'Maverick will be no match for the Corium's magic. Your mother will be with us soon. We'll go back to Kirkwood Forest together, rebuild the Witch House there, and never have to worry about Maverick again.'

'I need to be distracted,' said Naldy, pressing her fingers against her temples. 'My mind is all a jumble, and this waiting is torture. We shouldn't have left.'

'I have just the distraction for you,' said Ralph, reaching into his rucksack and pulling out two iron cups. He leant over and placed one in front of each of them. 'Let's see how you go.'

Ralph's cup floated instantly, without a single word spoken aloud, and he smiled, clearly pleased with himself.

'I'm not an Effangale, Ralph.'

'Well, your mother seems to think you are. She said so, and she's the Corium, so she must be right.

Just give it a good go.'

Naldy tried to concentrate, repeating the floating spell *Arcesso* in her mind, but nothing happened. Her cup remained stubbornly on the wooden planks. She tried again, and then again, but her thoughts refused to focus on the cup.

Instead, she could only think about her mother and Maverick, picturing them locked in battle, the Witch House looming eerily behind them. She imagined spells striking the ground, sending bursts of sand into the air while their intended targets leapt swiftly out of harm's way, their cloaks billowing in the wind.

'*Arcesso*,' said Naldy aloud, and her cup lifted from the ground, floating up to join Ralph's.

'That's cheating,' said Ralph, grinning as he bumped his levitating cup against hers.

The two of them laughed.

Then, the cups dropped to the deck with an ominous clang, and the ship's wheel spun wildly. The vessel tilted sharply to the left. Naldy jumped to her feet as Ralph dashed to the wheel, gripping it tightly and struggling to steady the ship.

'*Arcesso*,' said Naldy aloud, but the cup didn't move. 'Ralph?'

He spun the wheel frantically, fighting to keep the ship from capsizing.

'Ralph?' cried Naldy, worry etched across her face as the boat slowly straightened.

She could see tears rolling down his cheeks. She closed her eyes, picturing her mother helpless in the cold, moonlit sand, with Maverick standing over her.

'Can you do magic, Ralph?' asked Naldy desperately.

Ralph turned his attention to the metal cups on the slatted floor. They didn't float but only rolled slightly in time with the ship's sway.

'Please, Ralph, try.'

'I am trying,' squeaked Ralph anxiously. 'It's gone.'

They were right all along, thought Naldy. *Maverick had always intended to end all magic.*

'The list Mortous gave you,' said Naldy, trying to quell her worry.

Ralph stuffed a hand into his cloak pocket.

'I don't have it,' said Ralph. 'I left it in my old travelling cloak. We left in such a hurry—I'm so sorry, Naldy.'

'We have to go back,' said Naldy in a panic, clutching the boat's railing. 'Turn the boat around, Ralph. We have to go back.'

Naldy imagined witches and wizards everywhere, unexpectedly stripped of their powers: brewpots—once floating mid-air—crashing to the ground; broomsticks carrying witches plummeting from the sky; candles lit by magic flickering out; and spells across the land suddenly ceasing to work.

'Turn the boat around, I said!'

Ralph didn't move. He simply returned a forlorn expression, his hands clutching the ship's wheel.

'We must go back, Ralph, before Maverick destroys the... before he—'

Naldy's words faltered as a strange sensation overtook her. She collapsed to the deck, her entire body tingling as an overwhelming wave of euphoria surged through her. The feeling coursed through her like fire. Even the tiny hairs on the back of her neck prickled as though energy was rushing through them.

Naldy gasped as the sensation abruptly subsided —the euphoria gave way to a pang of anguish. The truth struck her: she had become the Corium, and she knew this meant her mother had been killed.

'Are you okay?' asked Ralph, rushing to help Naldy to her feet as the ship tilted slightly.

'She said she was going to follow us, Ralph,' said Naldy, a hollow feeling settling inside her. 'We shouldn't have left. Why did we go? We should never have left.'

Ralph threw his arms around Naldy, pulling her into a tight hug—but she broke away. Anger swelled inside her as she stepped into the open centre of the deck.

The ship rocked, cutting through the endless swells of the sea. Naldy looked up at the clear night sky, where countless stars winked peacefully above.

She had no idea how the Corium's magic worked, but something deep and instinctual stirred within her. Ralph took a step towards her.

'Stand back, Ralph,' said Naldy, her voice filled with fierce determination. 'This one is for everyone left behind along the way.'

She threw her head back as a gust of wind surged,

whipping her black hair wildly. The sails filled with air, and her travelling cloak fluttered around her body. When Naldy opened her hazel eyes, it wasn't the glimmering stars above that she saw, but a montage of familiar faces.

She saw Odorf, her satchel of potion bottles secured at her waist; Oak with his mossy eyebrows; Rupert's broad smile; and her father, his brown, unkempt hair framing his kind face.

The Witch House flickered into view, its windows issuing streams of hot, red fire. Then, the Devante appeared, each flashing by in turn—the vibrant red of her family's prized spellbook, Rubrum; the peacock engraving on the orange Aurantiaco; the deep blue of the Caeruleum; the unremarkable, tattered, faded pink cover of Rosea; and the lustrous silver and gold surfaces of Metallum and Aurum.

Finally, she saw her mother standing proudly, her long black hair cascading to her waist.

The stars returned to view. Naldy lowered her head and found Ralph watching her with such fondness that she couldn't help but smile a little.

She turned her gaze to the iron cup, rolling back and forth with each sway of the sea. The cup lifted off the ground and glided over to Ralph.

He caught the cup from the air and smiled. A creaking sound drew their attention, and they noticed the ship's wheel turning slightly, correcting their course.

'I wish I could see Maverick's face,' said Ralph, stuffing both hands into his cloak pockets. 'He must have been so proud, thinking he'd succeeded in destroying magic. And now, I imagine, he's standing dumbfounded in the desert—without any Devante, too.'

From one of his pockets, Ralph pulled out the list Mortous had given them.

'It was in the other pocket,' he said. 'Tarren must have put it there... I'm sorry about your mother, Naldy. I'm so very sorry.'

He handed the list to her. She looked at the parchment. Once, it had been so full of Devante, but now, below the 'H' at the top, only the 'Corium' remained.

'We need to stop him, Ralph,' said Naldy seriously, the image of her mother's face etched in her mind. 'Maverick needs to be stopped.'

'We will,' said Ralph confidently. 'I promise you, Naldy, we will.'

Naldy took a deep breath of the salty sea air.

'We have one then,' she said, bittersweet. 'A Devante.'

www.ingramcontent.com/pod-product-compliance
Lightning Source LLC
Chambersburg PA
CBHW032139190626
46814CB00005BA/1751